TERRA

Mitch Benn

TERRA

GOLLANCZ

LONDON

Copyright © Mitch Benn 2013

All rights reserved

The right of Mitch Benn to be identified as the author of this
work has been asserted by him in accordance with the
Copyright, Designs and Patents Act 1988.

First published in Great Britain in 2013 by Gollancz
An imprint of the Orion Publishing Group
Orion House, 5 Upper St Martin's Lane, London WC2H 9EA
An Hachette UK Company

A CIP catalogue record for this book
is available from the British Library

ISBN 978 0 575 13208 5 (Cased)
ISBN 978 0 575 13209 2 (Export Trade Paperback)

1 3 5 7 9 10 8 6 4 2

Typeset by Deltatype Ltd, Birkenhead, Merseyside

Printed in Great Britain by Clays Ltd, St Ives plc

The Orion Publishing Group's policy is to use papers that
are natural, renewable and recyclable products and made from
wood grown in sustainable forests. The logging and manufacturing
processes are expected to conform to the environmental
regulations of the country of origin.

www.mitchbenn.com
www.orionbooks.co.uk
www.gollancz.co.uk

Hello

I'm a bit nervous right now.

As I write this it's April 2013, and publication of this book is still three months away. I finished writing it a year ago and I've just written the sequel. This means I've now spent over two years of my life working on a story that, at this moment, I still don't know if anyone will ever read ...

But now you're here.

So this book is dedicated, with gratitude, and not a little relief, to YOU, the reader. Whoever and wherever you are. Whether you're thumbing pages, cradling your eBook or just dawdling in a bookshop (in which case, do crack on and buy it, it gets better than this, and look, it's stopped raining).

You're the reason I wrote this and I am SO pleased to see you.

I've been on an interesting journey and it's not over yet.

Thanks for coming with me.

Mitch Benn

April 2013

- Before we begin, a note on notation:

'Dialogue presented as it is spoken will be rendered in the Anglo-American way, like this.'

- Dialogue that has been translated from the languages of the planet Fnrr will be presented italicised and in the Continental format, like this.

- Hope that's clear.

M x

PART ONE

When Worlds Collide

I.I

Mr and Mrs Bradbury had been married for six years, and neither of them could remember why.

Some married couples are lucky. They agree about everything. They like to do the same things and go to the same places. They have the same opinions and ideas. Their lives are peaceful and harmonious and they bring happiness to each other and all around them.

Mr and Mrs Bradbury were not one of these couples.

Many married couples disagree about lots of things. Sometimes these disagreements turn into arguments, and on occasion these arguments can become quite heated. But underneath it all, they love and care about each other enough to overlook the things they disagree about, or at least to find a compromise they can both be happy with.

Mr and Mrs Bradbury were not one of these couples either.

The Bradburys argued. All the time. About EVERY-THING.

They would argue about what to do, where to go, what to eat, what to wear, what to watch on TV, what words to use, what books to read, what to think about the books they read, whether to read books or watch TV, whether the TV was too loud or too quiet, the weather, whether or not the weather was what they wanted the weather to be, what they should want the weather to be whether or not the weather was whatever they'd wanted before ... Anything you could possibly argue about, they argued about. Even some things you couldn't argue about, or at least things that nobody had ever thought of arguing about. Once they had an argument over whether full-fat mayonnaise was better than 'light' mayonnaise which ended with Mr Bradbury slamming the fridge door right off its hinges and Mrs Bradbury chasing him into the street throwing eggs at him.

That's the kind of couple the Bradburys were.

You may know a couple like this. You probably spend a lot of time wondering: *Why do they stay together if they're always arguing?* The Bradburys' friends – a small and diminishing group, as you can imagine – used to ask themselves this question a lot. Some of them came to the conclusion that the Bradburys must like it that way; arguing all the time was the thing that made them happy. But it didn't seem to make them happy at all, and it certainly didn't make anyone else happy. So their friends abandoned this theory, and one by one they abandoned the Bradburys as well.

Then one of the Bradburys' few remaining friends gave Mrs Bradbury an idea. They'd met one afternoon in the supermarket – quite by chance; people didn't tend to choose to spend time with the Bradburys. 'Have you ever thought about a baby?' Mrs Bradbury's friend asked her. 'Babies bring love and harmony to a family. Trust me, if you have a baby all your arguments will seem so unimportant. Having a baby will bring you closer together.'

Mrs Bradbury mentioned this conversation to her husband in a rare moment of domestic truce, and they considered the idea. They had always thought it might be nice to have a baby (this was one of the few things they'd ever agreed on) and the more they thought about it, the more it did seem that having a baby would indeed help them to stop arguing.

It didn't.

It gave them a whole new fascinating range of things to argue about.

When the baby was growing inside Mrs Bradbury they would argue about whether they wanted a boy or a girl. They argued about which doctor to visit for advice, and when they'd decided upon one, they argued about whether his advice was any good. They argued about which room of the house should become the nursery, and about what sort of cot to buy. As the baby took up more and more space inside Mrs Bradbury she would complain to Mr Bradbury about how tired she was and how he wasn't helping enough, and Mr Bradbury would retort that he was sorry he was at work all the time but SOMEBODY had to go and make some money, and so on and so on.

When it was time for the baby to be born, they argued about whether to have the baby at home or in a hospital, and even after their baby arrived – a beautiful baby girl, by the way – they argued over whether Mr Bradbury was holding her the right way, or if Mrs Bradbury was feeding her enough, or feeding her the right things, or enough of the right things, or feeding her the right things the wrong way, or whether Mr Bradbury was burping her properly, or hard enough, or too hard, or often enough, or too hard too often.

Their bitterest arguments were over what to call the baby. Mr Bradbury wanted to call her Jasmine – he'd had a cat called Jasmine when he was a little boy and he'd always liked the name – but Mrs Bradbury said that was disgusting, you couldn't name a baby after a cat, and anyway she wanted to name the baby Agatha after her grandmother, and Mr Bradbury said that was a ridiculous name for a baby, you couldn't be called Agatha unless you were at least sixty years old with white hair, pointy glasses and a fierce little dog. So it was that three weeks after their little girl was born, she still had no name.

What a sweet-natured little baby girl she was. While her parents frothed and fumed at each other high above her, this tiny girl with no name would lie back in her little bouncy chair gazing up at them with huge blinking blue eyes and a look of quiet wonder on her face, then she would smack her tiny lips, close her eyes and go back to sleep. She was indeed bringing love and harmony to her family, but her parents were too busy arguing to notice.

One evening Mrs Bradbury was having difficulty getting

the baby to sleep. She was trying to remember a lullaby to sing, but all the ones she could think of began with something like 'Hush little …' followed by the baby's name, and Mrs Bradbury's baby didn't yet have a name. Mrs Bradbury could, of course, have just sung 'hush little baby' but the fact that she and her husband couldn't even agree on their child's name made her feel silly and embarrassed, and she didn't enjoy being reminded of it. So the poor baby cried on until suddenly, to her own surprise, Mrs Bradbury began to sing a song neither she – nor anyone else – had ever heard:

'Do not cry
Do not weep
Floating gently off to sleep
You are loved and safe from harm
Sleeping sound in Mummy's arms.'

Mrs Bradbury was so taken aback by the simple beauty of the song – and by how well she'd sung it (she'd never sung like that before) – that it took her a moment to notice that her baby was now sound asleep. Perhaps, she thought, as she placed the quietly snoring baby back in the basket beside her own bed (she was still too tiny to sleep in the cot they'd bought), she was going to be quite a good mother after all. From the next room, Mr Bradbury shouted to keep that noise down because he couldn't hear the TV.

Then came the night the Bradburys stopped arguing for ever.

They had spent the day at Mrs Bradbury's mother's house. The visit had started awkwardly with Mrs Bradbury's announcement that the baby would not now be named Agatha after Grandma after all, which she had said while casting a fierce look at Mr Bradbury, and things only got worse from there. By the time they said a terse goodbye to Mrs Bradbury's mother, strapped their nameless baby girl into her very expensive car seat (oh, the arguments they'd had over buying *that*) and set off for home, both Mr and Mrs Bradbury were vibrating with bottled-up rage.

Mr Bradbury started things off by accusing Mrs Bradbury of ruining everything before they'd even sat down by dropping the whole not-naming-the-baby-Agatha bombshell, whereupon Mrs Bradbury countered that it wasn't her fault that her mother was disappointed, and Mr Bradbury said that Mrs Bradbury's mother was always disappointed, mainly with him, he knew she'd never liked him, and Mrs Bradbury told Mr Bradbury that her mother didn't dislike him, he just never gave her a chance, and Mr Bradbury said that was a bit rich coming from her, she never gave anybody a chance, it was no wonder they had hardly any friends, and now look you've made the baby cry with all your shouting, and Mrs Bradbury said that no, it was Mr Bradbury who'd made the baby cry by driving too fast ...

At that moment, everything changed.

I.2

Someone else who didn't have many friends was on the same road as the Bradburys that night. His name was Lbbp, and he was a long, long, long, LONG way from home.

Lbbp's home was a small but comfortable apartment in a very tall cone-shaped building in a busy district of the great city of Hrrng, on the beautiful island of Mlml on the distant orange-green planet of Fnrr. If you have a very very very powerful telescope and you point it at the space between the second and third stars on Orion's Belt on a very clear summer's night, you still won't be able to see the distant orange-green planet of Fnrr. It's pretty distant.

Lbbp didn't have many friends because he was very busy. He had little time to pay attention to the few friends he had and certainly no time to make new ones. The thing that kept Lbbp so busy was his work. Lbbp loved his work, and, though he was too modest to say so, he was very good at it.

Lbbp was a scientist. On our world he would have been called a biologist. Lbbp was fascinated by living things. All his life he had studied the plants and animals of his own world; going on surveys and expeditions, conducting experiments, writing books and essays until at last he became one of the few scientists on Fnrr permitted to study the plants and animals of other worlds. And of all the worlds he had ever visited, by far his favourite was the one known in the clipped, clickety language of Fnrr as *Rrth*.

Lbbp loved Rrth. It had some of the most beautiful plants and fascinating animals of any of the hundreds of worlds Fnrr's scientists had surveyed, but there were rules

8

to be followed when visiting Rrth. In particular, it was strictly forbidden for a Fnrrn to have any contact with the dominant species of Rrth, the strange and noisy bipedal primates known as Ymns.

Ymns, it had been decided, were simply too stupid and primitive to be bothered with. Even when they weren't fighting each other or making a disgusting mess all over the nicest bits of their own planet, they seemed to spend a lot of time smashing into each other in those funny little land vehicles they whizzed round in (but didn't seem to be very good at controlling). Given the chaos that Ymns already caused with the simple, clumsy machines that they'd thus far managed to invent for themselves, the damage they could do to their planet – or, far worse, to other people's planets – if they ever got hold of any proper technology did not bear contemplation. They were off-limits. To everyone.

Besides, as the Fnrrns knew from watching the episodes from Rrth history the Ymns told each other on their picture screens, any time someone from another planet did visit the Ymns it didn't go very well. Either the visitors would start killing and enslaving the Ymns in their millions, or the Ymns would invent some new weapon and blow the visitors up with it. Usually both.

Lbbp had his own reasons for distrusting the Ymns. Over a number of visits to Rrth he had studied and catalogued many fascinating life forms; towering trees, dazzling blooms, magnificent beasts and beautiful delicate flying creatures. It saddened and angered him that every time he returned he would find another species gone, another vast area of natural beauty ripped up and destroyed to make way for the Ymns and their nasty square buildings and ridiculous little vehicles, or just blasted bare and left barren for reasons Lbbp couldn't begin to guess at.

Lbbp was careful never to express these feelings to his colleagues at the Hrrng Preceptorate, the vast teaching and learning establishment in his home city where he held the post of Postulator. As a scientist he was supposed to be cool and objective in his studies and writings. Still, Lbbp couldn't help but feel that the Ymns didn't deserve such a planet as Rrth. Or at least that Rrth deserved better inhabitants than the Ymns.

In any event, the rule was that any Fnrrn spaceship entering Rrth's atmosphere had to have its invisibility shield switched on at all times, to avoid attracting unwanted Ymn attention.

Most Fnrrn scientific expeditions to Rrth would consist of a group of five or six scientists, but Lbbp liked to go alone. He enjoyed his own company and there wasn't much room for anyone else in his little lemon-shaped spaceship. Lbbp was proud of his little lemon-shaped spaceship, although, since they don't have lemons on Fnrr, as far as he was concerned it was just spaceship-shaped. In fact, the first time he'd seen lemons, on an earlier visit to Rrth, he'd logged them in his field journal as 'small yellow spaceship-shaped fruits'.

On this evening, the evening of the Bradburys' uncomfortable day at Mrs Bradbury's mother's house, Lbbp's little spaceship was hovering invisibly over what, in the darkness, looked to Lbbp like a dried-out river bed. Since there aren't many roads on Fnrr (not since they invented gravity bubbles) and since Lbbp tried not to pay much attention to the Ymns or their little land vehicles (it just got him tense and angry, and that didn't help him work) he didn't really know what roads were or how to recognise them. If he had, he might not have been content to let his little spaceship hover just a few metres above the surface of one.

Right now, Lbbp's mind wasn't on Ymns or their vehicles anyway. His attention was fixed upon the fascinating little Rrth animal his ship's life-detectors had picked up a few minutes earlier. It was about the size of a small ksks (a Fnrr fruit which tastes almost nothing whatsoever like a melon) with soft grey fur, a twitchy little nose and two long furry flaps sticking straight up from the top of its head. Lbbp was transfixed by these flaps. Were they ears? Lbbp found ears particularly interesting, not having any himself, and he'd never seen such amazing ears before. The animal must have incredible powers of hearing, he thought. Lbbp was just noting in his field journal that the animal's superior hearing must help it to evade predators with ease, and that, as such, it probably had very few offspring to prevent over-population, when the little animal started suddenly, flattening its ears to its head. Had the animal sensed his presence? Nervously, Lbbp glanced at the switch controlling the ship's invisibility shield. Relieved to see that it was still in the 'on' position he gave it a comforting pat with a long, grey four-fingered hand. A comforting, clumsy, ever so slightly just a bit too hard pat. Just hard enough to switch the invisibility shield off.

Had Lbbp's attention not been so fixed on the ksks-sized big-eared animal, he might have noticed the Ymn land vehicle speeding towards his ship from the other direction. But as the ship's instruments started making angry chirping noises at him, he definitely did notice it. Moreover, he realised with a sick feeling in his chest (where his stomach was), the vehicle's Ymn occupants would notice him too.

Mrs Bradbury finished accusing her husband of making the baby cry by driving too fast, and was just turning round in her seat to check on the baby, when she heard Mr Bradbury screaming. A high-pitched scream of terror she'd never heard him make before. Turning back around, she saw what he was screaming at, and started screaming too.

Hovering impossibly a few metres above the road ahead was a huge lemon-shaped object. It seemed to crackle with a mysterious energy and bright light glared out from the many little windows along its surface. One beam shone fiercely through the car's windscreen, blinding the Bradburys. Mr Bradbury, still screaming, slammed his foot on the brake and wrenched the steering wheel to the right. Mrs Bradbury clutched at Mr Bradbury in panic, succeeding only in putting one hand over his eyes while grabbing the steering wheel with the other, pulling it to the left. The car, very confused now, went into a flat skid, turning through a complete rotation as it passed under the hovering lemon thing, with Mr and Mrs Bradbury in the front seats clawing at each other and screaming all the way.

In the back seat, their baby girl had now stopped crying, but it was impossible to tell.

The car continued to turn, passing through another half rotation before sliding sideways off the road and into a field, coming to a bumpy halt in the long grass. Immediately the front doors of the car flew open, and Mr and Mrs Bradbury leapt out and ran, ran away across the field as fast as they could, screaming, screaming and never casting a look behind them.

Lbbp crawled out from beneath the control console and, rather pointlessly now, switched the invisibility shield back on.

He peered into the darkness, in the direction in which the two Ymns (Lbbp assumed they were Ymns) had disappeared. There was no sign of them; even his ship's life detectors couldn't pick them up. Lbbp wondered why Ymns needed those vehicles at all if they could move that fast on their own.

He refocused the life detectors back on the spot where the small furry animal had been. To his annoyance, but no great surprise, it had gone. Just as he was about to shut down the life detectors and set off back into space (it occurred to him that the two fast Ymns might have been running to alert the Ymn authorities, and this meant it was time to leave) the life detectors made a faint pip-pip sound.

What had they found?

Pip-pip.

A small reading, no bigger than the furry little animal, but why such a faint trace?

Pip p-pip pip.

The signal was muffled, as if the life-form was being shielded by something, but there was nothing he could see that would—

P-pip pip pip-pip.

The vehicle. Something was still inside the vehicle.

Lbbp's mind whirred into action. On the one hand, that was a Ymn vehicle, contact with Ymns was prohibited … on the other hand, he hadn't become one of Fnrr's leading scientists by denying his curiosity, and those two fast Ymns didn't look as if they were going to come back in the near future …

This is a really bad idea, thought Lbbp as he engaged the gravity beam. *I shouldn't be doing this,* he thought as he stepped into the gravity beam. *I could get into all sorts of trouble,* he thought as he descended through the floor of the spaceship. *Oh well, too late now,* he concluded as his feet touched the ground.

If anyone had been around, they would have seen a shaft of bright light appear out of nowhere, and then a tall thin figure with a large bald grey head, large shiny black eyes and a lipless mouth, clad in a shimmering blue one-piece garment, sliding down this beam to the ground almost like a child on a playground slide. So it's just as well that no one was around, as Lbbp confirmed with a quick sweep of his hand-held field-scanner. No one except whatever was inside the vehicle.

Lbbp had to bend low to peer through the vehicle's windows. He was marvelling at the huge, clumsy-looking controls when a tiny noise from the back of the vehicle caught his attention. Turning, he saw – what was it? A small, almost hairless creature staring back at him with large, blinking blue eyes. Lbbp experienced a moment's anxiety as he noticed that the creature was bound securely in its seat by means of firm-looking restraints. Odd; it certainly didn't look dangerous to him. Its tiny hands had only the merest suggestion of claws, far too small and blunt to do any damage, and, as it suddenly opened its mouth wide, he could see that it had no teeth at all. A wave of Lbbp's field-scanner confirmed that the creature's limbs weren't even strong enough for it to stand up unaided, never mind attack anything.

Lbbp realised what he was looking at. It was a Ymn infant, probably the offspring of the two Ymns who had fled. Lbbp felt a surge of concern and indignation at the tiny Ymn's plight. It was just a newborn; their newborn, and not only had they lashed it in restraints like a dangerous animal, they'd abandoned it to its fate at the first hint of peril. Lbbp was angry; it was true what they said on Fnrr. Ymns were indeed foolish, brutal savages. They couldn't care for their planet, they couldn't care for each other and now it was clear they didn't even care for their own children. They were disgusting.

And yet … this tiny Ymn didn't seem capable of brutality or savagery as it sat in its little chair, peering at him. Seeing it now, in its newborn innocence … Was it really destined to grow up to be as stupid and unthinking as the rest of its species? Ymns had a basic intelligence, this was well understood. You needed at least a degree of intelligence to mess things up as completely as Ymns did.

It deserved better than this, Lbbp thought. It deserved to be raised by someone civilised, someone who would give it an understanding of the true value of things, someone who could show it the wonders of the universe and who would never EVER leave it to perish, helpless and alone, someone …

Lbbp suddenly saw where this train of thought was leading him. *Don't be ridiculous,* he thought, *it'd be dangerous, it'd be impractical, unethical, really REALLY illegal, it'd …*

The little Ymn made a contented gurgling sound and reached out to Lbbp with a chubby pink hand. Without thinking about it, Lbbp reached out his own hand. The little Ymn grabbed his outstretched finger.

As the five tiny pink digits squeezed his long thin grey finger, Lbbp knew what he had to do.

* * *

Neither Mr nor Mrs Bradbury were especially fit, and running is hard work even when you're not screaming at the top of your lungs. Nonetheless, they covered quite a considerable distance before they simply had to stop to get their breath back.

Once they had their breath back, naturally they started arguing with it. Strangely, given that this was the last argument Mr and Mrs Bradbury would ever have, it began much the same way as all their others: why did you grab the steering wheel; I had to, you had your eyes closed; I didn't have my eyes closed, you had your hand over my face; I told you you should have let me drive, and anyway what have you done with the baby; what do you mean what have I done with the baby, you've got the baby, no you've got the baby, no you've got—

A moment's silence.

A moment's silence in which the sheer unimportance, the utter trivial pointlessness of this argument and every argument they'd ever had hit them like a dozen buckets of icy water, and all their anger disappeared, to be replaced by a dread that clutched at their insides like a cold hand.

Without another word to each other, the Bradburys ran. Back the way they'd come, back towards the danger they'd just fled, unaware now of tiredness or breathlessness, unaware of anything except the wet grass dragging against their legs and the freezing dread clenching ever tighter in their guts. They ran and ran, without a sound except a whispered please please please please as they went.

As they approached the road there was no sign of the floating lemon thing, nor was there any sound except their own footsteps and panting. No traffic noises. No animal sounds. No baby crying.

They saw the car. They saw that its lights were still on. They saw that its front doors were still open. Its back door was open too.

They looked into the car. They saw their bags. They saw their coats. They saw the highly expensive, and quite empty, baby seat.

For a second they stared at the baby seat, still and

wordless. Then a sound came from inside Mrs Bradbury, a howl, a wail, a great animal bellow of horror and despair. Mr Bradbury stood motionless, his mouth moving silently, his eyes reddening. Then they fell like stringless puppets into each other's arms and cried, and cried, and cried as if they would never stop. They cried for their own foolishness and for the baby they'd been too busy to name, who was now gone, they knew with a terrible, terrible certainty, somewhere they would never ever find her.

Mr and Mrs Bradbury never argued about anything ever again.

I.3

This is going to be complicated, thought Lbbp as he studied the small pink wriggly creature in his arms. Rrth – and anyone who might have been able to offer him any practical Ymn child-care advice – had already faded from the little spaceship's screens. The ship was equipped to transport live specimens; its internal scanners had immediately gone to work analysing the Ymn infant's anatomy and nutritional systems, and its automated chemical lab was now busily synthesising a gloopy yellowish liquid which, it had determined, would best sustain the little newcomer.

Very complicated, thought Lbbp. *Very complicated indeed.* Then the Ymn infant smiled up at Lbbp with such a trusting, innocent expression that Lbbp suddenly felt that maybe everything would be simple and easy after all. Then a sudden look of furious concentration passed across the little face, and, as a noxious smell drifted through the ship's hitherto sterile internal atmosphere, Lbbp realised that everything had just become extremely complicated. He put it – or since the ship's scanners had already determined the child to be female, rather he put HER – into a small clear tank he'd found under the console (it had been used to carry plant specimens back on his last visit; he'd been relieved to see that he'd remembered to clean it) and began rummaging through his ship's first aid box for wiping and wrapping materials. Having found some sterilising cloths and bandages, he steeled himself, and set about unfastening the Ymn infant's clothing.

Oh dear, thought Lbbp. *Oh dear dear me.*

The Ymn child smiled up at him. Lbbp held his breath and got on with the task at hand. He caught a glimpse of a readout on the forward wall of the spaceship giving an estimated time for the journey back to Fnrr, back to his home, back to the Preceptorate.

I'm going to have a lot of explaining to do, thought Lbbp.

I.4

- You have a lot of explaining to do, Postulator Lbbp.

The voice was that of Preceptor Shm, head of Hrrng Preceptorate. It echoed around the shining quartz walls of the Preceptorate's main conference chamber, to which Lbbp had been rather ominously summoned.

His return had, at first, gone unnoticed. Everyone at the Preceptorate knew about Lbbp's fondness for Rrth and its various life-forms, so the news that he was coming back with a new live specimen didn't raise much interest. It was only when – as was required – he brought the specimen to the Life Science Hub to have it catalogued and registered that alarm bells began ringing. Literally.

They weren't bells so much as high-pitched pinging sounds, but they did start almost as soon as Lbbp entered the building carrying the strange pink creature in his long thin arms. The first of Lbbp's colleagues to notice the bundle thought it was a Fnrrn baby, which caused a small ripple of intrigue, as everyone knew Lbbp lived alone and had no children. (Fnrrns, like humans, come in male and female varieties and they get together to have children much as humans do. It's actually quite a common way of doing things in the universe.)

It was only when they came to get a closer look at the infant – and perhaps ask where it had come from – that they noticed the pink skin, the wisps of hair, the curious protrusion in the middle of the face and those odd little flaps on the side of the head. Lbbp never found out which of his 'friends' had been first to press the alarm button (it was more of a paddle than a button, but it did the trick) but soon the usually serenely peaceful building was resounding to the high-pitched pinging noise and the whooshing and clanking of metallic doors and crystal windows sealing shut. The Life Science Hub had quarantined itself.

Uniformed security guards, who had they been humans back on Earth would probably have been wearing black but were instead dressed all in orange (Fnrrns find orange a very intimidating colour, whereas black, being the colour of night, strikes them as restful and calming), appeared from all corners of the building and surrounded Lbbp and his bundle.

- *Don't move!*

- *She's harmless!* shouted Lbbp.

- *What is?* said one guard.

- *The thing he's holding is, or so he says,* said another. *He called it a 'she'.*

- *Doesn't look like a she to me,* said a third. *Definitely an 'it'.*

- *She's a Ymn infant! She's under my care!* insisted Lbbp.

- *Well, whatever it is, hand it over,* said the biggest of the guards.

There was a pause.

- *Who to?* asked Lbbp. None of the guards had attempted to take the baby, or even come close enough to try.

- *You. Grab it,* said the big guard to one of the others.

- *YOU grab it, I'm not touching it,* came the reply.

- *Or me,* said another. *It might be bitey or stingy or something.*

The baby gurgled contentedly in Lbbp's arms.

- *We are not trained to handle dangerous alien specimens!* pointed out the littlest of the guards.

- *Or paid enough,* observed the one next to him. The biggest guard decided to take charge.

- *RIGHT,* he said. *You* (pointing at Lbbp) *come with us and bring that whatever-it-is with you. And the rest of you, get behind me if you're scared.*

Lbbp did as he was told, and so did the other guards, much to the biggest guard's disgust.

After a brief and, Lbbp thought, unnecessarily rough

medical examination which established that neither he nor the baby were carrying any dangerous contaminating agents, they were locked in a small waiting room while, Lbbp imagined, various authorities were informed and consulted as to what to do next.

Lbbp reached into his bag for a bottle of the gloopy yellow liquid. He fixed a small flexible nozzle over the cap and began to feed the baby.

- *We're in trouble now,* he said. *I only wonder how much ...*

The baby sucked away happily.

1.5

- You have a lot of explaining to do, Postulator Lbbp. Your actions have placed your academic future and possibly your liberty in jeopardy. Perhaps even the welfare of this whole institution.

Preceptor Shm's voice was full of sadness and concern rather than anger. Lbbp had known and admired him since his days as a student at the Preceptorate. He was wise, fair, and utterly devoted both to the Preceptorate and to science and learning in general. The thought that Lbbp might have endangered the Preceptorate itself had not occurred to him before now; upon hearing the Preceptor's words he lowered his eyes in shame.

Lbbp was seated on a small raised platform in the centre of the high-domed chamber; Shm, dressed in the long purple gown that many Preceptors had worn before him, was seated opposite him in the first rank of a raked bank of seats, arranged in semicircular rows. In these seats sat the Academic Council; the heads of all the various departments and Lycea of the Preceptorate. As Lbbp glanced up at them, they seemed to be having a frowning competition. He looked down at the floor once more as Shm went on:

- Still, you have always shown respect for the principles and tenets of science. It may be that you have your reasons for doing this. Whatever those reasons may be, it is time to share them with this council.

- Reasons! snorted another voice, from behind Shm. This was Compositor Vstj, who now rose to his feet.

- Postulator Lbbp, the purpose of this extraordinary meeting of the council was to read a list of the many violations and infractions of the Academic Code you have incurred by

bringing this ... thing onto the premises, but frankly we got up to twenty-six and stopped counting. Have you quite lost your mind, Postulator Lbbp?

Compositor Vstj was also an old acquaintance of Lbbp's. They had been students together at the Preceptorate many orbits previously. Lbbp had been something of a star pupil in his day; he'd won many prizes and awards and had graduated with one of the highest grades that the Science Lyceum had ever recorded. By contrast, Vstj's academic career had been undistinguished, but he still succeeded in rising to the post of Compositor – a senior administrative position – after graduating. The fact that Vstj came from a well-connected family who had given many generous donations to the Preceptorate over the orbits – exceedingly generous in the time leading up to his appointment, in fact – had played no part whatsoever in his success in landing the job, and no one present in the council chamber would be so spiteful or petty as to claim otherwise. It hadn't done him any harm, though. Vstj spoke on:

- Article 22.4 of the Academic Code explicitly prohibits contact with species number 676, otherwise known as 'Ymns'. Now I'll grant you that 'contact' is a rather vague and general term, Postulator, but I think most would understand it to include, say, abducting a Ymn infant and proposing to raise it as one's own child, wouldn't you agree?

Shm motioned to Vstj to be silent and then went on wearily:

- Postulator. This Preceptorate – this COUNCIL – is the most influential body in the whole nation of Mlml. Far more so than the government itself. The people understand that politicians will always be petty, shallow and emotional, but they look to us – the thinkers, the teachers – to be calm, rational, scientific. Time and time again, when elections are held, we see that the politicians that the people favour with their votes are precisely the ones they trust to follow our recommendations most faithfully and competently! Do you have any concept of the damage that could be done were it to be known that a senior member of

this institution had done something so impetuous, so capricious, so — oh, what's the word . . . ?

- *Stupid?*

- *Yes, stupid, thank you, Compositor — as to bring into this very building a member of a species with which not only has formal contact never been established but whose very presence on this planet is interdicted by academic AND civil law?*

- *She would have died,* objected Lbbp weakly. He was immediately annoyed by how whiny his voice sounded as it echoed around the chamber.

- *Oh, well, that changes everything.* Vstj's voice oozed sarcasm. *In that case, you should consider yourself at liberty to drag home every creature in the galaxy which you happen to find in a spot of trouble. That shouldn't cause much disruption once we've converted half the country into your own private petting zoo and destroyed the ecosystem!*

- *Silence, Vstj.* Shm closed his big black eyes and rubbed his temples with his long fingers. Fnrrn brains are nearly twice the size of human brains so when they get a head-ache, they really get a headache.

- *Stand up, Postulator Lbbp.* Lbbp did so and swallowed. The baby made no sound.

The council members had been making notes all this time on small crystal slates. They now submitted individual judgements on Lbbp's case which were compiled instantly by the Extrapolator, the Preceptorate's main computer, producing an overall 'verdict' which was relayed to Shm's own slate. He read from it in an expressionless voice.

- *It is the decision of this council that Postulator Lbbp be stripped of the position of Postulator and re-designated Dis-seminator.*

- *Would have demoted him to Ponderer myself,* muttered Vstj.

- *It is further decided that the Ymn specimen be placed into indefinite biostasis.*

Lbbp gasped. Biostasis meant the baby would be biologically 'frozen' – all her vital systems locked and unchanging for ever. She would never die, but she would never truly live again. He clutched her tightly to his chest.

- *No! Please! I'll take her back! I'll take her back to her own people! I'll find a way of getting her back! The Ymns needn't know about us!* Lbbp looked around himself in panic. Orange-clad guards were entering the chamber and advancing towards him.

- *I'm sorry, Lbbp,* said Shm and sat back down.

Suddenly, there was a chiming sound, like that of a great glass bell. Not many in that chamber had heard the sound before. Those who had, the oldest members of the council, were struck silent for a moment, then turned to their companions and explained what was happening, and soon everyone understood, though few could believe it.

The Extrapolator was intervening. The Extrapolator had something to say.

1.6

The Extrapolator was the biggest and most powerful computer on the planet Fnrr. In fact, as far as it or anything else on Fnrr was aware, it was the most powerful computer anywhere in the galaxy, and had there been a more powerful computer elsewhere in the galaxy, the Extrapolator would have known about it.

The Extrapolator was almost as old as the Preceptorate itself; beginning life as a simple electronic data retrieval system, it had been expanded and developed, having been rebuilt and rehoused countless times (generally according to its own designs) until it was now the single biggest repository of information anywhere. It was connected to every system on the planet; all information that passed through any computer or other device on Fnrr also passed through the Extrapolator's vast artificial brain. This information was collated, compiled and cross-referenced to give the Extrapolator the most complete picture of events, past, present – and even future. So total was its command of all known facts that it was capable of extrapolating (hence its name) all possible outcomes, predicting the future with almost total accuracy.

Since one of the facts of which the Extrapolator was aware was that it's generally not a good idea for simple life-forms (such as Ymns and indeed Fnrrns) to know too much about their own future, it was careful to ration this knowledge. From time to time, the leaders of Mlml society (and even, on occasion, leaders from the other nations of Fnrr) would consult the Extrapolator for advice on the wisest course of action. It was far, far more unusual for the Extrapolator to take it upon itself to intervene in Fnrrn affairs and steer events in a specific way, but that – to the consternation of the Academic Council – was exactly what was happening right now.

- *Silence, all of you.* Preceptor Shm's voice was stern and commanding. He touched his slate and the chiming noise ceased.

There was a tense hush as Shm read his slate. The guards who had been about to seize Lbbp and the baby kept their distance, but didn't take their eyes off them.

From its current home in a bunker hundreds of metres below the Preceptorate, the Extrapolator relayed its recommendations to Shm's slate. Shm studied them and then said in a voice devoid of emotion:

- *Postulator Lbbp is to remain in his present position* (a gasp went around the chamber, most audibly from Vstj); *the Ymn child is to be placed in his custody until further notice. It is to be raised as if it were a Fnrrn child and accorded the same rights and protections granted to all our children.*

The guards backed away. Lbbp wanted to flee but found he couldn't move.

- *That concludes this session*, said Shm. *Thank you.*

The council members filed out, muttering excitedly. An exasperated – *But ... But ...* was heard coming from Vstj as his colleagues ushered him away.

Shm strode over to Lbbp as the guards returned to their posts.

- *She's all yours, Postulator. I'd say I hope you know what you're doing but it's obvious that you don't. Still, it seems the Extrapolator knows something unknown to you or me. That's its job, after all.*

- *I suppose so*, murmured Lbbp.

Shm peered down at the baby with his huge black eyes. She gazed up at him with her little blue ones. Shm grunted.

- *You're going to need help, that's for certain. Don't be too proud to ask for it.*

- *Yes, Preceptor. I mean no, Preceptor. Thank you, Preceptor.* Lbbp turned to go.

- *Lbbp* …

Lbbp stopped. He couldn't remember the Preceptor addressing him just by his name before.

- *We've all done and said things we've come to regret in time*, said Shm. *Just be careful you don't try to make up for a minor misjudgement by committing a major one.*

Shm turned and left. Lbbp was alone in the chamber. It had never felt so huge, empty and cold. The gleaming white walls themselves seemed to be gazing at him in disapproval.

The baby gurgled. Lbbp looked down at her and felt much better.

- *Let's go home*, he said.

I.7

That evening, Lbbp was in the main room of his small but comfortable apartment, sat on a smooth bench seat, cradling the baby in his long thin arms and feeding her another bottle of gloop when his windowbell sounded. He said - *yes?* and the tinted window pane faded to transparency, revealing his friend and co-worker Bsht hovering outside his window, hundreds of metres above the ground.

- *It's not too late, is it?* she asked. The sky behind her had dimmed to its usual evening colours of russet orange and deep red. Three of Fnrr's ring of six moons shone with a yellowish glow above the cones and spires of the Hrrng skyline.

- *No, no, come on in,* replied Lbbp, and the crystal pane slid aside.

Bsht glided to the window ledge; there was a shimmer as she deactivated her gravity bubble and she stepped neatly into the room.

- *How is she?*

- *Sleepy, I think. I'm going to try to put her to bed once she's finished this.*

- *Bed?*

- *It's how they sleep. Lying flat on a padded surface. I tried her in a sleep-well but she made the most horrible noise until I took her out …*

Bsht sat beside Lbbp. On a low glass table in front of the bench seat sat a bowl of warm gssh – a soothing drink much favoured by Fnrrns to aid a restful night – and a reading slate. She picked it up and looked at the text and images displayed on the crystal surface.

- *What's this? Rrth customs and history?*

Lbbp wobbled his head slightly – a gesture roughly equivalent to a human shrug. - *She's going to have questions one day. Thought I'd start reading up on her people.*

Bsht scanned through the pages of information on the slate. It told of wars, violence and ignorance. She shuddered and put it down.

- *Do you think she'll understand? Why you did what you did?*

- *I'll do my best to explain,* said Lbbp, handing the baby to Bsht. Bsht studied the tiny pink face.

- *I suppose she is quite pretty when you get used to her. Does she have a name yet?*

Lbbp picked up the slate. - *I wanted to give her a Ymn name but they're nearly all unpronounceable. Then I came across this; it's an old name for Rrth in one of their ancient languages, and it's relatively easy to say . . .*

Lbbp pointed to a word on the slate.

- *T'r?* asked Bsht.

- *Terra,* said Lbbp. *I think I'll call her Terra.*

PART TWO

The Thing From Another World

2.1

Terra dreamed.

In Terra's dreams the sky was blue instead of its usual pink.

Great white shapes passed across the blue sky, obscuring a fierce yellow sun.

In Terra's dreams she was tiny, and content to be so. She would float through rows of towering blooms and shrubs, hearing voices from high above her. Sometimes the voices were soft, tinkly and soothing, but often they were grating and harsh.

Terra's dreams would always end the same way: colours, flashes of light and bursts of sound in darkness and silence, voices growing louder and harsher, a whirl of colours, a thin screeching sound, a blaze of light and a cold hard surface pressing against her face—

Terra's sleep-well had completed its deactivation sequence and lowered her to the floor of her room. She groaned, blinked and rubbed herself. She'd been using the sleep-well since she was two orbits old but she still didn't feel like she'd ever truly got the hang of it. In theory, the 4th Generation sleep-well, the latest word in domestic GravTech, would rouse the sleeper gently and gradually to full consciousness while releasing them from gravitational suspension, slowly returning them to wakefulness and weightfulness, leaving them refreshed and ready to face the day with renewed energy and focus. In practice, it generally crashed into Terra's dreams at their deepest point before depositing her face down, groggy and cross, onto the tiled floor.

Like almost everything else in Terra's world, the sleep-well hadn't been designed with her in mind.

* * *

Lbbp consulted the clock; it was mauve. Time to get moving.

He gripped the fattest tendril of the ndt plant and gave it a good squeeze. Fresh ndt juice gushed from the tendril into the bowl he held in his other hand. From behind him the protein manipulator beeped its readiness and dispensed two hot slices of configuration 6 onto a waiting hexagonal plate. Lbbp reset it for himself; he preferred configuration 11 in the morning, but 6 had been Terra's favourite since she'd been old enough for solid food. She'd want something familiar and comforting today, thought Lbbp. Big day, daunting day. Lbbp didn't envy her the prospect; he wished he could go in her place, but at least he could make her special breakfast.

He snapped the bowl magnetically to the side of the plate and carried them down the corridor to Terra's room. He stroked the door; it tinkled.

- *Are you awake?*
- *I think so ...*

The door slid away. Terra was sat in the middle of the floor, her long bronze-yellow hair covering her face. Lbbp had often contemplated shaving it all off, but it caught the light in such an appealing way, and it wasn't as if the hair was the only thing that made Terra stand out in a crowd.

She shook her hair back and stretched. Orange morning light streamed in through her window as it faded to complete transparency; it lit up her blue eyes and rosy skin. Lbbp knew that Terra's appearance startled many Fnrrns, but to him, at least, she was beautiful.

Terra stood up; her shiny blue garment smoothed itself out and began gently steaming her clean. She sniffed the air.

- *Number six!* she said happily.

- *Of course,* replied Lbbp, handing her the plate and bowl.

* * *

A little while later, Lbbp and Terra sat on the floor of her room, finishing their breakfast.

- *Do you have everything ready?* asked Lbbp.
- *Yes,* said Terra through a mouthful of configuration 6.
- *Slate all loaded up with the session one pre-sets?*
- *All loaded up. I got them from the Source last night.*
- *Are you nervous?*

Terra smiled. - *Not as nervous as you, I think.*

- *The Lyceum isn't just bigger than the Pre-Academy, you know ... It's a completely different experience. It can take a long time to adjust. It did for me ...*
- *It'll be okay. All my friends from the Pre-Ac are starting today as well, and Bsht will be there to look out for me ...*

Bsht, Lbbp's dear friend since his own days as a student, taught at the Lyceum. She'd been Terra's babysitter, protector and instructor all her life, and was the closest thing she had to a second parent. The thought of her presence was making the Lyceum a much less intimidating place. For Terra, anyway. It didn't seem to be helping Lbbp much.

- *Now, now, Bsht takes her responsibilities as lector far too seriously to give special treatment to anyone, even you,* he said, tidying away the plates and bowls. *If anything you might find she's stricter towards you by way of over-compensation. Even if she doesn't mean to be. There was this child when I was at the Lyceum whose mother ...*
- *Lbbp ... I'll be fine.*

Lbbp looked embarrassed for a moment, then his lipless mouth curled in a smile. Smiles, it turns out, are almost universal. - *I know. I know you will,* he said. *Now come along, the clock's almost violet.*

* * *

35

Terra tied her long hair back into what she would have called a pony tail back on Rrth, but she'd never seen a pony, and since hers was the only hairstyle on the planet, she hadn't ever felt the need to come up with a name for it. She packed her slate into a shiny fabric bag, slung it over one shoulder and stood at the window.

Lbbp tapped the window pane and it slid silently open. The air was crisp and bracing, the sky a clear pink, and orange sunlight glinted off the crystal and metal towers of the city. A beautiful Fnrrn morning.

- You remembered to charge up your bubble?

- When have I ever forgotten to charge up my bubble? Terra tapped the oval pod on her belt.

There's a knack to using a gravity bubble when taking off from a window. You have to activate the bubble at the exact moment you step off the ledge; too late and you get a moment's lurching drop followed by a nasty jolt; too soon and you can end up bobbing about on the ceiling. Terra had made both of these mistakes more than once, but now, at eight orbits old (just over eleven in Earth years) she had the procedure down to a fine art. She was about to touch the illuminated switch on the pod when Lbbp made a hurt little noise.

- I'm sorry . . .

She held up her hand; Lbbp touched his fingertips to hers.

- Always here, said Lbbp.

- Always here, smiled Terra.

Then she stepped off the ledge while activating her bubble in one smooth movement, and floated away towards her first day as a student of the Hrrng Preceptorate Junior Lyceum.

Lbbp watched the glittering sphere containing his pride and joy drift away into the morning. He shed no tears. He had no tear ducts.

2.2

Terra floated silently above the city in her bubble, joining streams of similar bubbles, which in turn gathered together to form rivers in the air, a great current of airborne bodies held aloft by the little gravity-nullifying devices on their belts. This was morning traffic in the great city of Hrrng, the shining capital of the peaceful island nation of Mlml.

To any other pair of human eyes, Fnrrns would look identical. The smooth grey skin, the large domed hairless heads, the black oval eyes, the short bodies and long slender limbs ... Terra had grown up among the Fnrrns. She saw the differences in skin tone, bone structure and demeanour; to Terra, every Fnrrn face was unique and distinctive. She recognised her friends in their own bubbles as they drifted alongside her. Here came Pktk, his brow wrinkled with worry. He'd been more scared than any of her friends at the prospect of moving up from the cosy Pre-Ac to the big bewildering Lyceum, and he didn't seem any less so now that the morning had arrived. Terra held up a hand with splayed fingers, the customary greeting gesture. Pktk's expression brightened a little as he returned it, a little too enthusiastically as it happens, causing his bubble to shift slightly to the right and bounce into the bubble of an older pupil, who didn't look happy to be returning to class and was even less happy to be boinged off course by a little newcomer. He corrected his trajectory and glowered at poor Pktk, whose facial expression now plummeted straight through worry and into fear.

Terra let out a little chuckle of sympathy at Pktk's plight, whereupon many heads turned towards her. She was briefly the centre of attention in the traffic flow. Terra's laugh was unlike that of her neighbours. They would laugh when something amused them, but their tight Fnrrn speech mechanisms produced only a hissing titter. Terra's Ymn throat produced a full tinkly laugh, and while her close friends had long since grown accustomed to it, other Fnrrns found it a strange, even alarming sound.

As the stream of bubbles drifted on, Terra heard excited whispers passing between travellers; - *That's the Ymn child;* - *I heard she was starting today;* - *Do you know what class she'll be in?* and thought little of it. She'd been hearing such murmurs all her life, and knew that they were caused by genuine, and inevitable, curiosity, rather than fear or mistrust. With one or two exceptions.

- *Don't pay them any attention. You'll be just fine.* The voice of Fthfth came from above and behind Terra. Fthfth deftly manoeuvred her bubble alongside Terra's and gave her a reassuring bounce.

- *I know I will!* said Terra, returning the bounce with a chuckle. Fthfth had been the Pre-Ac's star pupil and everyone expected her to perform with equal excellence at the Lyceum. She and Terra had been fast friends since their first days at the Pre-Ac; while some of the little Fnrrns had been disturbed by the presence of an alien in their midst, Fthfth had found it fascinating and challenging. Then as now, nothing motivated Fthfth like a challenge and no one was motivated by challenges like Fthfth. She'd made a special effort to befriend Terra and they'd become inseparable.

- *How was your break?* asked Terra. *Do anything fun?*

- *I've been practising gshkth with my father. I'm going to try for the team. What about you?*

Terra wasn't sure how to respond. She hadn't been much of a gshkth player at the Pre-Ac, and everyone knew that the gshkth they played at the Pre-Ac was just baby gshkth. At the Lyceum they played REAL gshkth, with a hard bdkt and proper gfrgs. She was mulling over her response when Fthfth pointed down and said excitedly - *Look! Tnk!*

Below them stood the statue of the great scientific pioneer and benefactor, Tnk. It had been Tnk, many eras before, who had cracked the secret of gravity manipulation, paving the way for the conquest of space and making everyone's morning commute considerably easier. Moreover, when the Mlml government and military had attempted to take control of his invention, he published all his findings on the Source, Fnrr's planet-wide information network, so that no nation or army would ever monopolise the technology to the detriment of their rivals. Rather than enrich and empower himself, he had chosen to enrich and empower the world. Mlml, and specifically the Preceptorate of Hrrng, became famous as the birthplace of GravTech, and after Tnk's death, a grateful populace had erected a great cobalt alloy statue of him in front of the Preceptorate's main atrium. There it stood, many orbits later, hovering approximately one metre above the ground.

Like a cloud of wind-borne seeds, the students drifted towards the Lyceum building, a twisting spiral horn-shaped tower in the middle of the Preceptorate complex. Light poured from open portals across its surface, and the students divided according to academic orbit, steering themselves towards the appropriate level of the tower. The senior students ascended towards the upper floors, the younger pupils towards the middle floors and Terra and her fellow novices swooped down to the lowest level.

Terra and Fthfth glided through the portal into a brightly lit chamber, deactivated their gravity bubbles and stepped gently to the floor. Pktk clipped the frame of the portal, ricocheted off the ceiling, bounced to the floor, accidentally switched his bubble off and skidded to a halt in a seated position at the feet of a tall female Fnrrn dressed in the grey garment of a lector.

- *Pktk, isn't it?* said Bsht.

- *Yes,* said Pktk quietly.

Bsht reached out a hand and helped Pktk to his feet.

- *I've heard so much about you.*

2.3

Terra and Fthfth exchanged excited glances and stifled giggles of delight. Since early childhood they'd heard so much about the wonders of the Preceptorate's council chamber that it had become something of a legend for them ... the way the daylight filtered through the high quartz ceiling, illuminating holographic portraits of Preceptors and Postulators from eras gone by ... the sense of calm and focus which was said to sharpen and clear your mind as soon as you passed through the doorway ... Now they, and all their classmates, were actually seeing it all with their own eyes, and they weren't a bit disappointed.

A few shades earlier, Bsht had checked all the new pupils' names on her slate as they arrived, then arranged them into a single line and led them out of the Lyceum building, across the courtyard, past the hovering statue of Tnk (- *Do NOT touch it, Pktk, there's a good boy.*) and towards the domed council chamber. Fthfth had been first in line, naturally, and Terra had been right behind her, their anticipation growing as they realised where they were headed.

Now the new pupils sat in the seats usually occupied by the council members, the curve of the rows directing their attention towards the centre of the chamber. As they watched, a round section of floor slid silently away, and a small circular stage rose up through the hole. On this stage stood Preceptor Shm, and three other distinguished-looking Fnrrns in ceremonial robes. The pupils burst into a chattering hiss, the Fnrrn equivalent to Ymn cheering.

- *Well, that was a bit unnecessary,* whispered Fthfth to Terra. *What's wrong with coming in through the door?*

- *Quiet!* giggled Terra.

- *Students* … began Preceptor Shm. *Today your world becomes just a little bit bigger, a little bit brighter, a little bit more exciting.*

Fthfth sat up straight in her seat. Pktk sank into his.

- *It also becomes a little harder and more demanding. We will ask much of you during your time here, and you must also demand much of us. Each and every one of you.*

At this, Shm's gaze swept along the rows of new pupils, as if he was trying to make eye contact with every one of them in turn. As his eyes met Terra's, he seemed momentarily taken aback. Then his expression relaxed. - *Of course,* he said quietly.

At this, one of the distinguished-looking Fnrrns behind Shm – the one in the green robe – fixed his eyes on Terra. Terra did her best to pay attention to the rest of Shm's speech – stuff about the common purpose of education, the virtues of hard work and co-operation, nothing particularly surprising – but the way this Fnrrn in the green robe stared at her made it impossible to concentrate. She was well used to being stared at – she'd been stared at all her life – but this was different.

- *Who is that?* she whispered to Fthfth. But Fthfth was listening intently to Preceptor Shm's speech, her face rapt with academic fervour. Whatever Shm had been saying, it was working on Fthfth.

At last Shm drew to a conclusion, something about *those values of excellence and diligence which have made this Preceptorate a beacon of* something or other … Terra guessed (entirely correctly) that this speech had been an inspiring piece of soaring rhetoric when Shm had first written and delivered it many orbits previously, but now it was just The Speech He Gave At The Beginning Of Every Session, and his weariness at trotting it out one more time was obvious. Nonetheless, his young audience and their lectors hissed appreciatively, and Bsht began marshalling her class for the walk back to the Lyceum.

Bsht led the pupils across the centre of the chamber, past the little round stage. Shm and his fellow dignitaries had not, much to Terra's disappointment, descended back through the floor after the speech but instead were now standing on the stage, deep in conversation with each other. As she passed the stage, she felt a tap on her shoulder. Turning, she saw the green-robed Fnrrn peering down at her with what might or might not have been a friendly smile.

- *You've been here before, you know.*

- *Excuse me?*

- *It is Terra, isn't it?*

Odd question, thought Terra. Unless there are a few more Ymn pupils here whose presence they're keeping a secret. Still, best be polite.

- *That's right.*

- *My, but you've grown. You must be eight orbits now?*

- *Er, yes,* said Terra, wondering where this was going.

- *I was here too, that day. The day your father brought you to us.*

Terra was about to say - *He's not my father* – Lbbp had been careful never to refer to himself as such – but something told her that this wasn't a conversation she wanted to have at that moment.

- *I'm sorry,* said the stranger. *My name is Vstj, I'm an old friend of your father.*

Terra began to suspect that this 'Vstj' had noticed her discomfort at hearing Lbbp referred to as her father and was now doing it on purpose. She said nothing and waited for him to continue.

- *Quite the scientist, your father. Always was, even when we were students. Are you going to be a scientist? Like your father?*

- *I don't know ...*

- *Experiments ...*

- *What?*

- *That's what they do, scientists. They conduct experiments. Sometimes the experiments work and sometimes they don't.*

- *I suppose . . .*

- *You know what scientists do when an experiment doesn't work?*

- *What do they do?*

- *They throw it away and start again.*

- *Terra! Come along!* Bsht and her classmates were waiting for Terra.

- *Sorry, but I've got to . . .*

- *Of course. Delighted to meet you properly at last, Terra. I'm sure we'll be seeing lots more of each other from now on.* With that, Vstj turned to speak with his distinguished colleagues, and Terra, unsettled, hurried to join her classmates.

* * *

- *Well, that's nonsense for a start,* Lbbp said later that evening. *Typical of Vstj, he never had any grasp of the scientific method. Experiments don't 'work' or 'not work'; sometimes they yield unexpected results but that's every bit as valid as . . .*

- *Lbbp, I don't think that's the point he was making.*

- *No, no, I shouldn't think it was.*

- *So what was he getting at?*

Lbbp sighed. - *Look, the thing to remember about Vstj, is he's . . . well, he's . . .*

- *What?*

- *He's a sh'znt,* said Lbbp. *He was a complete sh'znt when we were younger and he's an even bigger sh'znt now.*

- *Lbbp!* gasped Terra in alarm and delight. She'd never heard him use that sort of language.

- *Well, he is,* smiled Lbbp. *Forget him. How was the rest of your day?*

2.4

The rest of Terra's day had gone as follows:

After Preceptor Shm's address, Bsht led them out of the council chamber, across the square, past the hovering statue of Tnk (- *I said DON'T touch, Pktk, you'll ... Oh, now look*) into the Lyceum tower and back to the novice lectorium. Terra took her place in the front row of seats (she hadn't particularly wanted to sit at the front, but Fthfth had insisted) and clipped her slate into the arm of her chair.

The first spectrum had been spent on what Bsht called 'orientation'; basically a detailed description of the Lyceum's layout, which bits were and weren't off-limits, and the timetable of the coming session's classes. Terra was doing her best to take it all in, but she noticed that not only was all the information flashing up behind Bsht on the lectorium visualiser (a semi-intelligent display screen which monitored and illustrated the topics under discussion in the room), but also that the important bits were automatically loading themselves onto her slate as Bsht spoke. It didn't really matter if she didn't manage to memorise all of this as long as she didn't lose her slate, and there was no way she was going to lose her slate. NOBODY ever lost their slate. Not even Pktk lost his slate. Apart from that one time. And the other time.

After orientation came the morning interlude. The children walked (- *Don't run! There'll be plenty of space to run when you get outside*) out into a five-sided yard, where they spent a few shades playing hsk-hskt or tb-tb-tff, reading (Pktk) or organising their classmates into proper dfsh teams in order to play proper dfsh, properly (Fthfth). Terra played along; she quite enjoyed playing dfsh (it was much simpler than gshkth) but had to be careful; her denser Ymn bone and muscle structure both gave her an unfair advantage and made it more likely she'd accidentally injure someone ... There had been an 'incident' in her first orbit at Pre-Ac; no lasting damage and no real hard feelings but still a nasty experience for all concerned and an unpleasant memory for Terra (and, she imagined, a boy called Dv, if she remembered his name correctly).

A steady pinging noise signalled the end of interlude and the children filed back into the lectorium. The next session was to be given over to 'familiarisation'; Bsht called upon each pupil in turn to tell the class a bit about themselves and their family. Most of the pupils already knew each other from the Pre-Ac, but there were a few newcomers, and it was always nice to find things out about people. Some people more than others.

Fthfth had gone first; Bsht asked her because she was at the front of the class, and also because she was obviously so desperate to have her go that she wouldn't be able to sit still until she'd spoken, so Bsht knew it would be best to get her out of the way. Bsht was getting the hang of being a lector.

- *Hello, fellow students!* said Fthfth. *My name is Gkst-sh-Hbf-sh-Fthfth but you can call me Fthfth. I am eight orbits, three cycles and fifteen rotations old. My father's name is Knkt-sh-Dstnk-sh-Hbf and he is EXTREMELY clever. He is Director of Applied Science at the Hrrng GravTech Research Hub. My mother is called Hskth-sh-Fnl-sh-Gskt and she is EVEN CLEVERER. She is Chief of Cellular Surgery at Hrrng Nosocomium.*

- *Thank you, Fthfth. Now, would ...*

- *My favourite things to do are playing dfsh and gshkth and conducting experiments. When I grow up I want to be the first Fnrrn to demonstrate Thnrkl's Final Theorem and invent time travel.* Fthfth sat down.

There was a pause.

- *I've finished,* said Fthfth.

- *Thank you, Fthfth. Who would like to go next?*

Another pause.

- *Nobody? How about you, Pktk?*

Pktk had been having difficulty getting his slate into its slot. He was fiddling with it, a look of furious concentration on his face, when Bsht said his name. - *What?* he said, looking up suddenly and dropping his slate to the floor.

- *I'm ...* he began, reaching down for the slate, and finding his arm wasn't long enough.

- *I'm ...* he continued, trying to scoop the slate towards him with his foot and succeeding only in shoving it further away.

- *I'm ...* he said from beneath his chair as he reached under his neighbour's chair and retrieved the slate.

- *I'm P ...* he began, before sitting up too quickly, banging his head on the arm of his chair and dropping his slate again.

He sighed. - *I'm Pktk,* said Pktk quietly, sitting on the floor.

Bsht smiled. - *Yes, yes you are,* she said, helping Pktk to his feet.

A few more pupils took their turns to speak. The class listened politely to tales of mid-orbit breaks spent constructively in practising this or that game, visiting one or another site of natural or archaeological interest, reading some improving text ... For all their patient attention, there was a restlessness in the room. This wasn't what they wanted to hear.

At last, the moment they'd been waiting for.

- *Terra,* said Bsht. *Perhaps you'd like to tell the class a bit about yourself.*

An excited hush. Even those pupils who'd been with Terra at the Pre-Ac had never quizzed Terra directly about her background. They'd been far too polite, and those who hadn't been too polite had known to pretend to be too polite.

Terra stood up.

- *Well ...*

The room, already silent, became somehow more silent.

- *My name is Terra, and ...*

Silenter still.

- *... I'm not from around here.*

The class burst into a hiss of appreciative laughter. Terra smiled.

Terra gave them the short version – the stuff most of them knew already – Lbbp's discovery of her abandoned infant self, his brave decision to raise her as his own, the Preceptorate's sage benevolence in allowing him to do so ... The class listened appreciatively, and thus emboldened, Terra asked - *So, any questions?*

- *Do you eat animals?*

The mood of the room changed abruptly. The voice was that of Shnst, who, while at the Pre-Ac, had always sat at the back of the room next to her twin sister Thnst. They'd immediately staked their claim at the back row of this new lectorium and resumed their customary habit of muttering private jokes to each other. It was quite unusual for either of them to speak to anyone else; this and the indelicate nature of the question caused the atmosphere to thicken.

- *No*, said Terra after a moment's hesitation. *No, I eat the same things as every ...*

- *Because that's what Ymns do, isn't it? I read about it on the Source. They kill animals and eat their insides while they're still warm.*

- *No, no*, interrupted her sister. *They kill animals and then set FIRE to them, and eat the burnt bits.*

Uneasy glances passed between the pupils as quite a few stomachs turned over at the thought of this. Bsht decided to intervene.

- *Now, now, it was only a few eras ago that we Fnrrns ate animals as well; then we invented protein manipulators and we didn't have to any more.*

- *The G'grk still eat animals!* said Thnst, clearly warming to the topic.

- *The G'grk don't count as Fnrrns. They're barely better than animals themselves,* muttered Shnst.

This was greeted by murmurs of consensus, but not a consensus which made Bsht especially happy. - *Shnst,* she began, *that's hardly ...*

- *The G'grk could use protein manipulators if they wanted to, they just like killing things too much,* continued Shnst regardless. *They'd rather keep on living like savages.*

- *They wouldn't know how to use a protein manipulator even if they had one,* giggled Thnst. *They'd just grunt and stare at it then stab it and try to eat it.*

Everyone laughed now, except Terra and Bsht. Terra kept an intimidated silence. Bsht didn't.

- *The G'grk aren't dumb beasts, Thnst, and there may yet come a day when we would all do well to remember that.*

The lectorium fell quiet once more. Not a hush of anticipation this time but a queasy, fearful silence. Bsht went on.

- *Over the eras the G'grk have shown great ingenuity and organisation. It's just a shame that their culture still prizes war and conquest above other, nobler things.*

As Bsht spoke, the lectorium visualiser, registering the topic of conversation, began flashing up images and text illustrating the history of Fnrr's most bellicose civilisation.

While the other nations of Fnrr had long ago embraced reason and science as the foundations of society, the G'grk still clung to ancient codes of honour and bravery. They worshipped invisible overlords they called 'The Occluded Ones' and believed that domination of Fnrr – and elsewhere – had been promised to them as their inevitable destiny. The G'grk's homeland occupied the whole of the vast Central Plain of Chsk-Tshff, the continent from which Mlml was separated by a thin strip of ocean. They had conquered many surrounding nations over the eras, but their more recent attempts at expansion had been contained thanks to the superior technology of other nations' defences; the G'grk's rejection of science meant that such 'tech' as they possessed had been plundered from other countries, and as such they tended to use it rather inexpertly.

A shudder of fear passed through the rows of pupils as the image of the G'grk leader, Grand Marshal K'zsht, appeared. Old, scarred and war-painted, he clutched in his fist the ceremonial lance which served as the Grand Marshal's emblem of office. This lance was held to be so sacred that, once won (the G'grk's culture of conquest extended inwards into their own society as well as outwards; advancement came through duelling, challenges and sometimes straightforward assassination), the incumbent Grand Marshal would never let it out of his grasp, even in his sleep ... and given the process by which new Grand Marshals were often 'appointed', sleeping with a weapon in his hand was a practical as well as ceremonial necessity.

- *They belong in the past,* said Shnst angrily. *Hey, Fthfth, I hope you do invent time travel so we can send the filthy G'grk back to the pre-rational epoch where they belong ...*

- *Where they belong,* said Bsht, *is the Central Plain, and as long as they stay there they're none of our concern.*

- *They should stay where they belong,* said Shnst bitterly. *Why can't people stay where they belong?*

There was a chorus of horrified gasps. Even Shnst realised she'd said a dreadful thing and fell silent. All eyes turned to Terra, whose own eyes stayed fixed upon the visualiser. Fthfth discreetly put her hand over Terra's.

- *I'm okay,* whispered Terra.

- *Terra, I'm ...* began Shnst ... *I'm ...*

Rarely had the pinging sound heralding the end of the session been so gratefully received.

2.5

- *Oh dear. That sounds like it was awkward,* said Lbbp later over dinner.

- *It was. Very,* replied Terra, tucking into configuration 5 with some fresh pt-ssh on the side.

- *Well, if it's any consolation, I'm sure Shnst felt just as bad for saying it as you felt for hearing it.*

- *Maybe,* said Terra, wrinkling her nose. Lbbp loved it when she wrinkled her nose. *It's impossible to tell with those two.*

Terra finished another mouthful.

- *Lbbp, why does everybody hate the G'grk so much?*

Lbbp put down his plate, thought for a moment.

- *We've built such a world here on Fnrr. No one's hungry, no one gets ill any more, not seriously anyway, and it wasn't easy, I can tell you. You've read the history files ... we had our share of wars, famine and disasters, but we overcame our differences and looked for answers and found solutions together. And now we work in peace towards common goals.*

- *Except the G'grk?*

- *Exactly! Except the G'grk! They just can't let go of their old ways. It's absurd.*

- *Well, they have their own traditions,* said Terra. *It can't be easy for them.*

- *I'm sorry, but if your traditions consist of pretending the last few eras never happened and bludgeoning each other to death on a regular basis, then your traditions are rubbish and you need some new traditions,* snorted Lbbp. Terra laughed.

- *They're a bunch of hypocrites anyway,* Lbbp went on as he tidied the dishes away. *They can denounce science and technology as foul and unholy as much as they like, but they're perfectly happy to use tech once they've stolen it. Or try to use it, anyway. They're just too lazy and ignorant to develop their own stuff.*

- Or it could be that they have to steal it because the other nations won't trade with them, mused Terra.

- *They're impossible to trade with!* retorted Lbbp. *And what would they have to trade? Spears?*

- *I guess I'm just wondering if everybody hates the G'grk because they're so angry and violent, or whether they're so angry and violent because everybody hates them, that's all,* said Terra quietly.

It was Lbbp's turn to laugh. - *When did you become such a little philosopher? It's like having dinner with Hshft the Elder or something. Now come on,* he said, tossing the dishes into the matter scrambler. *Just time for a quick game of tb-tb-tff before sleep. Another big day tomorrow.*

Terra sighed and followed Lbbp to the main room. It was indeed another big day tomorrow, as Bsht had reminded them at home-time. Tomorrow, the class would have its first session using the Interface.

2.6

Children keep secrets. Even good children.

Not necessarily big secrets or bad secrets, not the sort of thing that would get them into trouble were it to be discovered, just things that are, well, none of anybody else's business.

Children on Fnrr keep secrets too.

Sometimes, after finishing his evening meal, Pktk would go to his room. He'd tell his parents he was going to do a little extra studying before sleep-time; reading up for a test the next day or something like that.

Once alone, Pktk would activate his slate and access the Preceptorate's history files, specifically the military history of Mlml. It was many orbits now since Mlml had been at war, but Pktk thrilled to read accounts of campaigns and battles from eras past. He would imagine himself leading troops into combat, rescuing helpless civilians, picking off enemy soldiers with his pulse-orb with devastating accuracy, defeating numerically superior and better-armed foes before returning to Hrrng and a hero's welcome. When his parents would call on him to go to sleep, he would activate his sleep-well and drift happily into unconsciousness with the hissed cheers of a grateful populace still ringing inside his head.

Everybody knew that Fthfth did her homework the very instant she got home. Her slate would be activated almost before her gravity bubble was switched off. What nobody, not even her parents, knew was that having completed her homework, she would access her own academic file from the Preceptorate's records. She was entitled to do so, as were all her fellow students, but she was the only one who did it on a regular basis.

Fthfth would reread her test grades, displayed as an almost unbroken list of double-stars. Almost unbroken. On two occasions, once when she'd been a little unwell but still determined to take the test that day, and once when she'd read up on the wrong topic by mistake, she'd scored a single-star. Fthfth would glower at those two single-stars, those two disgusting blemishes on her otherwise spotless record, and clench her little fists in anger and frustration. No matter how well she did in future, however many double-stars she achieved, those two marks could never be overwritten. Her record would never be perfect.

When her parents would call on her to come and eat, she would switch off her slate and promise to herself one more time never to underachieve so badly again.

Terra also had a private little habit. Not something she did very often, and she knew Lbbp would be upset, even alarmed, if he ever caught her at it, but sometimes, when she felt a certain way, she would feel the need to do it once more.

At sleep-time, she would bid Lbbp goodnight, go to her room and shut the door. She would switch her sleep-well on (Lbbp would hear the hum of the gravity field generator kicking in from the next room) but rather than step into it, she would open her window. As the cold night air washed into her chamber, she would activate her gravity bubble and step out into space.

Up and up Terra would float, careful to avoid being seen through the apartment windows of the upper floors of the building. Even in the climate-controlled environment of the city, the air was colder once you got this far above the ground ... Terra's garment, detecting the drop in temperature, would gently warm her as she ascended the hundreds of metres to the top of the tower. At the very apex of the building there was a small flat roof; Terra would land carefully on this surface and switch her gravity bubble onto standby mode.

Looking upwards into the clear night sky (Terra would

only do this on bright starlit evenings), high above the light pollution of the city, Terra would pick out the constellation known to Fnrr's astronomers as 133-4/77. Having identified its pattern, she would stare intently at the space between the two stars at its centre.

Somewhere between those stars, too impossibly distant to see, was the small yellow star designated 6-66-724-41, around which orbited a blue-green planet known as 6-66-724-41/3, or more commonly, Rrth.

On exceptionally clear nights, the haze of light generated by stars too distant to be seen as individual bodies would be just about visible behind the constellation. Terra liked these nights; she could peer at the haze and imagine that somehow her eyes had fixed upon the bit of it that contained home.

Home.

Odd, Terra would reflect, that she still thought of Rrth as 'home'. She had no memory of the place and everything she'd learned about it suggested that she was far better off away from there, but still ...

Then she would remember Lbbp, and consider how terror-stricken he'd be if he knew where she was. She would reactivate her gravity bubble, cast one last glance at the stars, and float back down to her room.

Terra didn't do this very often. Only when she felt a certain way. Like tonight.

Terra stared glumly at the object on the table.

It resembled an ornate lamp with a hemispherical glass shade. A series of illuminated touch controls was clustered around the metal base. The stem was made of a semi-flexible alloy so as to make its height adjustable. To Terra, it looked a lot like the sort of thing that you should never ever on any account stick your head in, but, before the morning was over, that's exactly what she would have to do.

- *This*, said Bsht, *is an Interface.*

The rest of the class seemed not to share Terra's apprehension. Rather, a crackle of excitement passed around the lectorium at Bsht's words. They'd been looking forward to this.

- *The Interface*, Bsht went on, *is a telemnemonic information transfer system. Does anyone know what that means?*

Fthfth knew.

- *It means it sends information directly into the memory centres of the brain. You can learn things that used to take cycles of reading in less than a shade.*

- *That's right*, said Bsht, *and you will be the first Lyceum novices to be allowed to use it.*

What Bsht didn't mention was how controversial a decision this had been. Terra only knew because she'd overheard Lbbp and Bsht arguing about it a few cycles previously.

She'd been writing a short piece for the Pre-Ac's end of session bulletin; a little vote of thanks for the work of the Pre-Ac teaching staff to which all the other pupils would add their names in due course. She'd wanted to ask Lbbp's opinion on how formal her language should be (Mlml society – in particular academic society – sets great store on striking the correct 'tone' in one's writing) and so had skipped out of her room and into the corridor. To her surprise, when she reached the door to the main room she heard Lbbp speaking in a very animated fashion. She stayed outside the door and listened.

– *It's outrageous!* Lbbp was saying. *It's unethical, it's reckless ... What on Fnrr does the Preceptor think he's doing?*

That made sense, thought Terra. Lbbp only ever got this worked up about academic matters.

– *I don't know why you're complaining to me,* said Bsht, *it's the council's decision. If you've a serious objection you should have taken it up with them.*

– *I DID take it up with them. They called me retrograde! Retrograde! Me! Can you believe that?*

Bsht said nothing, but even from the other side of the door Terra could guess at what her facial expression was.

– *Knowledge can't be injected like some sort of vaccine,* said Lbbp, calming down a little. *There's no point knowing something if you don't even know WHY you know it. And how are you supposed to appreciate knowledge that took no effort to acquire? That's not education, it's programming. It's disgusting.*

– *For what it's worth,* said Bsht soothingly, *there a quite a few of us on the staff at the Lyceum who agree with you.*

– *Still going to do it though, aren't you?* muttered Lbbp. *Still going to initiate the programme. On children! The Interface was developed by the military as a speed-briefing system and we're using it on children!*

– *Are you going to resign from the Preceptorate?* asked Bsht.

– *No. There'd be no point,* sighed Lbbp.

– *Fine,* said Bsht tersely. *Well, don't give ME a hard time then.*

At this point, Terra had tiptoed back to her room, deciding that maybe she didn't need Lbbp's help just now after all. But she'd made a mental note of the word 'Interface', and, as such, when Bsht had announced at the end of the previous day's classes that today would be their first day working with one, she'd felt a twinge of panic. Now she was looking at the machine itself, and the panic was creeping back.

Bsht talked the class through the basics of the device's design and use. The touch controls selected the required texts (the device would then access these files from the Source) and the user would fit the crystal dome over his or her head. The device would give a three-blip countdown and then begin stimulating the memory centres of the user's brain, transferring the information as quickly as if one were loading files onto a slate. Terra thought it sounded absolutely terrifying.

Bsht knew it was almost pointless asking who wanted to go first, but for procedure's sake she thought she'd better. She got as far as - *Who would like to go f...* before Fthfth ran down to the front of the lectorium and jammed her head into the dome.

- *What can I learn? What can I learn? What are the choices?* said Fthfth's voice from inside the dome.

- *Steady on,* said Bsht. *It takes a moment to programme it.*

- *Something difficult!* shouted Fthfth. *Something really massive like the complete history of the J'shfsk-G'grk wars!*

- *One thing at a time,* said Bsht. *This is the test programme. See how you do with this.*

Bsht's long fingers moved smoothly over the illuminated keys. The machine throbbed gently, a low blue light pulsing from the glass dome.

- *Come on!* said Fthfth.

- *Try to keep still,* said Bsht.

The machine gave three loud blips and activated itself. A deep hum came from the dome as it glowed with a fierce yellow light.

- *Hkh hkh hkh!* laughed Fthfth. *It's tickly!*

- *DO hold still, Fthfth,* said Bsht anxiously, wondering what would happen if the dome became misaligned. Did it overwrite existing memories? She didn't want to have to tell Fthfth's distinguished parents that their highly gifted daughter had absorbed vast amounts of facts and figures but forgotten how to walk.

The machine completed its sequence and shut down. Fthfth emerged from the dome, beaming. - *How did I do?* she asked eagerly.

- *Well, let's see.* Bsht took her slate and brought up a list of test questions.

- *Who was Preceptor from orbit twenty-four to seventy-seven in the twenty-first era?*

- *Jksh! Jksh the Younger!*

- *Correct. When did Tnk successfully identify the cohesion field?*

- *Orbit fifty-four of the twenty-seventh era!*

- *What invention made it possible to break the energy barrier?*

- *The phased neutrino shunt! Invented by Kltnt! Orbit sixteen, thirtieth era!*

- *Which planet is the primary source for grav-matter?*

- *Planet fifty-five dash four six six dash two three one slash four, sometimes known as Shth-Shnn; it exists in gravitational suspension between two stars and as such is uniquely ...*

- *Thank you, Fthfth. The test programme seems to have been a success.*

Fthfth frowned. - *But I already knew all that.*

Fortunately, the rest of the class had rather more and bigger gaps in their general knowledge than Fthfth, and as they took their turns with the Interface they found it filled these gaps swiftly and painlessly. Even Pktk managed to use the device successfully and without incident (apart from a moment's difficulty extricating his head from the dome, and this hardly counted as an incident by Pktk's standards).

Terra hung back and kept quiet, trying to make herself as inconspicuous as the sole representative of an alien species is ever likely to be. Perhaps, she thought, she wouldn't have to take a turn at all. Perhaps some edict had been handed down by the council that Ymns were too primitive to use the Interface, or too savage to be trusted with access to all that information. That would be good. She could bear the insult if it got her out of having to put that ... thing on her head.

- *So, Terra, your turn.*

Oh well.

Terra crept reluctantly to the front of the lectorium.

- *It's fine!* said Fthfth. *It's tickly!*

- *I can tell you're nervous,* said Bsht calmingly, *but the manufacturers have assured us that the Interface should be entirely safe and compatible with the Ymn brain.*

How do they know? thought Terra. *There's only one Ymn brain on the planet and I'm fairly sure I'd know if they'd been running tests on it.* She contemplated pointing this out but decided it would be futile.

- *Now put the dome over your head and try to relax,* said Bsht as Terra bowed meekly before the machine.

The crystal dome was disconcertingly warm, even though it didn't fit as snugly over Terra's head as it had over her classmates'. Her ears brushed against the insides. *Nowhere to put my ears, of course,* thought Terra. *There wouldn't be.*

- *I'm starting the programme now,* said Bsht. There was the sound of three blips, and then ... nothing.

- *Ah,* said Bsht. *Just a second.*

- *Can I come out?* asked Terra.

- *Hang on,* said Bsht, *I'm bringing up the user manual on my slate.*

- *Is there anything in there about using it on Ymns?* asked Terra hopefully. *Or maybe NOT using it on Ymns?* she added, more hopefully.

- *Well, there's a trouble-shooting section ... Here we are. It didn't sync with your brain because your head's slightly too small, that's all.*

Terra heard a brief burst of titters, which ceased abruptly.

- *So now what? Can I come out?*

- *No, it's fine,* said Bsht, *I just have to compensate by increasing the sensitivity a little ... There. Let's try again.*

Terra waited forlornly. Her neck was starting to stiffen up. She heard the three blips, and then ...

* * *

- *I think she's coming round.*

Terra opened her eyes. Her head ached appallingly and her vision swam. She could just see a ring of concerned-looking faces peering down at her.

- *Take it easy,* said Bsht. *There's been ... an incident.*

Terra sat up. She was at the back of the lectorium. Between her and the front desk, on which sat the Interface, a path seemed to have been cleared straight down the middle of the room, the chairs shoved out of the way.

- *Have I been ...?* Terra croaked.

- *It was incredible!* enthused Fthfth. *You got blown right out of the dome all the way back here!*

Terra blinked. She was sore all over and there was the most horrid smell coming from somewhere.

- *It was pretty amazing, actually,* said Pktk. *I wish I'd recorded it on my slate so I could show you.*

- *What do they call that fibrous stuff that grows out of her head?* Shnst asked Bsht. Bsht was busy speaking to someone on the Lyceum's internal communication system.

- *What was that?* asked Bsht distractedly.

- *What do they call that fibrous stuff that grows out of her head, Lector Bsht?* asked Thnst.

- *Oh. Hair. It's called hair.*

- *Right. Only it's on fire, that's all.*

* * *

- *I'm so sorry. I should have made them exempt you from using that thing.*

Lbbp and Terra sat on the smooth bench seat in the main room of their apartment. After the regrettable Interface incident, Lbbp had been sent for and had taken Terra home immediately. Though the Lyceum's resident physician had found no lasting damage to any of Terra's vital systems (although by his own admission he wasn't entirely sure what he was looking for), it had been decided to give her a day off to recover.

- *It's all right. It wasn't your fault,* said Terra, pretending not to know anything about Lbbp's earlier misgivings with regard to the Interface.

- *Well,* said Lbbp, thankful that Terra didn't know anything about his earlier misgivings with regard to the Interface, *if it's any consolation I don't think they're going to make you try to use the Interface again.*

- *What? Oh no!*

Not the reaction Lbbp had been hoping for. - *I thought you'd be relieved,* he said.

Terra sighed. - *Don't you see? Everyone else will just be pouring information into their heads using that machine while I'll have to read it all up the old-fashioned way. I'll get completely left behind!*

Terra got up off the bench and stomped across the room to the window. The sun was setting over the city. The towers and spires glinted pink and orange against the deep red sky. It was, by any standard, a breathtaking sight, but at that moment, it filled Terra with an aching loneliness. It was a beautiful world. But not her beautiful world.

- *I already feel so ... different. This is just going to make things worse.*

Lbbp stood behind her and put a slender grey hand on her shoulder.

- *And what's so wrong with being different? Doesn't make you less important, or less clever, or less ...*

Terra turned. - *Aren't I? Aren't I less clever?* she asked angrily. *Aren't Ymns stupid and primitive? Wasn't that the whole point of bringing me here? So I wouldn't grow up like them?*

There was an awkward silence as Lbbp took the time to frame his response as carefully as possible.

- *It was a spur of the moment thing. You were in danger and I made the decision to help you. It wasn't any sort of judgement on the Ymn race in general or even on your parents in particular. I just found an abandoned baby. The fact that it was a Ymn baby was a secondary consideration.*

Lbbp breathed heavily. That seemed to come out all right. Terra was still staring out of the window. Lbbp needed to cheer her up and, if at all possible, change the topic of conversation, and at that moment he suddenly thought of a way to stun two drftgrf-bgshns with one bdkt, as the saying had it.

- *Look,* he said, *they don't particularly need me at the Life Science Hub for the next day or two. Those cell cultures can develop themselves without my help. How do you fancy a trip somewhere, just you and me?*

Terra turned towards him, smiling. He already knew what she was going to suggest.

-*Rfk?* she asked.

Lbbp smiled. - *Rfk it is!* he said. *Tomorrow, first thing.*

I think I got away with that, thought Lbbp.

2.8

The nature reserves along the coast at Rfk had been Terra's favourite place on Mlml ever since Lbbp had first taken her there at just three orbits old. Lbbp had watched, beaming with pride, as the tiny Ymn girl had capered through the forest and along the shore, agog with fascination at the plants and wildlife. How gratifying that she should share his love of nature. A parent always hopes that their children will share their passions, but it's by no means a certainty that they will. This is doubly true of adopted children, and several thousandly true of adopted children from different planets.

Lbbp had made a point of taking Terra to Rfk at least once an orbit ever since. Several times an orbit, if work and other commitments permitted. The place had many guises, all beautiful in their own way. During the hot season, towering tree-sized flowers and delicate flower-sized trees would be in full bloom, a festival of colour around which bird-sized insects and insect-sized birds would buzz and flutter. During the cooling season, the foliage would turn a deep blue as it dried and fell, forming great cushiony piles which Lbbp would expressly forbid Terra to jump into, before joining her in jumping into them. During the cold season, icicles and frost would decorate the land and vegetation like glittering baubles, which Terra found curiously moving for reasons neither she nor Lbbp could guess at. During the warming season, the tree-sized flowers would punch their way through the ice like deceased warriors of legend, resurrected by their ancient gods to fight another battle. It was all especially fascinating because the climate within the city had been artificially controlled since eras past, so one had to venture out into nature in order to experience 'weather' at all.

That morning, Terra had set her sleep-well to wake her early and had Lbbp's configuration II ready for him by the time he woke up. They had made up a bag of food – slices of configuration 9 (it tasted better cold than the other configurations) some wsht rolls, pt-ssh paste and a flask of hot zff. They fitted their gravity bubbles (- *Did you remember to charge your bubble? - YES, I remembered to charge my bubble*) and packed spare power cells; it was almost a whole cell's journey to Rfk. They set off just as everyone else was floating to work and study ... Lbbp and Terra exchanged mischievous grins as they floated off in the opposite direction to the flow of traffic. No work for them today.

The sun was high in the sky by the time they arrived. They set down on the beach, a stretch of crystal sand which refracted the light in rainbow patterns along its length. The sea, reflecting the sky, was a deep pink. Terra gazed out towards the horizon and breathed deeply, all thoughts of Interfaces, gshkth practice and singed hair cleansed from her mind.

- *Wonderful, isn't it*, said Lbbp.

- *It is, it is indeed*, replied Terra.

They sat in silence for a moment, drinking it all in.

- *Lbbp*, asked Terra, *what's Rrth like?*

There was a heavy pause.

- *Well*, said Lbbp, *a lot of it is very beautiful.*

- *As beautiful as this?*

- *Some of it is pretty close, yes*, said Lbbp. *At least it was the last time I was there.*

- *How do you mean?*

- *It's the Ymns. They're not as ... careful as they could be with regard to their planet*, said Lbbp, choosing his words with care. He knew that the way Ymns were perceived by Fnrrns – primitive, savage, stupid even – had become a difficult topic for Terra, and this Interface business hadn't helped one bit. He didn't want to make matters worse by

65

launching into some bitter diatribe about Ymns despoiling their home world. He'd got most of that out of his system many orbits ago, he recalled with a shudder.

- *Is there hope for the Ymns?* Terra asked, with genuine curiosity.

- *There's always hope,* replied Lbbp after a moment's thought. *Culturally and technologically they're about where we were five or six eras ago and we turned out all right. Mind you, we'd never developed the sort of weapons they have on Rrth now.*

- *Weapons?*

- *Weapons that can destroy a whole city in one go,* said Lbbp. *They've actually used the things, too. I've seen pictures. And no you can't see them, it would scare you out of your wits. They've made enough of these weapons to kill everyone on Rrth several times over.*

- *Why?* asked Terra, distressed.

- *Who knows? By the time they'd set off the first few there'd be nobody left to set off the rest. There doesn't seem to be much logic to it. And given that they seem to be willing to go to war over the tiniest thing – minor tribal variations, ancient superstitions, even differing economic theories, if you can believe that – it seems pretty inevitable that they'll wipe each other out sooner or later. That's assuming,* said Lbbp, rather hitting his stride, *that they haven't done already.*

- *What?* Terra was genuinely alarmed now.

- *Well, think about it; we can see Rrth from here using astro-scopes and the like, but the light we're seeing left Rrth many orbits ago. It could all be over on Rrth already and we wouldn't be able to tell.*

Terra's face fell and Lbbp suddenly realised how stupid he was being. The implication of what he'd just said hit him too late; he could see that it had hit Terra already. She'd come to terms with being the only Ymn on Fnrr (although it seemed to be weighing rather more heavily on her these last few days); the idea that she might actually be the last Ymn left alive was truly disturbing. *You fool,* thought Lbbp, *letting your scientific enthusiasm run away with your mouth. You're talking to a child, not addressing a symposium.* He decided to change the subject.

- *Hungry?*

- *Starving.*

They went to eat their food in the shade of the forest, the sun being quite fierce now. Fnrrns turn a bright blue if they get sunburnt, and Lbbp didn't want to turn up to work with a blue face in the morning, since he'd made no mention of trips to nature reserves, but rather had told his colleagues he'd be working at home today.

They found a clearing with a carpet of soft red grass and made themselves quite comfortable. Lbbp leaned his back against the stem of a giant lgsh-chr flower and chewed blissfully on his configuration 9. The stem swayed in the breeze, with an almost hypnotic effect.

* * *

Lbbp's eyes snapped open suddenly. Had he been asleep? He felt weirdly vulnerable; it was the first time he could remember being asleep out in the open. Fnrrns had been using gravity-wells to sleep in for eras and found the notion of lying down to sleep, as animals do, to be slightly degrading. Lbbp himself hadn't just dozed off like that for a long time.

- *You were asleep!* giggled Terra. *Flat on your back like a jrrg or a big grey gff-gff.*

- *Or a Ymn,* reminded Lbbp. *You're having a Ymnising effect on me.*

- *Don't worry, I won't tell your clever Postulator friends that you fell asleep in the forest and lay there snoring away like a big—*

- *I do not snore!* protested Lbbp.

- *How would you know?*

Lbbp got up and stretched. The slice of configuration 9 was still in his hand. He took another bite, then asked - *How long was I asleep for?* Fnrrns don't dream, not adult

Fnrrns anyway, so they can have difficulty keeping track of time while sleeping. For all Lbbp knew, he could have been unconscious for six shades or half a cycle.

- *About half a spectrum. Don't worry, I kept myself busy.*
- *What have you been up to?*

Terra was holding her slate. She'd sketched the flower that Lbbp had been leaning on. The flower was three times her height and was changing colour, almost like a clock; purple, red, orange, red, purple, blue.

- *It does that to attract lots of different birds and insects,* said Lbbp. *They all have a different favourite colour, so this way it gets them all sooner or later. Look, the hjj bugs like the red best.* Terra noticed a little swarm of blue insects hovering around the flower. *Ingenious,* Lbbp went on. *Makes it difficult to draw, though.*

- *Look,* said Terra holding up her slate. She'd animated her drawing so that it changed colour like the flower.

- *Clever,* said Lbbp.

- *And here …*

Lbbp looked at the bottom of the drawing. Terra had sketched him, leaning against the stem with his eyes closed. With a giggle, Terra tapped the figure of Lbbp on the slate and it began to make little snoring sounds.

- *A bit TOO clever,* said Lbbp.

Terra laughed and tapped the slate to make the sound stop. The sound didn't stop. Or rather it did, but a similar sound carried on. A snorting sound, then a rustling sound. Terra and Lbbp exchanged curious glances.

The sound was coming from behind a hedgy patch of purple bush. - *What is that?* asked Terra. She put her slate down on the grass and skipped off to investigate.

- *Just a moment,* said Lbbp, but Terra was gone. He put down his slice of configuration 9 and went after her.

Terra found herself in a clearing overgrown with tall reedy grass. She looked through the grass towards the rustling sound. She saw nothing. She was about to decide that whatever she'd heard had already gone when a great section of undergrowth moved. She gasped and kept very still.

What had looked like a grassy mound was in fact an almost perfectly camouflaged animal. Twice Terra's size, it crawled along the forest floor, visible only when it moved. Terra couldn't quite make out its shape; it was covered in long purple quills which were almost indistinguishable from the grass. She couldn't tell which end was the head, or even if it had such a thing as a head. A brightly coloured sknth, a small furry arboreal creature, was scampering down a tree trunk about an arm's length away from the creature; at that moment, the creature settled the question of which end was its head. It reared up and bared a set of sharp yellow teeth, taking the sknth with one swift chomp.

Terra froze in fear. She watched the creature chewing its prey in horror and fascination. Something touched Terra on the shoulder. She started in fright. It was Lbbp. She wanted to punch him but was afraid to make any noise.

- *A znk! A wild znk! Fantastic!* whispered Lbbp.

- *Fantastic?* hissed Terra. *I know at least one sknth who wouldn't agree with that.*

The znk spat out a ball of multicoloured fur.

- *Isn't it beautiful?* enthused Lbbp, getting a little louder. *These were almost extinct an era ago, you know. It's so good to see them re-establishing themselves in the wild.*

- *Shouldn't we, er, be keeping quiet?* whispered Terra, remembering those teeth.

- *Don't worry,* said Lbbp, *their sense of hearing is terrible.*

The znk raised its head and made a sniffing noise. It swung round to look directly at Lbbp and Terra.

- *Their sense of smell, however, is excellent,* said Lbbp, who knew he'd forgotten something. *Terra, listen to me and do exactly as I say. That flower you were sketching?*

- *Yes?* whispered Terra, trembling.

- *Look at it. Look directly at it. Whatever you hear, don't take your eyes off that flower.*

Terra turned her head slowly and fixed her eyes on the

flower. It continued to change colour; blue, purple, red, orange, red ... She could hear sniffing and shuffling, but did not turn her eyes away from the flower ... orange, red, purple, blue, purple ...

- *It's gone,* said Lbbp.

Terra exhaled. - *Why did I have to look at the flower?*

- *You didn't. Well, not the flower specifically, anyway. I just needed you to focus your attention on something that wasn't the znk.*

- *Why?* asked Terra, as they walked back to the clearing.

- *Well, like a lot of predators, znk are only interested in other animals if they're a threat, or possible prey. It has just eaten so it's probably not hungry at the moment, but if it felt threatened by us it would attack to defend itself. That's why I needed you to keep still and look away. If you'd looked right at it, it would have taken it as a challenge, and if you'd tried to run, its hunting instinct would have taken over and it would have chased you whether it was hungry or not. As it was, it decided you were irrelevant so it left you alone.*

Terra wasn't sure she liked being referred to as 'irrelevant' but she was glad Lbbp knew his animals. Lbbp gave a proud little smile. - *And people say scientists are useless in a crisis,* he said happily.

- *Is it time to go home?* asked Terra, hoping that it was.

- *It is indeed. You're back at the Lyceum in the morning. Better get an early night.* And besides, Lbbp had noticed that something had eaten the slice of configuration 9 he'd left lying around and he wasn't keen to find out what.

* * *

Lbbp and Terra arrived back at the apartment building just as the sun was setting and the moons were coming out. The main room window shutter slid open; Terra was about to step inside when she was startled by the sight of Bsht sitting on the bench seat. She didn't look happy at all. - *And were have you been all day?* This was addressed to Lbbp, who was hovering behind Terra. For a moment

Terra thought he was actually hiding behind her.

- *What? Oh, out ... We've been, you know, out,* said Lbbp innocently as he floated into the room. *I didn't know you had a key to ...*

- *I've been trying to get hold of you since this morning,* interrupted Bsht. *Your friends at the Life Science Hub said you were working at home.*

- *Home? No, no, field trip, that's ... that's what I told them, field trip. They probably weren't listening. You know what us scientists are like. Can I get you anything? Bowl of gssh?*

Terra listened in silence, trying not to find Lbbp's discomfort amusing. It wasn't easy.

- *The sort of field trip where you don't answer your comm? The sort of field trip where you don't even take your comm?* asked Bsht, noticing Lbbp's little personal communicator lying on the glass table.

Lbbp sighed. - *What's the matter, Bsht?*

Bsht couldn't be bothered interrogating Lbbp about where he'd been all day. It wasn't important anyway. What was important was what she'd come to tell him.

- *Everybody's been recalled to the Preceptorate. It's the FaZoon. The FaZoon are coming back.*

2.9

The FaZoon are, as far as anyone can tell, the oldest civilisation in existence.

Their home world is – or rather, was – the legendary planet of Gagra-Sem-Gagra, which orbited a giant red star called Thoomm at the exact centre of the universe. This star had been one of the very first stars to form, coalescing in the immediate aftermath of The Expansion. On this ancient planet, the FaZoon had arisen nearly eleven billion orbits ago, and had survived in one form or another ever since. Their culture, their knowledge, their very beings had been developing and advancing almost as long as the universe itself had existed. When Thoomm had exploded (taking the legendary planet Gagra-Sem-Gagra with it) over a billion orbits ago, the FaZoon had taken to the stars, and had wandered the galaxies ever since, occasionally contacting younger and less advanced species (that is to say, all of them) and bestowing their gifts of knowledge. It was, in other words, a big deal when the FaZoon came to visit.

They roamed the skies in starships consisting of almost pure energy, becoming matter only when it, well, mattered. These starships were detectable by Fnrr's astroscopes at some distance, and so when a FaZoon vessel was spotted on an inbound trajectory, as had happened while Lbbp and Terra were enjoying snacks and avoiding znks at Rfk, all work would be suspended in favour of preparing for their arrival.

On one previous visit, the FaZoon had left information giving Fnrr's physicians the means to cure zg-zl, a fatal illness. On another, the FaZoon had taught Fnrrn scientists how to cause atomic fusion in a bowl of ndt juice. There were some who wondered why, if the FaZoon were so benevolent, they didn't just share all their knowledge in one visit and have done with it, but they were careful not to wonder this while the FaZoon were actually on the planet. Rumour had it that the FaZoon were so telepathically sensitive that all thoughts were known to them.

Fnrrns knew they had to watch what they were thinking during FaZoon visitations.

Curiously, although the FaZoon were believed to be highly telepathic themselves, they would not allow any telepathic communication technology to be used in their presence. Fnrrns, when communicating with alien species, would commonly employ psychic translation devices – this certainly sped things up, even if it did lead to moments of diplomatic tension (when the devices would translate what someone really wanted to say rather than what they actually said) but the FaZoon refused to allow anyone to know their thoughts. They possessed knowledge which no other species was yet wise enough to be trusted with, they said. As such, all communication with the FaZoon had to be done the old-fashioned way, by speaking their language. The FaZoon had been kind enough, on an early visit, to leave behind a phrase book.

Or rather, a phrase stone tablet.

Lbbp certainly had his reservations about the FaZoon. As far as he could tell, all the really important history-changing discoveries had been made by Fnrrn scientists working entirely without the assistance of almost infinitely wise and ancient alien benefactors. It annoyed him that sometimes people who hadn't read up on their scientific history would credit the FaZoon with discoveries like the light-bending camouflage technology which powered the invisibility shield on his little spaceship (invented by scientists in the nation of Dskt, just across the sea from Mlml) or interstellar travel (invented right here in Mlml, refined from Tnk's original gravity-nullifying techniques). And yes, what was the point of rationing out these great nuggets of scientific advancement? It seemed to Lbbp like the FaZoon were trying to keep the Fnrrns feeling indebted, obligated, needy. The FaZoon had never asked for anything in return, but Lbbp felt sure that such a day would eventually come.

Right now, Lbbp was just annoyed that what he'd hoped would be a relaxing evening had been ruined. He and Terra were sitting in the Leisure Hub of the Lyceum, a sort of auditorium, watching a presentation on the big visualiser they'd installed in there. It was a potted history of inter-actions between the FaZoon and Mlml, which all the staff and pupils had been required to watch. Lbbp had seen it many times before (he knew certain sections word for word, he was irritated to discover) but there was much that was new to Terra.

- *Have they ever been to Rrth?* she whispered.

- *What?* Lbbp whispered back.

- *The FaZoon; have they ever visited Rrth?*

- *No. No one has, not officially anyway. There's been a lot of secret trips to Rrth over the orbits – as you know – but nobody's made formal contact with the Ymns. They're not considered to be ready for it.*

- *I thought you said you'd seen Ymn histories about alien invasions of Rrth?*

- *Yes, lots. They seem to get invaded quite a bit, but, oddly, they've never been invaded by a species anyone's ever heard of. It's like they're in a different universe to the rest of us.*

Terra's nose wrinkled. - *That's a bit odd, isn't it?*

Lbbp shrugged. - *Space is big. There are certainly hundreds of civilisations out there that we haven't seen yet. Rrth does seem to attract the nasty ones, though.*

- *But the Ymns survived all these invasions?*

- *So far. These aliens, the ones no one's ever actually met except the Ymns, they're never very competent or organised. Whenever they decide to wipe the Ymns out, rather than just blast the planet from space, they go down to the surface and start trying to wipe them out one at a time. What sort of plan is that? It'd take ages. It always gives the Ymns time to figure out a way to beat them.*

- And the Ymns have always found a way?

- Well, sometimes they just get lucky, like the aliens all catch some horrid Rrth disease and drop dead. Funny thing is, that seems to have happened at least twice. You'd think they'd learn.

The presentation came to an end. Preceptor Shm, who had been sitting in a chair next to the visualiser, stood up and addressed the room, sounding even more tired than usual.

- As you know, the FaZoon always send their envoys to whichever nation is in the most total darkness at the moment of their arrival.

It was believed that the FaZoon were highly sensitive to light, and preferred to interact by night. Lbbp reckoned it was simply that the FaZoon, luminescent beings of almost pure energy, knew that they looked more impressive in the dark. Being impressive seemed quite important to the FaZoon.

- On this occasion, Shm went on, *that nation will be Mlml. They're coming here.*

A ripple of excitement. A faintly audible groan from Lbbp.

- It therefore falls to me to assign a delegation to meet with the FaZoon. I will deliberate upon this and announce my selection in two days' time. That is all.

Preceptor Shm turned and left without another word. *- That's it? That's it?* said Lbbp angrily. *He drags us all the way in here to show us an old info-gram and tell us he's got nothing to tell us yet?*

- Everybody else seems quite excited, said Terra quietly.

- I know, snarled Lbbp, stomping towards the exit. *Pathetic, isn't it?*

- I'm quite excited, said Terra inaudibly as she followed him.

* * *

75

One of the first decisions Preceptor Shm made with regard to the imminent arrival of the FaZoon was to organise the younger Lyceum students into a welcoming committee. They would recite a greeting to the FaZoon envoys (in the FaZoon language, of course) before the official delegates were introduced.

So it was that the next day, Bsht found herself standing in front of a lectorium full of students making some extremely peculiar noises.

- *I know it's not easy, but take your time over it.*

- *It hurts!* protested a young boy named Yshn. *It hurts my throat!*

Terra thought Yshn was being a bit melodramatic. It was just a lot of words in a different language, that was all. She listened to the guide reading that Bsht played over the lectorium sound system and repeated it. *'Kaa sem lo maa FaZoon. Kaa sem jay maa FaZoon.'* It was easy.

Looking around the room, she could see that while Yshn had been the only one to complain so far, he obviously wasn't the only one experiencing some discomfort. The pupils' Fnrrn speech mechanisms, accustomed only to making the clipped, clickety sounds of their own language, had to strain to produce the open, flowing sounds of the FaZoon words. Terra's Ymn voice box was finding it much easier.

After three or four recitations, the rest of the pupils began to cough and gasp. Terra found that hers was now the only voice to be heard. She kept going.

- *Kaa sem lo maa FaZoon. Kaa sem jay maa FaZoon. Kaa sem lo maa FaZoon. Kaa sem jay maa FaZoon.* She paused. Everyone was looking at her. *What?*

- *Have you learned FaZoon before?* asked Bsht.

- *I'd never even heard of the FaZoon before yesterday,* explained Terra.

- *You'd never even heard about them?* said Fthfth incredulously. Terra shrugged.

- *They just never came up in conversation. Sorry.*

- *So why are you so good at that then?* enquired Pktk with a hint of suspicion in his voice.

- *I'm not that good at it ...*

- *It's just that when you do it it actually sounds like the recording,* said Fthfth. *Say FaZoon ...* In Fthfth's voice it came out as *F'znnn.*

- *Faa–Zoon ...* said Terra.

- *Weird,* muttered Pktk.

- *It would appear,* said Bsht, *that Ymns have something of an advantage where speaking FaZoon is concerned.*

- *There you go,* said Fthfth, *you're finally the best at something.*

- *Fancy a game of dfsh later?* said Terra with a smile, reminding Fthfth of what was literally the only other thing Terra had ever been better at than her.

- *I think this should be brought to the attention of the Preceptor,* said Bsht.

Terra wasn't sure whether to be pleased or terrified. After a moment's consideration, she decided to settle on both.

* * *

- *Preceptor, I'm not sure this is appropriate. She's only eight orbits old.* Lbbp was pacing anxiously round Shm's reading room.

Terra was too busy being in awe of her surroundings to pay attention to Lbbp. She was in the Preceptor's reading room; the sanctum of sanctums, the privatest of the privates, the personal study of the very head of the whole Preceptorate. To see the inside of the Preceptor's reading room you generally either had to be in blood-curdling trouble, or actually be the Preceptor.

- *It's a responsibility, I know, but it's also an honour. And you've said yourself,* went on Shm in a low whisper, *that sometimes you worry about her feeling ... excluded.*

- *I'm not sure making her address an alien delegation in front of the whole city is the best way of making her feel included,* replied Lbbp in a similarly low whisper. *It's just going to point out to everybody how different she is, as if they needed reminding of it.*

Terra was dimly aware that Shm and Lbbp had started whispering, which meant they were talking about her and didn't want her listening. That was fine with Terra; she was perfectly content not to listen. She was happily gazing at the scrolls and tablets adorning Shm's shelves. Was that …? It was! A first edition of Tnk's thesis! She couldn't wait to see the look on Fthfth's face when she told her.

- *Terra …* Shm addressed her directly. Better start paying attention.

- *Yes, Preceptor?*

- *You are aware of the importance of maintaining good relations with the FaZoon?*

- *Yes, Preceptor.*

- *You are also aware of the FaZoon's aversion to telepathic communication?*

- *Of course, Preceptor.*

- *Now don't worry, I'm not asking you to converse with the FaZoon. Just recite a formal greeting, after which you'll hand over to the other delegate who will do all the actual talking, do you understand?*

- *Yes, Preceptor.*

- *Good. Well, if that's settled,* he cast a glance at Lbbp as if daring him to object, *we'll introduce you to the, er, grown-up half of the delegation.* Shm touched an illuminated pad on his desk. The door to the reading room swished open and a tall Fnrrn in green robes entered.

- *Hello again, Terra,* said Vstj, and he looked about as happy to see her as she was to see him.

- *Lbbp!* said Vstj, forcing a smile. *It's been a very long time.*

- *Yes, it has,* said Lbbp, trying to force a smile and not quite succeeding. *How's life in the accounts division?*

- *Oh, it's all pretty intense stuff,* said Vstj, still smiling, just about. *You know, trying to decide which departments to fund … and which ones not to …*

- Of course, I forgot that you two know each other, said Shm.

- Yes, very well! grimaced Vstj.

- Very well indeed ... grimaced Lbbp.

Vstj turned to Terra. - *And so, the fascinating history of Terra the Rrth child takes yet another thrilling twist. Who'd have thought that, at just, what is it, eight orbits?*

- That's right, said Terra.

- ... just eight orbits old, she would find herself addressing alien dignitaries, sharing the honour with someone who'd spent whole years of his life preparing for just that responsibility ...

- Have you? said Lbbp with genuine curiosity.

- You may recall from our days as students, Lbbp, that I had a natural aptitude for language.

- I remember you talking a lot, certainly.

- Indeed. Since then, I have immersed myself in study of the FaZoon tongue, mastering it – if I do say so myself – to a higher degree than any Fnrrn before me. I have made it my personal goal to take communication between Fnrrn and FaZoon to a new level. So you can imagine how pleased I was, said Vstj, his rictus grin starting to look a bit painful now, *to discover that there was someone in this very Preceptorate who, without even having to try, has even better FaZoon diction than my own!*

- Yes, yes we can, said Lbbp, *we can really imagine that.*

- Well, that's marvellous, squeaked Vstj, *I'll see you on the big day then. Preceptor* ... and with a last bow, he was gone. Shm watched him leave. Lbbp watched Shm watching Vstj leave. Shm noticed Lbbp watching him watching Vstj leave.

- What? asked Shm innocently.

2.10

Of course, when one is growing up in such an academically oriented society as Mlml, a simple thing like being selected to perform interplanetary diplomatic functions is never allowed to interfere with one's classwork. Immediately after being dismissed from the Preceptor's reading room, Terra found herself taking notes in the Practical Science laboratory.

- *So, once Tnk discovered the existence of grav-matter it was a question of harnessing its power in a safe and controllable way,* said Pshkf, the practical science lector. He had in front of him a containment field generator and a silver phial.

- *Now, watch this …*

Pshkf switched the containment field generator on and poured a drop of silver liquid onto the plate at its centre.

- *Is that …?* asked Fthfth

- *It is indeed. Purest quality grav-matter, fresh from the mines of Shth-Shnn. Now if we bombard the grav-matter with energy waves at just the right frequency …*

Next to the field generator stood a small bronze-coloured device; a crystal-tipped cylinder mounted on a flexible stand. Pshkf touched the base of the stand and the crystal began to pulse and glow. The droplet of grav-matter swirled as if stirred by an invisible spoon.

- *Here comes the good part,* smiled Pshkf. He slapped his hand down on the desk; the droplet rippled, bounced and then rose above the plate, hovering, a perfect rotating sphere of liquid.

- *There. Neutral mass. And before you ask, no, you can't have a go.*

- *Why not?* said Fthfth crossly.

- *Okay, who knows why not?* Pshkf addressed the class. *What would happen if I got the frequency of the bombardment wrong?*

- *If you set the frequency too low, nothing would happen. Too high and the grav-matter would invert, the containment field would collapse and you'd create a tiny black hole which would attract objects equal to its own mass before cancelling itself out.*

Everyone stared at Pktk. That was the most words anyone had ever heard him say in one go. He looked back at them.

- *What? I like GravTech.*

- *Good boy. Then there's something coming up which I think you'll enjoy. He's right, children, mess this up,* he pointed to the spinning grav-matter particle, *and everything in this room gets crushed into a little dot of super-dense matter. That's why,* he said, casting a glance towards Fthfth, *you can't have a go. Anyway,* Pshkf went on, addressing the whole class, *you all get to play with GravTech on a daily basis. It's exactly the same principle behind your little gravity bubbles. And it's the same principle applied on a much bigger scale which gives us this ...*

He led the class to the middle of the lab, where a gleaming metal ovoid, over a metre in length, sat on one of the workbenches.

- *This, my friends,* he gave a special little nod to Pktk, *is the infralight drive from an thirty-first era Rrsk-sh-Frrrg Starchaser, and in my learned opinion a finer piece of engineering you will not find.*

Pktk was in awe. - *Where did you find it?*

- *In a recycling yard, if you can believe that. They had no idea what it was. I'm restoring it, and the Lyceum have been kind enough to let me use their equipment if I let you lot look at it, so there it is.*

Pktk examined the beautiful simplicity of the infralight drive's design as Pshkf enthused on. - *I know everyone goes on about Tnk and his thesis, but if you ask me Kltnt was the real hero. He found a way to use Tnk's theories to open up the whole of space. This thing, when it's running, generates such a perfect void in the cohesion field that anything within that void exists as matter and energy at the same time. Total masslessness. Then all you need to do is give yourself a decent poke in the rear end with the neutrino shunt – not included – and you're off across the galaxy . . .*

A sudden pinging noise was heard over the Lyceum's announcement system, then a familiar voice:

- Right, so what do I – oh, it's on, is it, erm . . . Attention please, would Terra . . . is that all? Just Terra? Doesn't she have a full name? No, no, I don't suppose she would, now I come to – Ahem. Would Terra please report – no, not report, this isn't the army, what's the word? Would Terra please . . . proceed? Proceed, is that it? Oh forget it. Terra, it's me, Vstj, I'm in the Leisure Hub, could you come here please. Useless device, I don't know why I didn't just . . .

After a moment's pause, Terra said *– I, er . . . I think I'd better go to the Leisure Hub.*

- Yes, I think you better had, smiled Pshkf.

* * *

- Hello?

The Leisure Hub appeared to be deserted.

- Hello . . .? said Terra again.

- You know, young Terra . . .

Terra jumped. Vstj had been sitting in the back row of seats. She'd expected to find him on the stage. Vstj went on, *- . . . we have quite a lot in common, you and I . . .*

- We do?

- Hmm. Everybody thinks I'm stupid too.

Terra had genuinely no idea how to respond to this; fortunately Vstj wasn't finished.

- I know what they all say about me, you know. Oh, Vstj, only got the job because his family bought the Preceptorate a new holographic library, owes it all to his family, be nothing without his family . . . Well, you know what, little Terra?

- What?

- Frankly, if my family had bought me the Chancellorship of the whole country, it would barely make up for the orbits I spent growing up with the miserable fzfts. Still, he went on, striding towards the stage, *at least my lot didn't dump me in a burning vehicle and leave me to be carted off by aliens. One mustn't complain.*

- I don't think ... the vehicle wasn't actually on fire, I ... Compositor Vstj, are you feeling all right?

- Yes, said Vstj, hopping up onto the stage with a strange glint in his eye, *I'm feeling absolutely DANDY. Now, young Terra,* he said, pacing up and down the stage, *tomorrow night, you and I will stand on the steps of the Forum in front of the whole population of Hrrng, and address envoys from the wisest and oldest race in the universe. I will be there as the culmination of a lifetime of study and preparation, you will be there because of your freakishly massive larynx. It is funny how things turn out, isn't it. Slate, please ...*

Terra, struggling to follow Vstj's line of discourse, handed her slate over. Vstj tapped on it and handed it back.

- There. That is the text of the greeting you will read out. DON'T practise it here, do it when you get home. Give that father of yours something else to beam with pride about.

Terra glanced at the slate. There was a block of text consisting of phonetically transcribed FaZoon words, and then the same text translated into Mlmln.

- Just the usual diplomatic guff about honoured guests, mutual understanding, peaceful co-operation, blah blah blah, said Vstj, sitting down on the stage with his legs dangling off the front. *That is what it says, by the way. Feel free to have it checked. I wouldn't be so mean as to trick you into say-ing, 'FaZoon are ugly and they smell. Please vaporise me,' or anything like that. That wouldn't be funny at all ...* said Vstj, gazing into the middle distance.

- I'm ... going now, said Terra.

- Yes, yes, off you go, said Vstj without looking at her. Terra turned and headed for the exit. Vstj spoke again before she got there.

- *Of course, you know what I'm supposed to be doing at the moment ...? End of financial orbit budget reports,* said Vstj mournfully. *Can't imagine why the Preceptor would want to divert my attention from that, can you? Still, nice to be kept busy, I suppose ...*

- *Yes, yes, it is,* said Terra and hurried back to the Practical Science lab, where there were things she understood.

The night was unusually warm for the time of orbit. The climate control office had made sure of that.

In front of the Hrrng Forum – the seat of Mlml's civilian government – there was a great open square, paved with gleaming white stone and surrounded by cobalt alloy statues of previous chancellors and eminent senators from eras gone by. A visitor to Hrrng might be impressed by these statues, until they visited the Preceptorate a short distance away, saw the considerably bigger (and noticeably rather less attached to the ground) statue of Tnk, and drew their own conclusions about Mlml's cultural hierarchy. The government was in office, but rarely gave the impression of being in power.

On this occasion, although it was way past more or less everybody's sleep-time, the Forum Square was packed. Fnrrns of all ages, from all corners of Mlml and beyond, stood and waited. Some held little glowing lanterns, in the six-pointed snowflake-like shape of the FaZoon's starships (around the outside of the square, lantern vendors were doing a roaring trade).

There hadn't been a FaZoon visitation for over twelve orbits, and since one never knew when – or indeed, if – the FaZoon would return, nobody wanted to miss this. Excited discussions had gone on among Terra's friends about what possible gifts the FaZoon might bring this time. Some said it would be the secret of time travel (- *It better not be*, said Fthfth crossly, *that'd be my life's ambition ruined*); others thought that the FaZoon might bless them with the power to see the future (- *That'd be the Extrapolator out of business then*, said Lbbp); some thought that this time the FaZoon would tell the Fnrrns the secret. Just, you know, The Secret.

At the edge of the square where the Forum building itself stood, there was a wide set of stone steps leading up from the square to the building's grand front portal. At the top of these steps stood an odd-looking group: the Chancellor, in her black robes, two of her senior advisers, in red robes, Preceptor Shm, in his purple robes, Vstj, in his green robes, Lbbp, in his usual blue garment (feeling horribly self-consciously robeless), and, wearing a little purple robe made just for the occasion, Terra.

At the front of the crowd stood Fthfth, between her parents, the eminent scientist and the even more eminent surgeon, and Pktk, between his parents, who seemed to wear permanent expressions of worry and concern. It was hard to tell, pondered Terra, whether Pktk's parents worried about him so much because he was, well, how he was, or whether he was how he was because they worried so much.

The moment had nearly arrived. The Preceptorate's astronomers had calculated the exact point at which the FaZoon ship would enter the atmosphere. Shm really hoped they'd got it right.

- *Look!* someone shouted. All eyes turned skyward. What appeared to be a new star was growing in size and brightness. It became more distinct, it had a discernible shape, like a six-pointed snowflake.

Hissed cheers and cries of – *FaZoon! FaZoon!* rang out across the square as the glowing shape descended silently.

- *Nervous?* whispered Lbbp to Terra.

- *What do you think?* Terra replied. Lbbp gave her hand a comforting squeeze.

The FaZoon vessel completed its descent and hung over the square, filling everyone's field of vision with dazzling light. It was now too bright to look at directly. Some of the crowd shielded their eyes with their hands, others donned tinted goggles (around the outside of the square, goggle vendors had been doing a roaring trade).

- *Here we go,* said Vstj to Terra. *Stand beside me.*

Casting a nervous glance back at Lbbp, Terra stepped forward and stood alongside Vstj. The FaZoon ship, bright as it was, suddenly glowed brighter still. Everyone in the square, begoggled or otherwise, had to shut their eyes for a moment. When they opened their eyes again, six new figures stood on the steps in front of the Mlml delegation.

They were tall, thin and bright. That was as much as anyone could tell. Taller than the Fnrrns, the figures glowed almost as brightly as the starship. If they had such a thing as a 'shape', it was impossible to make it out.

The cheers and *FaZoon!*s subsided and a hush descended.

- *Go on,* hissed Vstj.

The figures stood, motionless and luminous.

- *Now?* whispered Terra.

- *YES!* hissed Vstj.

Terra produced her slate from under her robe, gave a little cough and began to read.

- *Kaa sem lo maa FaZoon. Maa sem ko jay saya Fnrr mo FaZoon.*

The figure nearest to Terra bent down as if to scrutinise her. Terra did her best not to be put off and continued.

- *Fo sem kaa mee FaZoon-shaa, ra-sa mo soom-kaa …*

The figure's face – or where the figure's face would be – was now level with Terra's own. The light it emitted made it hard for her to read, but feeling all the eyes upon her, she carried on.

- *Jaya fo maa, jaya fo soo, jaya sem ko-na-sem …*

The figure raised its … hand? Arm? Finger? and reached out towards Terra's face. Trembling now, she raced to finish the reading.

- *Mo sem ja doo kaa FaZoon-shaa! Gaa sem …*

The finger touched Terra's forehead.

* * *

Terra stood on the rainbow sand, gazing out over the pink sea.

Where is this?

A PLACE OF THE MIND.

I thought you didn't do this sort of thing.

Terra stood on snowy wastes. Icy winds whipped past. It wasn't cold.

WE ARE FAZOON.

I'm Terra.

Terra stood on a high mountain peak, looking down over forests and rivers. She wasn't afraid.

YOU ARE NOT OF THIS WORLD.

No, I just live here. I'm from Rrth.

Terra floated in space. Before her hung a familiar blue-green planet and its solitary moon.

That's the place.

THEY DO NOT KNOW US. THEY MUST NOT KNOW US.

Well, I'm not going to tell them.

Terra was in a place that was not a place, whiteness and silence.

THIS IS UNFORESEEN. YOU ARE UN-FORESEEN.

I'm sorry . . .

* * *

Terra sat on the stone steps, her slate in her hand. It was dark.

She could hear cries and gasps of alarm from all around her. Someone grabbed her shoulders.

- What happened? What did you do?

It was Vstj. Lbbp appeared behind him and pulled him away from Terra.

Terra began to stand up. *- They've gone?*

Lbbp helped her up. *- One of them bent down and touched you and then they all disappeared. FaZoon, ship, everything.*

Vstj was still shouting *- What did you say to them? What did you say?*

Terra was confused. *- I just read out what was . . .*

88

- *The Ymn child scared them away!* said a voice from the crowd.

- *Whose stupid idea was it to let the Ymn talk to them?* said another. Shm and the Chancellor exchanged awkward glances.

With angry murmurs and disappointed groans, the crowd began to disperse.

Terra looked tearfully up at Lbbp. - *I didn't do anything ... They spoke to me inside my head ... I don't really remember what they ... I didn't tell them anything I wasn't supposed to ... did I?*

Lbbp put his arm around her. - *Come on home. It doesn't matter. Nobody blames you.*

- *Are you sure?* asked Terra. She gestured to the retreating crowd. *I think some of them do.*

- *Well, nobody who matters blames you,* said Lbbp.

-*Look!* Fthfth shouted. *They did leave us a message!*

The movement of the crowd had revealed strange symbols, freshly carved into the white paving stones. The FaZoon had given the Mlmlns a gift of knowledge after all.

Vstj, who had been slumped despairingly on the steps, leapt to his feet.

- *Where is it? Where? Out of the way, let me see ...*

Vstj stared at the symbols. He produced his slate from under his robe and began translating.

- *Two whole pt-ssh ... one fnj, chopped ... one ch-fsh leaf, one pinch vshk ...*

Vstj sat down on the steps.

- *It's soup. They've given us a recipe for soup.*

Lbbp smiled. - *So it hasn't been a complete waste of an evening.* He took Terra home.

The next morning, the square was deserted. The FaZoon symbols remained carved into the stones.

Later that day, Pktk came back to the square. He diligently copied the symbols onto his slate, and carefully translated the whole inscription. He went to the fresh produce market, bought the ingredients, went home and followed the recipe to the letter.

It was really good soup.

The next few days passed smoothly enough, although Terra couldn't help but feel that a cloud of suspicion still hung over her with regard to the FaZoon incident. For all of Pktk's protestations that *no, seriously, you should try it, it's really good soup* the general feeling was that the Fnrrns had been collectively cheated out of something, and while no one was foolish or nasty enough to suggest that it was in some way Terra's fault while in her presence ...

The matter of the Interface was also unresolved. Given that there didn't appear to be a way for Terra to use the device safely, she'd been excused from Interface sessions and given the time to do extra reading. But, much as Terra had feared, she couldn't keep up with the sheer volume of information that her classmates were absorbing. For every text or article she read, her friends would simply programme a hundred or more directly into their heads.

Lbbp would do his best to cheer her up, but Terra was consumed with worry that she'd be held back an orbit, or worse, banished back to the Pre-Ac.

Sometimes, of an evening, Lbbp would pass Terra's room. He would peek inside and see the child peering furiously at her slate, scanning through screens and screens of information. He wondered if she could possibly take anything in at that speed. On other occasions he would pass outside her door and hear her crying quietly. The first time this happened, he hurried in to her, offering consolation and hugs, but her obvious embarrassment at having been caught in tears made him feel guilty at having added to her distress. After this incident he would stand outside the door, listening to her sobs and feeling wretched at his failure to help her.

This couldn't go on. Lbbp resolved to demand an audience with the Preceptor. He owed them a favour.

2.13

Terra ached all over as she floated towards home. Gshkth was not really her sort of game at all, she decided.

Fthfth's skill and enthusiasm in the gshkth pit were a sight to behold, but while her enthusiasm was infectious, her skill wasn't. She would wield her gfrg with strength and dexterity, and while Terra could swing a gfrg like the best of them, she always seemed to be half a blip too slow to receive Fthfth's passing zmms. The bdkt would ricochet maddeningly off the hddgs, sometimes coming to rest among the frkts, sometimes getting stuck fast in a nshp. Fthfth would call out - *Yk yk! That was definitely a yk yk!* and try to persuade the arbiter to play a jrf-jtt, but the arbiter would blow his pff, call ANOTHER tsh-tsh and play would recommence until Terra, inevitably, would ch-gss when she was supposed to ch-grr and they'd concede another mgmk.

Terra was beginning to suspect that Fthfth wished she'd chosen another gshkth partner. She approached the main room window of the apartment, felt in her pocket for the little metal tube, squeezed it and watched the crystal slide open. She deactivated her bubble, stepped into the room and flopped onto the padded bench. Just a moment, she told herself. Just a moment to get her breath back, then she would go to her room and start reading. And reading. And reading.

The door swished open and Lbbp appeared, smiling.

- You're home! Excellent.

- Is it?

- It certainly is. Wait right there. Lbbp disappeared again. Terra was too tired to be confused or even particularly interested.

After a few moments – or possibly longer – Lbbp reappeared. He trotted into the room, followed by another Fnrrn Terra didn't recognise, younger than Lbbp but still much older than herself. He wore a silver garment and carried a slate. She sat up and peered at them blearily.

- *This*, said Lbbp, *is Gftg. He works for the Brain Science Directorate. I think you may be familiar with some of his work.*

Gftg held up his hand and splayed his fingers. - *It's a real honour to meet you, Terra*, he said with what seemed like ... nervousness?

- *I–I'm sorry*, stammered Gftg. *I've been following your story with great interest ever since ... since you were ... since you ...*

- *Arrived?* ventured Terra.

- *Yes, arrived*, said Gftg. *I was so pleased when your – erm, when Lbbp* (Lbbp had asked Gftg not to refer to him as Terra's 'father'; he'd just remembered in time) *contacted me. I do hope I'll be able to help you.*

Terra had absolutely no idea what was going on.

- *Come into the servery*, said Lbbp, registering her confusion.

Terra followed Lbbp and Gftg through the corridor and into the small room where food was prepared.

- *Oh no*, she groaned.

There on the work surface, just next to the protein manipulator, stood an Interface.

Lbbp smiled. - *I thought you might say that*, he said, *but let Gftg explain.*

Terra sat down grumpily on one of the servery's stools, folded her arms and glowered at the Interface, her memory full of headaches and the smell of burnt hair.

- *I worked on the design of the Interface*, explained Gftg, *and between you and me, not only was it never intended for use by Ymns, it wasn't even supposed to be used by children at all.*

I know, thought Terra, but couldn't be bothered to explain how.

- *We'd already made some adjustments to the model we*

*supplied to the Lyceum, but it wasn't until we heard about your
... incident that we realised it was going to be used by anyone
... erm ...*

- *Differently evolved ...?* suggested Lbbp.
- *Exactly,* smiled Gftg.

So much for the 'manufacturer's assurances', thought Terra.

Gftg went on. - *There are obviously some fundamental
differences in cranial and cerebral structure between Ymns and
Fnrrns,* he said, *but without access to any, erm, detailed information on Ymn anatomy we didn't know exactly what these
differences were. But Lbbp here,* he gestured towards Lbbp
who smiled proudly, *granted me access to the medical scans
from your regular Nosocomium check-ups.*

Terra wasn't sure whether to feel grateful or disturbed.
Gftg had obviously gone to great trouble but the thought
of a stranger poring over images of her brain was a little ...
creepy.

- *Anyway, I've been studying the scans for a while now and
I've been able to construct this,* he indicated the Interface. *It's
your own personalised model.*

Terra approached the work surface and looked at the
machine. It was sleeker and newer-looking than the one in
the Lyceum, with a smaller crystal dome (to fit her smaller
head, she supposed).

- *Can we afford this?* she asked Lbbp. Lbbp smiled.
- *It's taken care of. The Preceptor said it was the least he
could do.* After Lbbp had pointed out at length and quite
forcibly (by Lbbp's standards) that, given the humiliation
he'd brought upon Terra with the FaZoon debacle, paying
for her to have her own Interface was, quite literally, the
least the Preceptorate could do.

Terra bent down to look up into the glass dome.

- *Want to give it a try?* asked Lbbp.

Terra wasn't sure.

- *Just see how it fits,* said Gftg.

Nervously, Terra inserted her head into the dome. She
smiled.

- *It has spaces for my ears,* she said.

- *It has spaces for your ears,* smiled Lbbp.

- *I'm just going to run a start-up programme,* said Gftg. *It's not going to transmit any information, it's just going to try to sync to your brain.*

Terra heard the sound of Gftg tapping instructions into the machine, then the three blips of the countdown.

She felt a warm sensation. Nothing unpleasant.

It was as if a distant voice were calling to her. Faint, indistinct. She strained to hear it.

It seemed that the voice was that of someone who knew her. Knew her, but wanted to know her better.

The voice was louder now. It called her name.

- *Terra?*

Louder still.

- *Terra, can you hear me?*

Completely clear and close now.

- *Terra, are you all right?*

The voice was Lbbp's. But it hadn't been.

- *I'm fine,* said Terra. *I think ...*

- *Yes?* said Gftg eagerly.

- *It's like it's trying to find me, but it can't.*

Gftg looked momentarily crestfallen, but shook off the disappointment. - *That's good!* he said brightly. *It's finding its way through your conscious pathways and trying to reach the memory centres. It'll take a few sessions to sync up properly but this is a good start.*

Anything beats being blown across the room with your hair on fire, thought Terra, but decided not to bring that up just now.

2.14

For the next few evenings, when Terra got back from the Lyceum, Gftg and Lbbp would be waiting and they would try again. Gftg's presence wasn't strictly necessary; he'd shown Lbbp everything he needed to know in order to operate the Interface, but he came anyway. He was still slightly overawed to be in the presence of the Ymn child. From conversations Lbbp had with Gftg, he got the impression that Terra had quite a few 'fans' in Hrrng's scientific community.

- *My friends at the Directorate are so jealous*, said Gftg on one occasion.

- *Really?* asked Lbbp, sounding slightly more interested than he actually was.

- *Well, yes. They can't believe I'm getting to work with a real live alien.*

- *I'm right here, you know*, said Terra from inside the dome.

- *Sorry*, said Gftg as the Interface powered down. He lifted the dome from Terra's head. *Any clearer this time?*

- *I think so*, said Terra. *Ask me something.*

- *Okay*, said Gftg nervously. He read from his slate.

- *What's the correct bombardment frequency for the activation of grav-matter?*

- *Four point two one three seven five six nanoblips divided by x where x is the gravitational constant of the planet.*

- *Which species can only reproduce extra-atmospherically?*

- *Species five five seven two, or sgth-k-shffs. They spawn in deep space and the spores drift until they find a host planet.*

- *Which star expanded to red category twelve on the seventy-third day of orbit forty-five, thirty-second era?*

Terra paused.

- *Do you need me to repeat the question?* asked Gftg.

- *No,* said Terra. She'd heard the question, she could remember the question, and she could almost remember the answer. It was as if someone were calling it out to her while walking away.

- *Star number thirty-two dash five four ... five four ...*

The imaginary person calling out the answer inside Terra's head turned an imaginary corner and was gone.

- *I'm sorry, it's not there,* said Terra sadly. Gftg didn't share her despondency.

- *Not to worry! The information went in, it's just not imprinting properly yet. It's still great progress, though! We'll try again tomorrow.*

Terra turned to Lbbp. - *It worked! I got it working, sort of.*

Lbbp smiled back, although inwardly he wasn't sure how he actually felt about this turn of events. On the one hand Terra's distress at the thought of being left behind at the Lyceum had been a cause of great concern; seeing that possibility recede a little (and Terra's relief at this) was something to be glad about, he supposed ... On the other hand, he still had serious doubts about the use of the Interface in general; secretly, he'd been quite pleased that it hadn't worked on Terra, and seeing her just now with her head crammed into the dome being 'programmed' like all the other pupils had made him uncomfortable.

Gftg made a promise to return the next day, and left, but not before handing his comm to Lbbp and asking him to record an image of himself with Terra. Lbbp obliged.

* * *

- *What do you think?* asked Terra after Gftg had left.

- *I think that picture's going to be all over the Source by morning,* muttered Lbbp.

- *No, I mean what do you think of the Interface now?* corrected Terra, who immediately realised she'd said too much.

- *What do you mean, what do I think of it now?* Lbbp said, suspiciously. *What makes you think I felt any particular way about it before ...?*

Terra sighed. - *I heard you. I heard you arguing with Bsht about it a few cycles ago. I knew you thought it was dangerous.*

I knew it, thought Lbbp. *I knew she was worried about it.* He spoke. - *Well, not dangerous exactly, I just thought it was, maybe ... or at least, potentially ... okay, I thought it was dangerous. And I'm still not entirely convinced that I was wrong, especially after you tried the one at the Lyceum, and it ... did that ... thing ...*

-*...with the flash ...* said Terra.

-*... and the bang ...*

-*... and the hair ...*

- *Quite,* said Lbbp. *You can imagine how guilty I felt that I hadn't said anything.*

Terra's nose wrinkled. Her lips pursed and her eyebrows became perfectly horizontal. Lbbp recognised this as her I'm Having A Thought face.

- *What is it ...?* he asked.

- *What if you HADN'T said anything? To warn me about the Interface?*

Lbbp was confused. - *But I didn't ...*

- *No,* said Terra, *you THOUGHT you hadn't said anything, but you had, you just didn't know I'd heard it ...*

- *I'm confused,* said Lbbp, who was.

- *You HAD said you thought the Interface was dangerous, you just didn't know I'd heard you saying it. You'd warned me about it without meaning to. Well, what if you hadn't? What if you hadn't put the idea in my head that the Interface was dangerous?* asked Terra animatedly. *What if the problem wasn't that I was the only Ymn trying to use it, but that I was the only one in the class who thought that using it was a bad idea?*

- *You think your brain might have rejected it?* Lbbp was intrigued.

- *Why not? If I was afraid of the thing – and I was – wouldn't my brain just shut down rather than let it in? Would that have made it ... do the thing, with the flash, and the bang, and the hair ...?*

- Yes ... and now you've got this new custom Ymn-friendly model, pondered Lbbp, *you're not scared any more, just a bit apprehensive, so it's working, but not properly ...*

-... but if I just relaxed and stopped worrying, it might work just fine ...?

Lbbp drummed his chin with his long grey fingers.

- It's a hypothesis, he said, *and quite a promising one. If perhaps a rather worrying one for me ...*

- How do you mean?

- Well, said Lbbp, *if you're right, it means there was never anything wrong with the Interface and this is all my fault for being such a big panicky old-fashioned g'shbk.*

Terra burst out laughing.

Lbbp smiled. *- I mean, I remember when slates were invented there were people who didn't trust them. I'm sure back when they created the Source there were those who said it was dangerous or evil or something ...*

- Yes, said Terra, *I bet a couple of million orbits ago there was a Fnrrn sitting in a tree saying I don't approve of all this cave-painting and tree-carving, in my day if you wanted to tell someone something you just grunted. What's wrong with grunting?*

Lbbp and Terra laughed until tears streamed down Terra's cheeks and Lbbp's sides ached.

- Well, come on then! said Terra once she'd recovered.

- Come on what? said Lbbp.

Terra bounded across to the Interface. *- Let's give it a go!*

- Now? said Lbbp wearily. *It's late! You have classes tomorrow, I've got ...*

- It's not that late! Let's test the hypothesis! Let's be scientists! Let's prove ourselves right!

- It IS that late, said Lbbp, *and I'd much rather test it while Gftg's here. At least then if it goes wrong we've got someone around who knows what he's doing.*

Terra looked crestfallen. Lbbp put his arm around her shoulders.

- *Look, it was a great piece of deductive reasoning and if you're right, you'll be just as right tomorrow as you are now, okay, my little scientist?*

Terra smiled.

- *And anyway,* said Lbbp, *science isn't about proving yourself right. A bad scientist tries to prove himself right. A good scientist tries to prove himself wrong, and only when he fails does he conclude that he's right.*

- *If it's too late for experiments, it's too late for lectures,* said Terra with a smile.

2.15

Terra switched the sleep-well off, did a gentle forward flip and came to a neat two-footed landing on her bedroom floor. She couldn't sleep.

The prospect of getting the Interface to work properly, of being able to catch up with her classmates, indeed, just the thought of all that knowledge flooding into her head was far too exciting.

She opened her bedroom door; wincing at how loud the swishing noise was in the silence of the night.

She crept past Lbbp's room. *You do snore, you know,* she thought.

She crept back to the main room, where the Interface was still set up.

Relaxed, thought Terra, *that's the thing. I've got to be relaxed.*

She placed the Interface on the floor at the end of the padded bench seat, and adjusted the stem so that the dome rose just above the end of the bench. Lying down upon the bench, she would be able to fit her head neatly inside it.

Terra set the test programme running, then hurried to get into position before the third blip.

She lay back with her hands clasped across her tummy and waited.

This is taking a while, thought Terra.

This is taking rather too long, she thought.

Did I set it up properly? I heard the blips.

What happens if I take the dome off just as it's starting up?

I'll give it another few moments, thought Terra, *then I'll get up and check it. I'll be okay as long as I don't fall asleep.*

Terra fell asleep.

2.16

Terra dreamed. White clouds, blue sky. Soaring.
She was a bird. She was a giant bird. She rode a giant green bird. She was herself, and she was riding a giant green bird.

Fields and valleys beneath her. Rolling purple hills. Raging sea. Calm, peaceful raging sea. The waves surged and roared, silently. She was alone. Someone was there, and she was alone.

Voices? Just sounds. The sounds of voices. Voices.

She swooped. She dived. She swam. She was a fish. She rode a fish. She was herself and she swam alongside a giant green fish.

She was not alone. She was watched. No one was there. No one was there, and they were watching her. She was not afraid.

There was a znk. She was not afraid of the znk. She made some undergrowth to hide in, then hid in the undergrowth, and was not afraid of the znk. No one was still there, watching.

The znk spoke. - *What is this place?*

- *It's Rfk, I think,* replied Terra to the znk. *It doesn't look like it but it is.*

- *This place is not recognised. Where does this information originate?* asked the znk, who was Lbbp.

- *It's not information, silly,* said Terra, growing now to the height of a lgsh-chr flower. She was a lgsh-chr flower, changing colour, red, purple, blue. *It's just a place.*

Hjj bugs came to pollinate her - *What is the source of this information?* they asked, rude little hjj bugs.

Terra did not want to speak to the hjj bugs, so she went

home. She was at home. The visualiser spoke. She spoke. Terra watched herself on the visualiser and she spoke.

- *You are Terra. You are the Ymn child.*

- *Yes, we are,* replied Terra to herself.

- *How are these images generated?* asked Other Terra on the visualiser.

- *They're not generated,* said Terra, *they're just here.*

- *By what means are you connected?* asked Compositor Vstj. Who had invited him? Terra shook her head and turned him into Lbbp. That was better.

- *Connected to what?* asked Terra, climbing into the visualiser.

- *These images conflict with accepted parameters,* said Lbbp. Terra peered out of the visualiser at him. *What is their point of origin? Security protocols are now in operation.*

Terra was annoyed by Lbbp, and by the room, and the questions. She made them go away, and soared through the air again.

Pktk was there. He rode a great blue bird. Terra decided it was her green bird's best friend. Pktk was not afraid. Pktk was always afraid, but not this Pktk, not now. He spoke.

- *This signal has been traced to the home terminal of apartment six-green-four, Shfs-Gs-Shfs Tower, Upper Blue District, Hrrng.*

- *That's where we live,* said Terra. *You've been there lots of times.* They swooped down together, skimming over a valley of purple grass. Terra laughed and kept on dreaming.

2.17

Lbbp was not used to being woken in the middle of the night. When Terra had been a tiny baby he had often been dragged from sleep by the sound of her crying, but these days it was very unusual, once he'd activated his sleep-well and drifted off into dreamless unconsciousness, for him to be disturbed before his scheduled waking time.

As such, when Lbbp's comm started beeping beside his sleep-well, just a spectrum or so after he'd dozed off, it took him quite a while to figure out where he was and what was going on.

Blearily, he tumbled to the floor, got up and groped for his comm.

- *Yes?* he asked.

- *You are Postulator Dfst-sh-Kshchk-sh-Lbbp?*

- *What? Er, yes, yes I am. I think.* It was very unusual for anyone to address Lbbp by his full name. He himself hadn't heard it spoken in orbits. He had to think about it for a little while to be sure it had in fact been his own name he'd just heard and not that of some other Lbbp. Lbbp wasn't a particularly unusual Fnrrn name. Not so as to be exciting or noteworthy. *Erm ... might I ask why? And who are you?*

- *This is an artificially intelligent vocal communication from Hrrng Preceptorate Information Traffic Control. Please wait while you are connected to an organic representative.*

Lbbp groaned and stretched. What could InTraCon want with him at this time of night? He hadn't been using the Source to do personal stuff at work ... Not much anyway. Nothing that would merit this sort of intrusion. He was mentally rehearsing the strong words he was going to have with whoever spoke next, when they spoke.

- *Is that Postulator Lbbp?*

No, it's the Grand High Emperor Of The Outer Galactic Rim, now g'shb off and let me sleep, thought Lbbp. - *Yes,* said Lbbp.

- *It's Chfl here from InTraCon, sorry about the lateness of the call . . .*

- *That's perfectly okay,* said Lbbp, who found he didn't have the energy to be angry. *What's going on?*

- *Well, Postulator, we were rather hoping you could tell us,* said Chfl apologetically. *Someone logged into your home network has opened a channel directly into the Lyceum data bank, but the thing is, they're not taking any information out. They're sending it.*

- *What?* asked Lbbp, starting to wake up.

- *That's not the strange part,* said Chfl, *it's the stuff that's coming in. It's like nothing we've ever seen before. It looks like . . . memories . . .*

- *Memories?* said Lbbp. *Memories of what?*

- *That's just it,* said Chfl. *It looks like memories of things that couldn't possibly have happened.*

- *Memories of . . . couldn't possibly . . .* Lbbp was beginning to wonder if he was properly awake yet. *I'm sorry, I don't . . .*

- *Perhaps I'd better show you. Do you have your slate there?*

- *My slate? Yes, yes, I . . .*

- *Just a blip . . . There, you should be seeing what we're seeing now.*

Lbbp stared at his slate. He was looking through someone else's eyes. The image blurred and flickered, phasing from full colour to monochrome and back again.

He seemed to be flying, high above unfamiliar and yet very familiar terrain. It looked like everywhere he'd ever been and nowhere in particular. He was following some sort of blue avian creature, which had . . . was that someone riding on its back? What was going on?

- *Are you seeing this, Postulator?*

- *Yes, yes I am, but I don't . . . That animal, it doesn't . . .*

There are elements from various avian species but they've just been thrown together into something that makes no evolutionary sense ... That creature not only doesn't exist, it COULDN'T exist ...

- *So what are we looking at then?*

- *I have no idea ...* And Lbbp genuinely didn't. He watched in utter bewilderment. The picture continued to phase and blur ... He set his slate to save mode, recording the pictures so that he could study them properly in due course.

What WAS that animal? There wasn't a single species of flying creature recorded anywhere in the galaxy that was big and strong enough to be ridden like a gnth-sh'gst. And who was that riding it? It looked like a child ... in fact, didn't he know that child ...? Wasn't he at the Lyceum with ...

A voice was heard. The voice of whoever owned the eyes through which Lbbp was now looking.

- *Pktk, have I ever shown you my planet?*

TERRA!

It was Terra's point of view he was seeing on the slate, confirmed now as the eyes glanced down at the speaker's own hands. She was also riding a great flying animal, green this time, and as she stroked the back of its head Lbbp saw those hands; small, pink, unmistakable, unique on the planet.

Lbbp ran to Terra's room. The sleep-well was inactive and Terra was nowhere to be seen. Seized with panic, Lbbp ran back to get his comm. He had to raise the alarm, to set out in search of her, to ...

He saw the image on his slate. It had changed. Pktk and Terra (through whose eyes he still saw) were now drifting in the vacuum of space, looking down on the planet Rrth.

- *Look, there it is,* said Terra's voice. *Just the one moon I'm afraid. Shall we make some more?*

Lbbp's mind reeled. Rrth? Rrth was over twenty opticals away! She couldn't have got there since last night! And no one could survive in space without an environment suit, you'd be dead in a few blips! This couldn't be happening! It just couldn't be happening! It couldn't …

It WASN'T happening.

It wasn't happening. Any of it.

The main room light was on.

Lbbp opened the door. There she was. Flat on her back, asleep with the Interface dome over her head. She was there, she was home, she was safe. The wave of relief almost banished Lbbp's confusion. It returned after a moment.

Lbbp's fingers fumbled with the comm.

- *Postulator? Are you still there, Postulator?* Chfl's voice had been squeaking from the comm all this time. Lbbp hadn't noticed. He answered him now.

- *I'm here. Look, I think I may know what's going on and it's nothing to worry about. I'll explain everything when I arrive in the morning.*

Lbbp switched off the comm and sat beside Terra's sleeping form. The dome of her new Interface pulsed away. *Couldn't wait, could you? Silly girl. Silly, brilliant girl.*

He glanced down at his slate. Rrth now had a whole network of moons, of various different sizes and colours.

- *Shall we do another one or is that enough?* asked the Terra on the slate. The one in the room slept on peacefully.

It's all going on in her mind as she sleeps, thought Lbbp. *She sees things and has adventures as she sleeps. She goes to places that aren't there, she sees creatures that have never existed. Things happen that don't happen. What an extraordinary concept.*

Fnrrns don't dream. Not adult Fnrrns anyway. Baby Fnrrns have visions in their sleep, sometimes happy ones, sometimes scary ones, but as their minds mature and develop into sensible, logical Fnrrn minds, they grow out of such things and sleep each night in a state of soothing oblivion. Lbbp remembered how Terra would sometimes wake up crying and frightened when she was tiny, but that hadn't happened for orbits now. Did she still dream? Do Ymns dream all their lives?

Lbbp was pondering how he might safely extricate Terra from the Interface when the machine itself solved the problem for him. With its test programme having long since run its course, and no further instructions forthcoming, it switched itself into standby mode. Lbbp's slate went blank.

Terra smacked her lips and blinked. She peered sleepily up at Lbbp.

- *Oh dear,* she said.

- *Oh dear indeed,* concurred Lbbp.

- *I couldn't wait,* said Terra pleadingly. *I just couldn't wait to test our theory. But I fell asleep before it started working. Nothing happened.*

- *Well, not exactly,* said Lbbp.

- *What?*

- *I'll tell you about it in the morning,* said Lbbp. *Now get back into your sleep-well and go to sleep!*

Terra slouched guiltily back to her room. Lbbp watched her go. Go where? Once she was asleep, what adventures awaited her?

Lbbp was more than a little envious.

- *So go on then, what did happen last night?* asked Terra as she settled down to eat her configuration 6 the next morning. *Am I in trouble?*

Lbbp put down his plate of configuration 11 and paused. - *Not in trouble, really, no ... it's just.*

There came an angry hammering sound. They turned to look towards it.

Pktk was hovering outside the window, and he didn't look at all happy. Pktk rarely looked happy, but this was a whole new level of not-happy that he seemed to be experiencing at the moment.

- *Well, you're not in trouble with me, anyway,* said Lbbp warily. *Shall we let him in?*

- *I think we'd better,* said Terra.

The window pane slid open and Pktk bounced angrily into the room, his bubble still active.

- *What did you do, Terra?* he asked as he bounced off the floor. *And how did you do it?* He bounced off the ceiling. *And most of all, WHY did you do it?* He bounced off the floor again, finally remembered to switch his bubble off and landed in a heap at Terra's feet.

- *I don't ... understand,* said Terra, feeling hurt, confused and trying desperately not to laugh.

Pktk sat up. - *Last night when we were all asleep, my father's comm goes off. Apparently there was some live visual feed coming over the Source, showing ME flying around on some sort of monster, then floating off into space! My mother wakes up screaming, running round the apartment shouting help help my baby's in space, I wake up, she sees I'm okay and THEN starts screaming at ME, asking when had I been off in space and riding flying monsters without telling her, and then I look at the pictures on my slate and it's me and YOU, you're in space as well and what is GOING ON?*

- *It's on the Source?* asked Lbbp, a note of panic in his voice.

- *It's all over the Source!* said Pktk.

- *WHAT'S all over the Source?* asked Terra, confused and distressed. *Could one of you please tell me what you're talking about?*

Lbbp sighed, picked up his slate and retrieved the recording from the previous night. - *This*, he said, and handed the slate to Terra.

Terra watched, Lbbp waited, Pktk watched them watching and waiting and fidgeted with anger and anxiety.

Terra watched the blurring, phasing images. It all looked weirdly familiar for something so indistinct. Then suddenly she knew where she'd seen these pictures before, and she felt horribly exposed, almost violated.

After a few moments, Pktk found he could contain himself no longer. - *Well?* he asked.

- *It's my dream. My dream from last night. Oh no, the Interface …*

- *You confused the Source*, said Lbbp. *Not an easy thing to do. You plugged your brain right into the Lyceum data bank and then started deluging it with images from your unconscious mind.*

- *You still dream?* asked Pktk, incredulously. *Terra, you still dream? Like a baby?*

- *Yes*, said Terra, *and that*, she said, pointing to Pktk, *is why I've never told anyone.* She turned to Lbbp. *When I was tiny, I learned how everyone dreams when they're very very young but that you're supposed to grow out of it as you get older. Well, I never did … I kept waiting for the dreams to stop but they kept coming. At first I didn't tell anyone because I didn't want people to think I was still a baby … you know what it's like when you're little, you want to grow up as soon as possible.*

Lbbp nodded. Terra went on: - *And by the time I realised*

that it's different for Ymns, that we just keep on dreaming our whole lives, well, then I didn't want anyone to know because there were already so many things about me that were different to everyone else. I didn't think they needed to know about this one.

Lbbp was saddened by the thought of Terra having to keep something so innocent a secret for so long. - *You could have told me,* he said. *I thought you knew you could tell me anything . . .*

- *I just thought you'd worry, or worse than that,* Terra said, with a pointed look at Lbbp, *I thought it might arouse your scientific curiosity.*

She knows me too well, thought Lbbp. *Much too well.*

- *I was afraid that if I told you about the dreaming, next thing I knew I'd be in your lab at the Life Science Hub with wires poking out of my head,* said Terra, with a smile.

- *So instead of that, you did it to yourself by accident. What a family,* laughed Lbbp. He looked Terra right in the eyes. *If there's ever anything on your mind, you can always tell me. We don't need to keep secrets from each other.*

Pktk had been silent for so long they'd both rather forgotten he was there. He spoke, and they remembered.

- *Wait,* said Pktk . . . *you've got your own Interface? How did you get your own Interface?*

- *It's a long story,* said Terra. *But yes, it does have spaces for my ears.*

2.19

Lbbp noticed the clock; epoch-shattering scientific breakthrough or no epoch-shattering scientific breakthrough, they were late for the Lyceum. The Lyceum had a list of circumstances under which lateness could be excused. Lbbp was fairly certain that epoch-shattering scientific breakthroughs weren't on that list.

They hurried to the window and floated away as quickly as they could. Lbbp came with them; it might be necessary to make some sort of excuse for their tardiness, he thought, and besides, he also had the distinct feeling he hadn't heard the last of this dreaming business. If the images had ended up on the Source, why by now they could have been seen by …

Everybody.

When Terra and Pktk arrived at the lectorium, late (to Bsht's evident annoyance), the rest of the class immediately forgot what they were doing and rushed to greet them (to Bsht's evident extreme annoyance).

- What were those flying things?!

- Where can I get one?!

- How did you get into space?!

- How did you get back?!

- EVERYBODY SIT BACK DOWN RIGHT NOW!

Everybody sat back down.

Lbbp let the silence bed in for a blip or two then whispered to Bsht.

- Have you got a moment?

Bsht turned to look at Lbbp with an expression combining all manner of emotions, none of them positive.

- Of course! Why not, it's not as if I have anything else to do right now . . .

Lbbp and Bsht retired to the corner of the room. The lectorium visualiser, which really was becoming too clever by half, Terra thought, had begun playing the recording of last night's visions. The class watched it all over again, fascinated and not a little envious.

Terra took the opportunity to address her classmates.

- It's a dream. That's all it is. It's a dream I had last night, and . . .

- A dream? asked Shnst.

- Like what babies have? asked Thnst.

Terra sighed. *- Fnrrn babies, yes. Ymns keep dreaming all their lives.*

General astonishment.

Terra explained the whole sequence of events, as best she understood it; how she was practising with her Interface (*- yes, I've got my own Interface, yes, it has spaces for my ears, no, it hasn't set fire to my hair again, not yet anyway*), how her dream made its way into the Lyceum data banks and onto the Source (no one was yet quite clear how that had happened) and how poor Pktk's parents had been awoken with terrifying reports of Pktk floating in space (Pktk smiled ruefully at the laughter this provoked – a lot of his classmates had met his parents).

Fthfth was thoughtful. *- So it didn't happen. Any of it. It just sort of pretended to happen inside your head . . .*

- That's right, said Terra.

- And you get this sort of thing happening inside your head every night? Must be terribly confusing.

- And tiring, mused Yshn. *What's the point of being asleep if you're still busy inside your head? Might as well just stay up.*

- That's . . . not really how it works, said Terra, who'd never had to explain all of this before and was finding that it wasn't quite as clear in her own mind as she'd thought it would be.

- How do you know when you've woken up? asked Fthfth.

- *You just sort of do,* replied Terra, immediately aware of what a weak answer that was.

At this point, Fthfth hit upon the vital question of the moment, the one no one else had thought to ask yet but which was, everyone realised upon hearing it, the thing that everyone ACTUALLY wanted to know.

- *Could you do it again?*

- *I expect so,* said Terra. *I don't see why it wouldn't work again. I'm not sure I want to try, though.*

- *Why not?* asked everybody.

- *Well, you see,* said Terra, thinking, oh dear, how to explain this, *dreams are sort of ... private. Seeing everybody else looking at my dreams, it's not ... it's not very ...*

- *Nice?* suggested Pktk.

- *That's it,* said Terra gratefully. *It's not very nice having everyone looking inside your head like this. When you're asleep you have whatever thoughts your brain feels like having. What if I did it again but this time I dreamed about something secret, or something embarrassing, or just something I didn't want everyone else looking at for ... whatever reason?*

- *But would you have to be asleep?* asked Fthfth. *What if you put the Interface on and just ... thought about things?*

- *What, thought about things that aren't real?* said Shnst.

- *How can you think about something when it's not real?* said Thnst.

- *Well, we can't, but it looks like Terra can,* said Fthfth with the air of a detective solving a mystery. *Just last night she invented a new species of flying creature and gave Rrth a whole new moon system. Terra can think of all sorts of things that aren't real when she's asleep. The question is, can she do it when she's awake?*

Bsht re-entered the lectorium and the class fell silent. Bsht seemed slightly less angry but still about as confused as when she'd left.

- *Right,* she began, *I've had the situation ... explained ... and it seems there's nothing to worry about. But I don't want to find anyone looking at this,* she indicated the dream still playing on the visualiser, *again today please.* She switched the visualiser off. Terra could have sworn the visualiser made a disappointed *aww* noise as it deactivated.

2.20

The rest of the day passed as without incident as could reasonably be expected. Yes, Terra was the subject of furtive glances and excited whispers wherever she went in the Lyceum, but if she wasn't used to that by now she was never going to be.

It was during the morning interlude that Terra had her own little revelation. She was pondering Fthfth's suggestion that she try to use the Interface to capture dream-images while she was still awake. It was an intriguing idea, she supposed, but it would be an altogether different process. Rather than let her unconscious mind go wherever it wanted, she would be steering the course of events herself. Would it be as interesting that way? Could she even do it?

She thought she'd give it a try. She closed her eyes. The end of the previous night's dream, the one everyone had now seen, seemed like a good place to start.

Terra thought about space. She tried to see herself floating in space, and there she was, inside her head, drifting in the inky void, looking down at stars and distant nebulae.

Terra's eyes opened. She could do it! She closed her eyes again; the picture was still there. She could summon up images at will.

I don't need to be asleep! she thought excitedly. *I can just think of anything I want, and then with the Interface I can ...*

It was at this point that Terra realised something. A little something that would, within a few short days, change everyone on Fnrr's life for ever.

I don't need the Interface.

Not to do this, anyway ... I could still use it for learning like everyone else does – I'm never going to finish this orbit if I don't – but I don't need it to record my dreams or anything else I think about.

I could just write it all down.

Terra found a quiet corner of the yard; the other pupils saw her go and decided to leave her alone, or at least Fthfth made this decision on their behalf and informed them of it. Terra had been having one of her 'interesting' days, after all, and probably needed some peace and quiet. Terra was lucky to have such thoughtful friends, Fthfth reminded them all.

Terra sat down and closed her eyes.

In her mind she saw ...

Space, still space. She was in space, floating ... no, not floating this time, she'd done that already ... she was ... Yes! Flying a spaceship. Much more interesting, and plausible, which suddenly seemed quite important.

So, what sort of spaceship? Lemon-shaped like Lbbp's? No, sleeker, like a l'shft dart, silver and pointy. She was ... alone? With friends? Alone. Alone in her sleek silver ship. She was ... what? Looking for something. What, though? Home? Another planet? What else is in space? She ran back through the last few days ... what had she seen, heard, talked about ...

Sgth-k-shffs! They live in space. They'd been the subject of one of Gftg's Interface test questions. Terra only knew about them because of the Interface; it seemed appropriate to incorporate them into this ... what would she call it?

That was a question for another time. Okay so, sgth-k-shffs it is then ...

Terra opened her eyes, made a few notes on her slate and closed her eyes again.

She was in space, alone in her silver dart spaceship, and there was a sgth-k-shff drifting in front of her. Bigger than the ship, it swam silently through space, ejecting bursts of plasma from the two vents on its back, propelling itself through the void.

Why am I here, though? thought Terra, opening her eyes.

Am I involved in these events or just watching? I should be involved; it's more interesting that way.

Let's see. What's so interesting about sgth-k-shffs? They spawn in space ... spores drift until they find a host planet ... Grow to maturity in seas and oceans ... Launch themselves back into space using natural plasma bursts ... absorb energy directly from stars ... unique life cycle ... protected species ...

That was it, protected species ... protected from what?

Terra closed her eyes again.

Daktavarian space poachers. That's what they're protected from. Hunters from the Silusirian system, preying upon the defenceless sgth-k-shffs for their plasma to power their pursuit ships.

Terra had no idea if there was such a race as the Daktavarians, such a place as the Silusirian system or, indeed, if you could actually power a spaceship with sgth-k-shff plasma, but it all sounded good to her ...

Here they came, four ships. Nasty metallic cylinders, bristling with weapons, closing in on the sgth-k-shff. And she, Commander Ksh-Gf-Trr of the Interplanetary Wildlife Protectorate (*that sounds great, write it down*) was the only thing between them and the poor sgth-k-shff. She primed her weapons systems and waited.

The lead Daktavarian ship attacked first, firing crackling energy bolts which scorched the surface of her dart-like ship as she evaded the incoming fire with extraordinary skill. She threw the ship into a hard spin, firing retro boosters (*that's what they're called, isn't it? Doesn't matter*) and pursuing the cylinder from behind. One perfectly aimed pulse-blast crippled its main engine and sent it tumbling helplessly into the void. Now for the others.

The three remaining Daktavarian vessels had arranged themselves in a triangular formation around the sgth-k-shff. Oh no! The attack upon her craft had been a diversion and she'd fallen for it (*that's good, don't want to make yourself too perfect, that would be boring*). She gunned the dart-ship's main grav-engines (*yes, I like the sound of that*) and raced back to the sgth-k-shff which she'd sworn to protect (*sworn? Really? Yes, why not?*).

The Daktavarian vessels had deployed an energy net (*nice*) around the sgth-k-shff; it struggled against the crackling threads. She had one chance at this. She aimed her ship at the space between two of the Daktavarians.

This was going to be difficult, dangerous and risky (*yes, that's important*). Too close to either of the Daktavarians and her ship would smash into a thousand shards, too close to the sgth-k-shff and she'd kill or injure it herself. An unthinkable possibility, given that she'd made a solemn promise to her dying grandfather, founder of the Interplanetary Wildlife Protectorate, to protect the galaxy's last remaining sgth-k-shffs with her life (*oh, yes, that's good, that's really good*).

Success! She flashed through the gap, Daktavarians above her and sgth-k-shff below, severing the energy net with the needle-sharp prow of her ship. Turning to attack, she saw that two of the Daktavarians were now tangled in the loose threads of the net ... Trying to power away, they instead swung around and smashed into each other (*ha! Serves them right!*).

One Daktavarian remained (*should think of an interesting way of getting rid of the last one, don't want to just blast him, that'd be boring. But why wouldn't I blast him?*). She got him in her sights, but then – oh no! Passing through the energy net had caused her weapons system to shut down (*there you go, that's why you can't blast him*)! Frantically she powered the weapons back up, but they'd never be ready in time! The Daktavarian bore down on her ... what could she do (*it's all exciting stuff, this*)?

Suddenly, the sgth-k-shff freed itself of the last threads of the energy net and turned as if to go ... Its plasma vents opened and, just as the Daktavarian's pulse-cannons fired, it let loose a stream of plasma which blew the Daktavarian into fragments (*oh, nicely done; you save the sgth-k-shff and then it saves you. That's very pleasing*).

She set off after the sgth-k-shff, and then saw something that made her heart leap and her eyes moisten (*moist eyes, eh? I guess I'm still a Ymn in this reality then*).

The sgth-k-shff had not been drifting aimlessly; it had detected a mate. Sgth-k-shffs communicate telepathically across immense distances (*do they? They do now*) and this one had been answering the thought-calls of another. And now here she (*he? Which one's which? Who cares?*) was.

She smiled as the two sgth-k-shffs floated away together, their species preserved for one more generation.

* * *

Upon opening her eyes, Terra was surprised to find that she actually had tears of happiness in her eyes, happiness for the safe and reunited sgth-k-shffs, which didn't even exist except in her head and, now, on her slate. None of what she'd written down was real, but if she imagined that what she'd imagined was real, it felt ... well ... real. Even though she knew it wasn't. That didn't matter somehow.

She looked down at her slate. There it was, the first exciting adventure of Commander Ksh-Gf-Trr of the Interplanetary Wildlife Protectorate. The pinging noise for the end of the interlude sounded and she trotted inside to show her friends what she'd created.

-*... and the sgth-k-shffs drifted away together, to be happy for the foreseeable future.*

Terra put down her slate and looked at her classmates faces.

There was a surprisingly long silence.

Even more surprisingly, it wasn't Fthfth who broke it.

- *And none of this is real?* asked Pktk. *None of it actually happened?*

- *No*, said Terra. *I just thought of it and wrote it down.*

- *Where did you get it from?* asked Pktk, intensely interested.

- *I just combined bits and pieces of ideas from all over the place, things I'd read, things I'd heard about and just mixed them all up into something that didn't happen, but might have happened.*

- *Well, yes, except there's no such race as Daktavarians and you can't power spaceships with sgth-k-shff plasma,* muttered Fthfth.

Pktk turned towards her. - *Well, how do you know? If Terra's invented a whole race of people called the Daktavarians, who's to say that THEIR spaceships wouldn't be powered by sgth-k-shff plasma? It's kind of up to Terra, it's her ... it's her ...* There wasn't a name for it. In the Fnrrn language there was no name for the thing that Terra had just created.

- *Story*, said Bsht.

- *What?* asked Terra.

- *That's what they call them on Rrth. Stories. I've been looking it up while you were talking, Terra. There's a Ymn word, 'story'. We've always thought it was just another word for 'history' – the two words are very similar, in fact they're the same* word in some *Ymn* languages. *But looking at these translations of Ymn broadcasts,* she held up her slate and showed Terra the blocks of text, *I think it has a different meaning. 'History' is an account of events that actually happened, 'stories' are accounts of events which may or may not have happened. Some of them are true, some of them are just . . .*

- *Thought up? Like I just thought that one up?* asked Terra, her eyes wide.

- *Indeed.* Bsht exhaled heavily and sat down. When you get a job as a Lyceum lector you don't expect major discoveries in the fields of xeno-linguistics and xeno-sociology to happen while you're teaching the novice class.

- *I'd better tell the Preceptor about this. This changes . . . a lot of things.*

Fthfth was still mulling something over. - *And sgth-k-shffs are NOT telepathic,* she grumbled.

2.22

Pktk finished his evening meal and went to his room to do his homework, or so he told his parents. He'd explained about Terra's dream, and told them about her story, and while his mother was still relieved that he hadn't in fact spent last night drifting through space with his Ymn friend (although it took her a long time to believe that), she was obviously rather perturbed by the idea of things that weren't real being talked about as if they were real. To her, such things seemed … distasteful.

Pktk sat down and looked at his slate. He accessed his favourite files, the files on military history. He read for a while; accounts of frontier skirmishes during the battle for control of the planet D'fng during the thirty-first era.

Pktk closed his eyes.

After a little while he opened them again. He smiled. He took up his slate, closed down the history files and opened up a new blank text file.

He wrote.

The Personal War Memoirs of Captain Vmk-sh-Gllg-sh-Fsst of the 12th Light Armoured Division, Last Survivor of the Battle of Chxx Ridge.

Pktk smiled. There had never been a Captain Vmk-sh-Gllg-sh-Fsst of the 12th Light Armoured Division, last survivor of the battle of Chxx Ridge. He had never existed.

But he did now.

2.23

The next few months were exciting times to live in Mlml.

The discovery, thanks to Terra's Interface accident, that Ymns could access their imagination – either consciously or unconsciously – to create non-existent but still thrilling and moving scenarios, these 'stories' (or st'rss as it came out in Mlmln), and, more importantly, the realisation that not just Ymns but Fnrrns could do this too if they tried, opened up a whole new world of possibilities.

Up until this point, Fnrrn culture in general and Mlmln culture in particular had consisted more or less entirely of two things: science and sports. Science was considered to be the bedrock of Fnrrn civilisation, and rightfully so. The peoples of Fnrr owed their prosperity, their health, their security, their very lives to science. Scientific advancement was the cause towards which almost all activity on the planet was dedicated, and when you couldn't take any more hypothesising or experimenting for one day, you could always go and thrash it all out of your system in the gshkth pit or on the dfsh field.

Even at home, one would relax by playing games. Games were important. They were fun, relaxing, and, crucially, they honed the mind and the powers of reason. All the better for when one returned to the important stuff: science.

Such broadcasts as people watched consisted of news (generally updates on the latest scientific discoveries), documentaries (generally histories of previous scientific discoveries) and coverage of sporting events. That was it, and up until now that had been perfectly sufficient for everyone.

Not any more.

Fnrr, and specifically Mlml, had gone literature crazy.

It had started modestly, with people writing short stories and publishing them on the Source, inviting critical appraisals and input. Most of them had been pretty awful, but the learning curve had been steep.

Novella-length stories had started to appear, along with, for the first time, full-length translations of Ymn stories and books, since Rrth was now renowned as the birthplace of *fk-shnn* (another new word; if nothing else the story-craze was having a dramatic effect upon the vocabulary of the language of Mlml). Popular titles included *Which Sister Will Die?*, *Sad Orphan Becomes Happy* (there were a few of these, actually) and *Crazy Monoped Can't Stop Chasing Sea Mammal* (Fnrrn story titles still tended to be rather literal rather than evocative, and the same applied to these translated works).

What no one knew was that Fnrr's very first home-grown author was in fact Pktk. He had never shown *The Personal War Memoirs of Captain Vmk-sh-Gllg-sh-Fsst of the 12th Light Armoured Division, Last Survivor of the Battle of Chxx Ridge* to anyone, or indeed any of Captain Vmk-sh-Gllg-sh-Fsst's other thrilling adventures (there were four in the series so far, taking Captain Fsst, or GENERAL Fsst as he now was, all the way to the end of the D'fng war and back to Fnrr where he was now fighting the G'grk at the battle of Gskkh-Sh'kkr). He saw the attention that successful authors were now getting. Pktk didn't like attention. He was happy for it to be paid to other people.

In any event, Pktk didn't think anyone would particularly enjoy reading stories about battling the G'grk in eras gone by when, for the first time in living memory, the G'grk were fighting battles in the here and now.

News had broken of a frontier dispute between the G'grk and Dskt, the nation which bordered the Central Plains on its landward side, and which faced Mlml across a narrow expanse of ocean on the other. As is always the case in such matters (not that anyone in Mlml was old enough to remember this) it was unclear who had started it, but within a few days of the crisis beginning, a small party of G'grk soldiers had been captured (on Dskt territory according to Dskt, on their own territory according to the G'grk High Command), a Dskt border station had been blown up (unprovoked, said Dskt; retaliation, said the G'grk) and things were suddenly very tense indeed. Not a time to put out a story about heroic wartime exploits, thought Pktk, showing more taste and restraint than anyone else in the entire history of publishing.

When the matter was discussed in Mlml at all, it was usually dismissed as the G'grk getting up to their old tricks, of causing trouble for the sake of it. Lbbp, for one, had his doubts about this. The G'grk were backward, superstitious and brutal, but they weren't stupid. They wouldn't go out of their way to provoke a war with a nation which was vastly technologically superior unless they wanted something. Or unless they knew something the Mlmlns and Dkstns didn't. Lbbp would reflect that if the sudden literary explosion that Mlml was enjoying proved anything, it was that 'primitiveness' was a very relative concept.

That was the best aspect of the whole thing, as far as Lbbp was concerned. If the populace had genuinely harboured any sort of resentment towards Terra because of how badly the last FaZoon visit had gone, then all such feelings had been well and truly forgotten now. She was feted as the founder of a cultural revolution, the little girl from another world who had introduced all of Fnrr to another world right here. There were rumours (baseless, Lbbp hoped) that a competition would soon be inaugurated, a prize for the best original work of fiction, and named in Terra's honour, and perhaps even with her being invited to judge the entries. No formal approaches had been made in that regard, but Lbbp was determined to turn them down if they ever materialised. Alien though she was, celebrity though she might be, she was still a little girl, his little girl and she had classwork to do.

There was another side to all this. Another factor which no one else had considered, perhaps because it was only really relevant in Lbbp's case. A much bleaker, more chilling implication.

Lbbp was alone one night when it hit him.

He'd seen Terra off to sleep, and was now staying up trying to finish a bit of work before retiring himself (he was getting a bit behind at the Life Science Hub, what with one thing and another). He stared at his slate; he was tired, the text was starting to become a meaningless jumble of characters and punctuation. He rubbed his eyes and got up to make himself a bowl of zff.

He couldn't resist looking in on Terra, to make sure she'd gone to sleep. It was an exciting time for her, he knew, and it was becoming a full-time occupation keeping her attention focused on the things that mattered.

She was fast asleep, rotating slowly in mid-air. Lbbp smiled. At least that business with the FaZoon had been forgotten. Ridiculous, pompous pretend demi-gods, he had no time for them. Maybe now they'd leave Fnrr alone. Maybe they'd go and check Rrth out, disrupt their lives for a change.

Lbbp's memory drifted back to the conversation he'd had with Terra, that day in the Leisure Hub, about why the FaZoon had never been to Rrth. About how no one was supposed to go to Rrth, not officially. He remembered talking about how those aliens who had visited Rrth often met a sticky – occasionally a snotty – end, and how weirdly they only ever seemed to belong to races that no one had ever encountered, as if they only existed –

Lbbp froze. His jaw dropped. His insides turned to ice.

They didn't exist.

The aliens who attacked Rrth in all those broadcasts he'd seen; they weren't real. The broadcasts were stories. Enacted, visually realised stories.

That was why none of the races were familiar, the Ymns had made them up. All of them. The huge, city-blasting disc-ships, the three-legged death machines (now he thought about it, they were obviously made up; who builds a machine with three legs? It'd fall over whenever it took a step), the lizard people in Ymn suits, even the little friendly one who got left behind, they were all just stories.

They've never met any real aliens, thought Lbbp. *They've never met any aliens at all. They tell all these stories about aliens but they're just imaginary. They're alone. As far as they know, they're completely alone. How awful for them.*

Lbbp felt a great wave of aching sympathy for the whole Ymn race. So alone, so desperate for contact with someone, anyone from beyond their own little blue-green world that they've invented a whole fictitious history full of encounters and invasions. They even fondly imagine themselves being conquered and decimated by beings from another world; it's as if even that would be better than the terrible loneliness of being the only civilisation in the galaxy.

Had anyone else realised this? Should he bring it up? To whom? Had the time come to propose making official contact with the Ymns again? He was aware of at least two occasions on which that had been suggested, and rejected. Could it be done now? The prejudice against Ymns was still widespread and deep, and he himself had played a part in this, he recalled with a shiver of guilt. But now, surely, Terra's presence and this new discovery of Ymn creativity had challenged that. Was it enough?

There was also the question of how the Ymns would react. *They've built up so many different expectations of what form alien contact might take,* Lbbp pondered, pacing the room, *both positive and negative, that how they would respond to one of us actually turning up is impossible to even guess at. They might be full of awe and wonder, they might take up their weapons and try to repel us before we'd even said hello, they might be gripped with fear and panic . . .*

Lbbp's knees weakened. He sat down heavily on his

bench seat. There was a dreadful, churning feeling of guilt in his chest, where his stomach was.

They were scared.

That night, on the road, in the dark, when he'd appeared out of nowhere.

They'd been scared quite literally out of their minds.

Those two Ymn forms that he'd barely even glimpsed as they ran away into the night. They didn't abandon their baby. They didn't (as he'd occasionally considered) leave her behind as some sort of sacrifice to the alien sky-god to save their own skins. He'd scared them so much that they'd forgotten everything but the need to get away. Everything. Even what they'd left behind in the vehicle.

For the first time in the eight orbits since that night on Rrth, Lbbp understood the fear that the two Ymns felt. And suddenly, he knew with an absolute certainty that as soon as they'd realised their terrible mistake, they would have gone back for her. And he knew how they must have felt when they found her gone. Just how he'd feel.

Lbbp found himself standing at the window. He found his eyes searching the skies for constellation 133-4/77. Locating it, he gazed into the space between the two centre stars, and whispered. Whispered to the Ymn race in general and to those two Ymns in particular.

- *I have wronged you. I have wronged you, and I'm so so sorry.*

Lbbp didn't get any more work done that night.

Terra's pet project for that orbit, however, was the Lyceum play.

Since Mlml had immersed itself in Ymn literary traditions, it was with glee and delight that the existence of the theatre was discovered. Stories could not just be written down, they could be read aloud and even acted out. The possibilities!

Preceptor Shm had taken some persuading to allow the play to go ahead. He listened to Bsht, Fthfth and Terra's proposal (mainly Fthfth's) with an even greater degree of weariness than was his custom. He expressed deep reservations about Preceptorate time and resources being spent on something so wilfully frivolous, until Bsht explained to him that frivolity was the whole idea. Shm eventually conceded. He did not regard himself as being in a position to judge the merits or value of frivolity. He was a scientist, and science and frivolity are most definitely non-overlapping magisteria. He yielded to Bsht's evidently superior knowledge of all things frivolous, and bade them good afternoon.

Pshkf, the practical science lector, was happiest of all about the idea of putting on a play. From what he understood about such matters (which wasn't much so far, but he was enjoying himself reading up on it), plays required sets to be built, props to be made, special effects to be generated. Pshkf was never happier than when he was building things. He set to work immediately. The play itself had yet to be decided upon, but he set to work anyway.

Which play to perform became quite the vexed question. The obvious thing to do, of course, was to select a Ymn play and produce that, but when Bsht researched the matter, she discovered that the most popular play in Ymn history was a rather depressing little piece about two grumpy adolescents from rival families who fall in love and kill themselves. Bsht decided against this play; as far as she could tell, its entertainment value was minimal, and besides, the title of the Fnrrn edition was *The Grumpy Adolescents Who Fall In Love And Kill Themselves*, so staging it seemed a bit redundant once you'd told people what the play was called. Bsht reflected that something needed to be done about the methodology used for titling works of literature. Giving the whole story away did seem to, well, spoil things.

It was Pktk who settled matters.

- *Why don't we do Tnk?*

He was at a meeting convened after class by the hastily formed Play Committee, consisting of Bsht, Terra, Fthfth, Pshkf, Shnst (or Thnst; they took it in turns and it was hard to tell which one was there at any given time) and himself.

There was a pause as his suggestion sank in. The meeting had been going nowhere; with no literary tradition of their own to look back through, and what appeared to be scant resources to be plundered from the Ymn archives, they'd been at something of a loss. Pktk, silent as ever, pondered the issue while the others spoke. They had no literary heroes, and no military heroes that anyone other than him cared about (or had heard of), the only historical character that everyone knew and admired was ...

- *Tnk?* asked Bsht.

- *Yes, Tnk,* said Pktk. *We all know the story, or most of it anyway, and it's the story of the Preceptorate and its greatest scientist, so even Preceptor Shm can't complain that we're wasting our time.*

- *Well, I think it's brilliant,* said Fthfth. *We must start on it at once. I'll be historical adviser and Terra can write the script. Bsht, you can be, what do they call it, director?*

- *Yes, that's it, I'll be the director, the person in charge,* said Bsht with irony that Fthfth in no way picked up on.

- *You can build the sets, Pshkf* (they were half built already) *and you can play Tnk,* she said to Pktk, who dropped the slice of ksks he'd been eating.

- *Me?*

- *Of course! Who else has the same inner strength, the same quiet resolve?* enthused Fthfth. *You won't just play Tnk, you'll BE Tnk ...*

- *But ...*

- All those in favour of Pktk playing Tnk!

All present said *yes,* except Pktk, who said - *But . . .* again.

The meeting broke up. Everyone hurried off to attend to their allotted task.

Pktk sat alone. When he'd suggested doing a play about Tnk, it had never occurred to him to actually PLAY Tnk. He hadn't intended to play anyone. They did know that, right? They didn't think they were acceding to his wishes?

Pktk floated home, his mind full of doubts and his stomach full of anxiety.

When he got home, he made himself some more of the FaZoon's special soup and felt much better.

2.25

Fthfth decided that since the play was now an official Lyceum project, and indeed a celebration of the life and works of the Preceptorate's greatest hero, then it was the solemn duty of everyone, that is to say, EVERYONE, to get involved.

She posted notices on the Lyceum's internal information network, reminding pupils of their duty to assist their colleagues in whatever way they could in this most urgent endeavour. She even printed out some notices, actual printed notices on thin sheets of something she'd found a box of in an old dusty cupboard, and stuck them up around the building. She would see pupils huddled around them. Whether they were reading them or just trying to figure out what they were, she couldn't tell and it didn't matter. The important thing was to get their attention, and she had.

Terra had started writing the script right away. She chose to start the narrative with Tnk's arrival at the Preceptorate as a Ponderer, rather than go all the way back to his Lyceum days. She didn't want to write a four-spectrum epic. She would write about Tnk's friendship with Kltnt, his rivalry with Spshnf (she would have to be careful not to make Spshnf too villainous; he had differing theories to Tnk's but that didn't make him a bad person) and end with his moment of triumph, the posting of his thesis on the Source. If that didn't get them up and hissing, nothing would.

Lbbp would watch her tapping away on her slate. It filled him with joy and pride to see her working away so contentedly. Even the occasional reports of further skirmishes between the G'grk and Dskt border patrols couldn't spoil his mood. Surely they'd sort something out; it was the thirty-third era, not the fifteenth, after all.

2.26

- *Let's try that again, shall we, and not so fast, Fthfth.*

Fthfth's enthusiasm was, as ever, boundless and infectious, but she wasn't the best at taking direction.

- *But there's so much of it! It'll take ages if I do it slowly.*

- *If you do it at the speed you've been doing it,* explained Bsht patiently, *nobody will understand a word you're saying. It's better to be slightly long-winded than unintelligible.*

Fthfth huffed and went back to her starting position on the Leisure Hub stage. She had, she reminded herself, volunteered to be the play's narrator. In fairness, she'd at some point volunteered for more or less every job that the play needed doing, but this was the one she'd ended up with and, being Fthfth, she was determined to do it perfectly. Not well; perfectly.

Of course, where the arts are concerned, there really is no such thing as objective 'perfection'; it's all a matter of taste and perspective. This was a new concept on Fnrr, and thus far it had been rather lost on Fthfth.

- *I could cut it down a bit,* suggested Terra from her seat in the front row of the auditorium.

- *Maybe you could look at that between now and tomorrow's rehearsal,* said Bsht, sitting next to her, *but for now we'll use the text as it is.*

Fthfth stood as patiently as she was capable of, and waited for Bsht's cue.

- *And ... off you go, Fthfth.*

Fthfth gave a tiny cough and commenced. - *In orbit forty-four of the twenty-seventh era, a young student arrives at the mighty Hrrng Preceptorate.*

Pktk wandered on from stage left, carrying a bundle of

papers (slates hadn't been invented back in the twenty-seventh era) and looking suitably bewildered. Pktk was good at bewildered.

- He had travelled far, from the small town of Jfd-Jfd in the province of Mntp. It had taken many days and he was tired from travelling.

Pktk rubbed himself all over and said - *There's got to be an easier way to travel than by rattly old omnicoach ...*

Ah yes, thought Terra. *You see? Portentous. I'm not cutting THAT bit.*

2.27

- It's called a proscenium. I looked it up. Good word, isn't it, proscenium ...

Pshkf was admiring his own handiwork, and waiting expectantly for everyone else to admire it too.

- It's an arch, said Bsht.

- A PROSCENIUM arch, corrected Pshkf. *It's been used in Rrth theatres for eras. It serves as a frame for the picture of the play, see?*

Pshkf's proscenium dominated the Leisure Hub stage; a gleaming white arc of shimmering plastic-lucite blend. He'd been up all night installing it; putting it up in sections and then molecule-bonding them to form a single expanse.

- What do you think, Terra? asked Bsht, who clearly had her doubts.

- It's certainly very imposing, said Terra, who hoped it wouldn't distract the audience's attention from the play itself. Not all of the cast had yet developed a particularly commanding stage presence and now they were going to have to compete with this huge white curve.

- It's not just imposing, said Pshkf excitedly. *Watch this.*

He tapped his slate; the auditorium lights dimmed. He tapped it again. The stage transformed. Suddenly, through the arch could be seen a diorama of the Preceptorate complex, as it had been in the twenty-seventh era. Another tap and the scene became rolling countryside, purple hills and green trees. One more tap and there was the council chamber in all its quartz-domed magnificence.

Pshkf beamed. *- Holographic backdrop. Infinitely pro-*

grammable. You could set your play anywhere you wanted. What do you think?

 - *It's amazing,* said Terra, and she really thought it was.

2.28

- *I don't see why I have to be the bad guy, that's all*, said Yshn. He was peering glumly at his slate.

- *You're not the bad guy*, sighed Bsht, *you're what's called the antagonist. You just come into conflict with the PROtagonist, in this case Pktk*. Yshn glanced across at Pktk, who gave him a cheery wave. *It's not about being good or bad.*

- *Yes, but Tnk isn't just the hero of the play, he's the hero of the whole nation, and I have to be the person who tries to stop him. It's not fair. They're all going to hate me.*

- *Cool*, muttered Pktk as he wandered past.

- *Cool?* repeated Yshn, confused.

- *Yes, cool*, said Pktk. *Looks like great fun, playing the bad guy. I get to play the great and wise Tnk, but, well …* (he glanced around to make sure Terra wasn't listening) *he's a bit … dull, isn't he? He's all a bit worthy and boring. Spshnf, on the other hand, that's a great part. He sneers, he plots, he grumps, he shouts … Much more fun. I'd offer to swap but it's a bit late now.*

Yshn considered Pktk's words. Now he thought about it, it was more fun to be the bad guy. What a thrill to go out of your way to be despised by the audience. Like most children, Yshn had spent the better part of his life thus far seeking the approval of adults. The thought of actively seeking their disapproval, even temporary make-believe disapproval, was suddenly very exciting.

- *Who knows*, said Pktk, *you might even get them to make that sound Ymns make when the bad guy comes on.*

- *What sound?* asked Yshn eagerly.

- *It's a sort of low oo sound, like …* Pktk tried to boo but it sounded all wrong coming through his tight Fnrrn speech mechanism – just a sort of bbhhh sound.

– *Hmm. That doesn't really work, does it,* mused Pktk. *Never mind, I'm sure they'll think of some way to let you know how much they hate you.*

Yshn, much encouraged, trotted off to learn his lines. Bsht, who had been listening to all of this, was genuinely very impressed.

– *That was … excellently done, Pktk. I think some of the wisdom of the Great Tnk is rubbing off on you.*

– *Maybe,* said Pktk happily. He was in an unusually good mood. But then, he remembered, there'd been some leftover FaZoon soup which he'd had for breakfast, and that always seemed to set him up well for the day.

2.29

*W*hy am I nervous? thought Terra. *I'm not even going on stage.*

Because it's your play, she reminded herself. *It's your play, you wrote it and if it's bad it's ultimately your fault. THAT's why you're nervous.*

Oh yes, she thought to herself, and then asked herself to be quiet now because she wasn't helping.

She sat in the front row of the auditorium – she'd thought about sitting backstage with her pals, but now that the play was finally about to start, she wanted to see it as the audience would see it, from the front, not sideways on. Besides, this way she could keep Lbbp company. If she was nervous, Lbbp was frantic, although he was doing a better job of hiding it than usual.

The auditorium was packed. The parents of every child involved in the production were in attendance, so were the pupils from the other classes, their lectors, friends, relatives, interested neighbours, total strangers … The atmosphere was one of anticipation and excitement; Terra had a brief and entirely unwelcome flashback to the night of the ill-fated FaZoon visitation. She banished the memory from her mind with a shudder as the lights dimmed.

Fthfth strode out onto the stage.

- *In orbit forty-four of the twenty-seventh era, a young student arrives at the mighty Hrrng Preceptorate.*

On came Pktk with his bundle of papers looking magnificently bewildered. He was wearing a very authentic-looking twenty-seventh-era Fnrrn costume which his mother had made for him.

- *He had travelled far, from the small town of Jfd-Jfd in the province of Mntp,* declaimed Fthfth, word-perfectly. *It had taken many days and he was tired from travelling.*

Pktk delivered his first line - *There's got to be an easier way to travel than by rattly old omnicoach …*

A knowing chuckle from the audience. They got that, then, thought Terra. Good.

As Pktk took a step forward, he tripped over the end of his slightly too long authentic twenty-seventh-era trouser leg, and dropped some of his bundle of papers. He looked fleetingly scared, then said:

- And once I've figured that out, I'm going to find a way of getting rid of these things, and he bent down to pick up the papers.

A big, warm laugh from the audience greeted Fnrrn theatre's first ever ad lib. The play was off to a good start.

And so it continued. The audience sat in rapt attention as Pktk re-enacted the fateful day on which Tnk first succeeded in activating grav-matter; Pshkf's mock-up containment field and pretend crystal projector flashing and crackling with light (the real thing, as he'd shown them in the practical science lab a few cycles previously, was nothing like so spectacular).

They gasped as Spshnf (played by Yshn using what sounded suspiciously like an impression of Compositor Vstj's voice) confronted Tnk across the council chamber floor (as depicted using Pshkf's holographic backdrop), challenging his theories and – horrors! – accusing him of plagiarism (which wasn't entirely historically accurate, but Terra needed to get some proper conflict into the story somewhere).

They sighed as Tnk told his wife Sftl (played by Shnst, or possibly Thnst) of his anxiety about his own discovery – was Fnrrnkind ready for such knowledge?

And finally they thrilled to the finale; with the generals hammering on one door of his study, demanding to be given exclusive access to Tnk's thesis, while the politicians hammered on the opposite door demanding the same

(Terra realised that this wasn't how it actually happened, not least because it seemed unlikely that Tnk's study would have doors on both sides, but it was symbolic – another of her new favourite words), Tnk, giving his final speech (- *I didn't do this for you! I didn't do this for me! I did this for everybody!*), pressed the key that published his thesis on the Source for all to read – at which point, the text and equations of Tnk's Thesis appeared in huge characters, scrolling away on the holographic backdrop behind Pktk in a stunning coup de théatre (not that anyone on Fnrr would have known to call it that – they'd have to come up with their own names for this sort of thing in due course).

The audience leapt to their feet, hissing and (this had become quite the thing to do after someone noticed that it's what Ymns do after a play) slapping their hands together.

The cast beckoned to Terra and she joined them on the stage. Lbbp cheered lustily and the applause (that was what it was called, applause) cranked up a notch.

Fthfth put her arm round Terra's shoulders from one side and Pktk from the other.

- *Is this where we bend over?* asked Pktk.

- *It's called BOWING, Pktk, and yes it is,* said Fthfth. So they did.

2.30

Terra and Lbbp sat on the padded bench seat, sipping gssh and sighing with happiness.

- *It was good, wasn't it? The play?*

Lbbp put his arm around Terra's shoulders and gave them a squeeze.

- *It was brilliant.*

A pause in which nothing was said because there was nothing that needed saying, then:

- *Are you going to write another one?*

- *Not yet, but yes, I'm sure I will one day.*

- *You could actually be in the next one,* suggested Lbbp.

- *As what?* asked Terra. *I don't exactly look like anyone else, and I'm not shaving my head and painting myself grey just for a Lyceum play ...*

Lbbp laughed, and said, - *Oh, you could play someone. Or something. I've been reading up on more Rrth legends. There are these creatures called angels who turn up in a lot of Rrth myths who look quite a lot like you. In particular, they feature in the plays they put on in their own Lycea, during this annual festival they have called ...*

- *Please, no history lessons now,* mumbled Terra. *It's too late and it's been a very busy day.*

Lbbp smiled. - *Of course. Time for sleep. Off you go.*

Terra got up and shuffled off to her room. She turned in the doorway.

- *Always here,* she smiled.

- *Always here,* returned Lbbp.

Lbbp relaxed back on the seat with his bowl of gssh. This was bliss, he thought. Terra was happier than she'd ever been. She had real friends, and she was proving herself every day in unexpected and wonderful ways. Though he would feel a stab of guilt whenever he remembered the night he'd found her (guilt which he was still keeping entirely to himself), he had no regrets at all. He was as content as he could ever remember being. He wished it could last for ever.

It lasted about another cycle.

2.31

The day had started much the same as any other day. Wake, breakfast, bubble, Lyceum. The first class of the day had been Linguistics; study of the phonetic structures of Mlmln. Not one of Terra's favourites; while she spoke Mlmln like a native and without accent, the language was not, nor could it ever be, natural to her speech mechanism. There were certain sounds which she could make perfectly well in passing speech, but if she tried to make the sounds in isolation she would struggle to reproduce them perfectly. It made her feel self-conscious and conspicuously alien, in a way she didn't often feel these days.

After the interlude, it was time for History of Science. More Terra's home territory, although there were still gaps in her knowledge.

- *Quiet please,* said Bsht and all hubbub died down.

- *Activate slates and access chapter four section six; refinements on Tnk's theory from orbit seventy-two of the twenty-seventh era to orbit twelve of the thirtieth era.*

Terra stroked her finger across her slate and the appropriate chapter appeared. Was she supposed to have read all this? It didn't look familiar at all.

- *We begin a new phase in the history of GravTech development today,* began Bsht. Terra breathed a tiny sigh of relief. - *We're going to be looking at the achievements and contributions of the scientists who developed and refined Tnk's initial theories. The first of these was Tnk's student, assistant and, eventually, greatest friend Kltnt. Although by orbit seventy in the twenty-seventh era Tnk had officially retired, he still maintained a keen interest in ...*

A low throbbing noise resounded through the classroom.

It seemed to be reverberating through the whole building. It made the floor vibrate and tickle Terra's feet, and made her stomach queasy. She wondered if it were having the same effect on her classmates' rather differently arranged insides; looking around, she saw that their faces wore the same perturbed expression as her own.

Bsht had fallen silent the second the sound began. Her face, pale grey at all times, turned paler.

The sound grew louder and more insistent. The children gazed at each other in confusion. Pktk's lip quivered. None of them knew what this sound meant but all of them instantly understood that whatever was happening, it was nothing good.

Above the noise now was heard the Preceptor's voice. There was a tension in the voice that Terra had never heard before.

- *All staff and students will assemble in the Leisure Hub immediately. All staff and students to the Leisure Hub immediately please.*

Bsht, as if suddenly shaken from a daydream, snapped into alertness.

- *You heard the Preceptor,* she said calmly. *To the Leisure Hub, now. No running and no gravity bubbles in the corridors ...*

Terra picked up her slate and followed her classmates into the corridor. All about her staff of all ranks and students of all ages were hurrying towards the Hub, their faces tight with worry.

- *What's happening?* she whispered to Pktk.

- *Something serious enough for them to cancel gshkth practice,* said Pktk, pointing at a group of older students hurrying along with everyone else, still dressed in gshkth smocks and carrying their gfrgs. *They NEVER cancel gshkth practice.*

Terra's little group of friends rounded the last corridor and entered the Hub. Some sort of meeting was already in progress but no one was speaking; the Hub's visualiser had been activated and was showing what looked like a news broadcast, but not the local Hrrng broadcast or even the national Mlml broadcast. A Fnrrm newscaster was speaking a language that Terra didn't understand; the visualiser was translating, Mlmln words heard over the newscaster's own voice. The picture phased and flickered, the newscaster shouted in panic, dark blue blood streaked across his grey face.

- ... *off the streets. All citizens are ... until further notice ...*

There was an explosion behind the newscaster. He flinched but carried on, his voice rising to a scream.

- *They're here! They're inside! Hide, wherever you can! Take what you can carry and—*

The visualiser went blank. A chill silence descended upon the Hub.

Preceptor Shm, seated on the stage in front of the visualiser, collapsed back into his chair and rubbed his eyes with his long fingers.

After a moment he stood and addressed the assembled crowd.

- *It is a dark day for all of us. A dark day for all Fnrrns.*

- *It's Dskt,* whispered Fthfth. *Dskt has fallen. The G'grk have invaded Dskt.*

- *What does that mean?* whispered Terra.

Fthfth looked back at Terra, her eyes full of fear and sadness. But it was Pktk who answered.

- *It means we're next.*

PART THREE
The Invaders

3.1

Everyone was doing everything they could.

The news of Dskt's fall had hit the people of Mlml with a shock that was almost physical. For longer than anyone now alive could remember, Mlml – indeed the whole of Fnrr – had existed in a state of serene calm. The G'grk had been fighting among themselves, tribe versus tribe, region versus region; nobody paid this much attention – it was no one else's problem and it kept the G'grk busy. The G'grk's expansionist past – when they had galloped across the Central Plains on their armoured gnth-sh'gsts, massacring neighbouring peoples and adding their territories to their ever-growing homeland – had receded into history so thoroughly that the G'grk themselves, as far as the Mlmlns were concerned, had become little more than mythical creatures, monsters from a fearful and forgotten age.

If the G'grk were mentioned at all these days, it was usually in a joke. Tidy yourself up, you look like a G'grk! Look at the state of this wiring! Did a G'grk put it in for you?

No one was cracking G'grk jokes any more. Some even wondered if the jokes had made their way to the Central Plains, if the G'grk had heard themselves mocked and ridiculed. Perhaps that was what had set them back on the warpath. Whatever had provoked them, their attack had stunned the whole planet with its suddenness and ferocity. Dskt, advanced, enlightened Dskt, whose armies had been far greater and better armed those of Mlml ... Dskt, whose technological superiority had, everyone had believed, guaranteed its security ... Dskt had been overrun in little more than a day. The G'grk possessed better weapons than anyone had suspected and had attacked in greater numbers than anyone could have anticipated.

In the cycle that had passed since the invasion, little news had been heard from Dskt. Some refugees had made it across the sea to Mlml; many more had perished in the attempt – some shot down by G'grk light-cannons as they fled, others trusting to their gravity bubbles, only to drown when their power cells failed them. Those who arrived safely told tales of mass disappearances, of whole civilian populations vanishing overnight, rumours of slave labour, and much, much worse.

So now, in Mlml, everyone was doing everything they could.

Young fit Mlmlns were volunteering for the armed forces – too many, in fact. So diminished was Mlml's military after so long without war, that there were barely enough officers to train the recruits, and no equipment for them to train with. For all that the sergeants drilled, and the munitions factories churned, few had any illusions that the Mlml defence forces would be ready in time.

In time for what? No one even knew if the G'grk were coming at all. There had been no formal declaration of hostilities, no contact at all with the G'grk since the fall of Dskt (or, for that matter, for many orbits previously). The hope that the G'grk would be satisfied, that Dskt was all they'd wanted, that crossing the sea to take Mlml would be more trouble than it was worth, was clung to throughout the land. That was all it was, just hope. Unlike the superstitious G'grk with their 'Occluded Ones', the Mlmlns didn't even have any gods to pray to. So they kept on hoping, and meanwhile, everyone was doing everything they could.

The stores began to run low on protein as people stocked up, hoping their manipulators would still work in the event of an attack. Few people even knew how to prepare fresh produce these days. Cooking was considered a fringe activity; a craft, a hobby, rather than anything to do with sustenance.

Escape routes were planned by city dwellers; those who inhabited the urban sprawls of Hrrng, and Shsst, and even the smaller towns like Jfd-Jfd and Fzkl, drew up plans to flee to ... where? And for how long?

Everyone was doing everything they could to take their minds off the fact that there was nothing anyone could do.

Except hope, and wait.

* * *

Life, as it does under such circumstances, went on as normally as possible. Routine serves a dual purpose in times of tension and impending crisis; it gets the things that need doing done and it gives people other things to think about.

Terra, sitting in the Lyceum yard at morning interlude, was thinking about Lbbp and how much she'd rather be with him right now. *This is stupid,* she thought, *I know that we have to keep going to class and Lbbp needs to keep going to work, but at any minute we could be at war and I might never see him again.* She wanted to spend every possible moment at his side. She entertained fantasies about the pair of them fleeing to Rfk and hiding out in the forest. Perhaps the war would pass them by completely and they could live together for ever among the flowers and trees.

Her reverie was shattered by the pinging sound which summoned her and her friends back to the lectorium. She sighed and got to her feet.

- *Come on!* said Fthfth. *It's practical science! You like practical science!* She bounded back into the building.

Terra slouched towards the door. The pinging stopped, to be replaced by what sounded like a high-pitched whine. *What does that sound mean?* thought Terra. *Is it an alarm of some kind? It's not starting, is it?* She looked to the skies, half expecting to see G'grk warriors descending like great flying beasts of prey.

It'd be louder than that, wouldn't it, she reasoned. *The alarm saying the nation was being invaded. It wouldn't be a little whining noise you could hardly hear at all.* She chided herself for being so silly, while commending herself for being so alert.

The noise continued. It wasn't a whine, it was more of a whimper. Someone was crying. Terra felt a pang of concern and decided to investigate.

Terra followed the sound. She found Yshn, tucked into the corner of the yard. He was sat down and curled up into himself, hugging his knees. His eyes were shut tight and he rocked back and forth, keening and sobbing.

- *Yshn ... Are you ...?*

- *They live in Dskt. My aunt and uncle. They live in Dskt. No one's heard anything from them since the G'grk arrived.*

- *Yshn, they might be—*

Yshn opened his eyes and turned angrily towards her. - *You know what they do to you? The G'grk? They enslave you. They convert all the factories to make weapons for themselves and then they make the people work for them in the factories. That's the best I can hope for! That my aunt and uncle are slaves rather than dead!*

He got up and ran across the yard, back into the building. Terra followed him into the corridor.

- *Listen, Yshn, there could still be ...*

Yshn spun round, furious. - *What do you care anyway? You're not one of us. You're more like them than you are like us. When the G'grk come you'll probably be on their side, so you can enslave all of us and then go off and eat burnt animals together! You've even got a G'grk name, T'r!*

Terra was struck speechless for a moment, then stammered, - *It's not T'r, it's Terra, it's just a bit difficult to ...*

- *It's T'r! And you're a stupid animal, just like them!*

- *That is ENOUGH!*

A new voice, a grown-up voice, a voice full of anger and disgust. Terra turned to see who it was who had intervened on her behalf. To her astonishment, she saw Compositor Vstj, his face set with fury.

- *Yshn, we're all very sorry about your aunt and uncle, and we're all concerned about the future, but what you have just said is almost unforgivable. You will apologise to Terra immediately and you will mean it. Do I make myself clear?*

Yshn was silent and open-mouthed. His anger abated and the horror and injustice of what he'd said to Terra struck him. He said, - *I'm ... I'm really ...* and then ran away down the corridor.

Terra made to follow him. - *Let him go,* said Vstj. *He needs some time to calm down and think things over.*

Terra gazed down the corridor after Yshn, stunned both by the conversation she'd just had and indeed by the one she was now having. Was this really Vstj, being so kind and supportive? What had come over him?

- *I'm so sorry for what just happened,* said Vstj. *No one has the right to speak to you that way.*

- *He's having a bad time,* said Terra. *It wasn't his fault.*

- *We're all having a bad time,* said Vstj, *it's no excuse. You're a very understanding person, Terra. It's quite remarkable, considering everything you've had to tolerate. And I'm afraid that one of the things you've had to tolerate has been me, hasn't it?*

- *Compositor Vstj, I don't know why ...*

- *We're going to need each other in the times to come, Terra. We're all going to need each other.*

- *Yes, yes we are,* said Terra. *Thank you, Compositor Vstj.*

Vstj turned to go. Terra called after him and he paused to hear her question.

- *You know the FaZoon better than anyone. Do you think the FaZoon are going to help us?*

Vstj pondered this for a moment, then:

- *I don't think we matter that much to the FaZoon. I don't think anything really matters to the FaZoon, do you?*

3.2

Compositor Vstj had a longer journey home than most of his co-workers at the Preceptorate. Every evening he would activate his gravity bubble and proceed through the fading light towards, and then beyond, the city limits of Hrrng.

Compositor Vstj's home was a commanding pyramid-shaped house which sat on a hill overlooking the city. It had been built many orbits before Vstj was born, by one of Vstj's many illustrious ancestors. Vstj himself had lived there as a child with his parents, and lived there now alone.

Most evenings upon his arrival, Vstj would let himself in by one of the smaller entrances at the rear of the house (the imposing front door had been locked for many orbits, and Vstj never saw the point of opening such a grand portal just for himself) and fumble around for the master light switch. The motion detector switches which, in most Mlmln homes, would activate the lights upon the occupants' return, had long since malfunctioned. Vstj would occasionally contemplate getting them fixed, but then decide not to bother; it was hardly a chore flicking on a switch.

As the lights flickered on, Vstj would always be greeted by the same sight. The lobby of his house was lined with holographic portraits of his deceased relatives. On one side, his father's family; eminent scientists, every one of them, for as far back as the family could trace itself. There was Gfn, the master agri-geneticist, inventor of crop-growing techniques which had made famine a distant memory on Fnrr. Here sat Chlgf, astronomer and astral spectroscopy pioneer; his methods were used to determine the atomic composition of distant stars even to this day. Next to him there was Dfn-Shfr, creator of the intelligent responsive fabrics which almost everyone in Mlml wore, and so on and so on.

Facing the scientists from across the lobby, Vstj saw his mother's family. Soldiers. Military leaders, generals, space admirals, defenders, champions. Legends. His own mother's portrait hung at the far end of the lobby. As Vstj proceeded along the corridor, she would stare down at him with the same look of disappointment she'd always worn in his presence while she was alive. Vstj would avert his gaze and shuffle on.

Vstj would make himself something to eat; generally configuration 4 or 12. He wasn't especially fond of configurations 4 or 12, but his protein manipulator was very old and had become jammed on those two settings. He knew it was time he replaced it, but it was a design classic, he would tell himself, and besides, there wasn't anything actually wrong with configurations 4 and 12.

Vstj would then spend the rest of the evening going over some work on his slate, or perhaps reading the news, before swallowing a couple of rather strong sleep-inducing tablets and activating his sleep-well. He did this because once in his sleep-well, in the darkness, silence and weightlessness, he would be alone with his thoughts, and Vstj didn't like his thoughts very much.

Tonight was different. Tonight Vstj's pill bottle remained unopened. Tonight Vstj was content to remain conscious for a little while before drifting naturally off to sleep. He thought back to his conversation with the Ymn child. He'd helped, hadn't he? He'd actually helped. He'd had a positive effect. He half wished his mother were still alive so he could tell her about it. Not that she would have been particularly impressed. The nation on the brink of war and here he was still shuffling numbers and fretting over budget projections. Well, maybe he'd show her. Maybe he'd never gone to war but now it looked like the war was coming to him. Maybe he'd finally have the chance to do something properly brave.

Wait, am I actually looking forward to this? wondered Vstj. *What sort of a person does that make me?*

Vstj's last thought before dozing off was that perhaps he should have taken the pills after all.

3.3

Terra had been looking forward to today. No Lyceum, and with work at the Life Science Hub temporarily suspended, she and Lbbp had planned a day of games. Tb-tb-tff and perhaps even dfsh, if she could persuade Lbbp to go out into the public gardens. Lbbp got embarrassed playing games in public; it was rather sweet, thought Terra.

She had a disappointment coming.

- *I'm sorry, Terra,* said Lbbp, switching off his comm. *They've convened an emergency debate at the Forum, and I've got to attend as part of the Preceptor's advisory panel.*

- *The Preceptor has an advisory panel?*

- *He does now, and I'm on it. Listen, Terra,* Lbbp sat down, took both of Terra's hands in his own and looked her in the eyes, *if there's any chance of averting this war we've got to take it. The politicians will never figure it out; all they care about is what makes them look good. They've invited the Preceptor to speak before the Forum. If anybody can think of a way out of this it's him, and if he says he needs me there I can't turn him down. Do you understand?*

- *I suppose,* said Terra sadly.

- *Good girl. Now look, I should be back before sleep-time; I'm sure you can find things to do with yourself until I get back. Play games on your slate, read some stories, hey, WRITE some stories, why not?* Lbbp got up to go. Terra had an idea.

- *I could come with you! I could come to the debate!*

- *I really don't think so, Terra,* said Lbbp, packing his slate into a bag. *It's not the sort of thing you'd enjoy.*

- *Why? Because I'm a stupid Ymn?* Terra surprised herself with her own anger. The conversation with Yshn had clearly upset her more than even she had realised.

Lbbp sighed, exasperated. - *No, because you're only eight orbits old!*

- *Fthfth's eight orbits old, I bet she's going,* retorted Terra.

- *I happen to know for a fact that she's not,* said Lbbp over his shoulder as he strode towards the window. *Now stay put, get some food from the manipulator, I'll be back before you know it.* And with that he opened the window, activated his bubble and floated off.

I bet they'd let Fthfth go if she wanted to, thought Terra. *She's the star pupil after all, and she's not a stupid Ymn like me...*

Oh terrific, thought Terra crossly, *they've even got ME thinking it now.*

Terra got up and stomped over to the table. She picked up her slate and started a game of one-player dks-wks but her enthusiasm failed her.

It's not fair, thought Terra. *They've all got this idea stuck in their heads that Ymns are dumb savages, but the only Ymn any of them has ever met is ME, and I'm not a dumb savage, am I? I'm as civilised as my friends, I'm as clever as my friends, I'm at least as polite as most of my friends ... How not-dumb and not-savage do I have to be before people get over the idea that all Ymns are dumb savages?*

She threw the slate down in frustration, and was immediately relieved to see it bounce harmlessly on the padded seat. Tantrums were all well and good but breaking her slate wouldn't help. She picked it up and checked that it was still working.

Just how did this idea become so deep-rooted? she wondered. *Why do Fnrrns dislike Ymns so much when they know so little about them?*

With nothing much else to do to stave off the boredom of a day without games, Terra decided to do some research.

She sat cross-legged on the floor, and stroked the slate to activate it. She began an archive search: Ymn/Fnrrn interaction to the present day.

The search went back further than she'd expected; the

astro-exploratory programme at the Ff-Shkrr Preceptorate in the nation of Gst-Sh-Kssk on the far side of Fnrr had first detected radio transmissions from Rrth nearly an era ago; since then the Ymns had been monitored by Fnrrn astronomers and xenologists from all over the planet.

She found articles filed by the first Fnrrn scientists to visit Rrth, including an accident report (and insurance claim).

She found a record of the first proposal to establish formal contact with Rrth, submitted by a team of scientists from Dskt some thirty orbits after the first discovery of the Ymns' civilisation. It was turned down by their own Academic Council on the grounds that Ymns were not yet sufficiently 'morally and culturally advanced' to be exposed to Fnrrn technology. A similar proposal submitted some orbits later to the Hrrng Preceptorate was rejected for much the same reasons.

She smiled to see Lbbp's name on a botanical survey. So long ago! He was older than he looked (or admitted to being). He had conducted a study of a densely forested area and enthused more than was entirely scientifically appropriate about the richness and diversity of life-forms he'd encountered.

Her face fell to read Lbbp's addendum to his own report. He'd appended it a few orbits later after returning to the same place and discovering it stripped, barren and deserted. He expressed his anger towards the Ymns who had done this in extremely unscientific language.

Terra read on; she found more and more reports from survey missions; papers by eminent Fnrrn sociologists and psychologists speculating on the possible underlying causes of the Ymns' propensity for violence and intolerance; proposals to 'rescue' various endangered Rrth species and preserve them in captivity on Fnrr (this idea didn't seem to have gone anywhere, to Terra's disappointment – the idea that there might be a secret zoological reserve full of Rrth animals somewhere on the planet appealed to her greatly).

But what was this? An article marked 'Secret' which nonetheless had opened right up when she'd touched the title on her slate. Secret but not secret? How did that work? Intrigued, she read the heading:

PROPOSAL

Submitted 3.2/7 33-29

To: Academic Council, Hrrng Preceptorate.

Copies to: Department of Extraplanetary Affairs,
Hrrng Forum

Specific Attention: Zft-sh-Ngst-sh-Shm, Preceptor;
Jsht-sh-Flgst-sh-Thn, Director of Extraplanetary Affairs

Proponents:
Gsk-sh-Bthtf-sh-Pskt, Senior Postulator
Hrf-sh-Tstk-sh-Sffk, Postulator
Dfst-sh-Kshchk-sh-Lbbp, Postulator
Fnng-sh-Glkn-sh-Bddf, Postulator

Proposal to initiate population control measures with regard to species 676, hereinafter referred to as Ymns, dominant life-form of planet 6-66-724-41/3, or Rrth.

A knot formed in Terra's stomach. She read on ...

Previously submitted reports (see appendix 1.0 for full reading list) have established, in our opinion, the clear danger to interplanetary peace presented by species 676.

Ymns have already caused irreversible damage to the ecosystem of their home planet (see attached reports 1, 2). Ymns have a history of violent conduct towards each other and the other species of Rrth. They persist in eating animal flesh despite having developed nutritional techniques which make this unnecessary. They have created weapons powerful enough to destroy all life on Rrth.

Formal contact with Ymns is prohibited by order of the Forum and the Preceptorate Academic Council. Their own attempts at space exploration have thus far been primitive and limited to their own planetary system (see attached report 3). However, projections of future Ymn technological progress (see attached report 4) concur that Ymns will achieve the capability for interstellar travel within the next era.

We contend that such a turn of events would be catastrophic for interplanetary relations.

A virus has been developed by the micro-biological research hub at Hrrng Preceptorate. If introduced to the biosphere of Rrth it will reduce Ymn fertility by approximately six eighths. All other life-forms will remain unaffected.

The Ymn population will decline generation upon generation; within an era there will be less than one quarter of the current number of Ymns alive on Rrth. This will reduce their capacity – and inclination – to expand beyond their own planetary boundaries.

This procedure will be painless and entirely non-lethal – no Ymns will die, but considerably fewer will be born. Our actions will go undetected by the Ymns; they have not yet eradicated disease from their species and this reduction in fertility will simply be ascribed to a mysterious epidemic.

For full technical and chemical specifications, see appendix 1.1

Terra's head spun. The knot in her stomach had become swirling nausea.

They were going to … They wanted to … The Fnrrns had considered *culling* the Ymn race. Not with traps or weapons, but with disease and sterility. The misery and confusion such a measure would have caused on Rrth ... They hadn't done this, had they? They hadn't actually gone ahead with this horrific scheme? It was dated from before her own birth – had she been one of the few Ymn babies born on Rrth at that time?

She scrolled frantically to the bottom of the document.

PROPOSAL REJECTED 2.3/7 33-29 For full
declaration see attached statement 1.1

She sighed with relief, although the nausea remained. Whose idea had this been? Who could ever have thought this was a good plan? She scrolled back to the top of the document.

Proponents:
Gsk-sh-Bthtf-sh-Pskt, Senior Postulator
Hrf-sh-Tstk-sh-Sffk, Postulator
Dfst-sh-Kshchk-sh-Lbbp, Postulator
Fnng-sh-Glkn-sh-Bddf, Postulator

Her eyes scanned across the names, the names of those 'scientists' who had wanted to purge her species like some sort of verminous infestation.

Her eyes stopped at the third name.

Dfst-sh-Kshchk-sh-Lbbp, Postulator

There was a metallic taste in her mouth and a buzzing in her ears.

Dfst-sh-Kshchk-sh-Lbbp, Postulator

The nausea rose up out of her stomach and into her throat. She dropped the slate, staggered to her feet and rushed towards the waste cubicle.

She vomited violently into the waste scrambler and fell to the cold floor.

Lbbp

Terra found that she was clinging to the smooth surface of the floor with her fingertips.

Lbbp

Everything she believed, everything she depended upon, everything she loved, seemed to be sliding away from her.

Lbbp

It was all true, everything Vstj had said, everything Yshn had implied, everything everyone had ever said about her behind her back. It was all an experiment. Take a member of the most brutal and despised race in the universe, dress it up like one of your own children and see if you can educate the little animal. Teach it to speak, maybe even to perform some simple tasks. What was it Lbbp had once said?

- *A bad scientist tries to prove himself right. A good scientist tries to prove himself wrong, and only when he fails does he conclude that he's right.*

So that was the idea. Propose that Ymns are so savage and primitive as to merit partial extermination, then test your own theory by trying to civilise one of them. Terra's whole life had been an academic exercise, a follow-up experiment, just Lbbp being thorough like the good scientist he was.

- *We don't need to keep secrets from each other.* That was something else Lbbp had said. - *We don't need to keep secrets from each other.*

The throbbing in her head subsided enough to allow her

to get to her feet. She wiped her eyes, sniffed and walked to the window. She tapped on the crystal and it slid open.

The city lay before her, illuminated by its own lights and three moons. It had never looked more alien to Terra.

She stepped out of the window.

3·4

L ater that evening, Lbbp floated back towards home, tired and stressed. The emergency debate had generated much in the way of fear and apprehension and little in the way of hope. Mlml's military commanders had declared themselves confident in their ability to repel a G'grk assault, but these assurances seemed hollow, perfunctory. The last hope now lay with the Dskt resistance; if they could keep the G'grk busy enough then the attack on Mlml might never come. Because if it did come, it was clear now that it would be unstoppable.

The debate would reconvene in the morning. Lbbp wasn't likely to get much sleep tonight.

Lbbp noticed Terra's bedroom window was open. He diverted his course towards it and stepped inside, deactivating his bubble.

- Terra? Why have you left your window open? It's freezing in here.

No reply. Lbbp looked round for the child but couldn't see her. There was a curious noxious smell in the air.

Terra's slate was on the floor. *She knew better than to leave that lying around*, thought Lbbp. It was then he had the first inkling that something was wrong.

Lbbp picked up the slate and read. He got as far as the heading 'Proposal'. With a sudden lurch of panic he knew what had happened. How had she found it? And why, WHY hadn't he mentioned it before?

He told himself not to be silly, he knew exactly why he'd never mentioned the proposal to her before. She would have reacted, well, pretty much how she HAD reacted.

She couldn't have been gone for more than a few

spectrums, and Lbbp was fairly sure he knew where she'd be headed. He just needed to find one thing first.

Rushing into his little reading room he found the shiny white travelling case. He wrenched it open and started to rummage through the contents.

Yes. Found it. His old field-scanner. And it was still working.

Lbbp passed the field-scanner's strap over his shoulder, grabbed a spare power cell for his bubble, ran back to Terra's room and leapt out of the window.

3·5

Terra had absolutely no idea what she was going to do next.

She'd been floating over the forests of Rfk when her gravity bubble's power cell had started to fail. It made its warning pip-pip sound and began to descend. The current generation of gravity bubbles made sure to return you to the ground before completely losing power; a mandatory safety feature installed after a few foolhardy Fnrrns had pushed their luck and chosen to ignore the low power warning. Unpleasant for all concerned, especially those poor unfortunates who'd been underneath them at the time.

She'd made it to the beach, her toes brushing the tree-tops as she descended. Now she sat on the rainbow sand and gazed out across the triple-moonlit sea.

She knew she could never go home again.

And where was 'home' anyway? Lbbp's apartment? Or 'the lab' as she now thought of it?

She peered up into the night in search of constellation 133-4/77. She found it easily in the clear black sky. Staring at the space between the two centre stars, she resolved to find a way back to her real home. Back to Rrth.

She had no experience with other Ymns, she didn't speak any Ymn language apart from a few words she'd picked up from watching Ymn movies (Ymn movies and TV shows were quite popular on Fnrr, now that everyone knew they were made up. Not only that, but some enterprising Fnrrns had started to make movies of their own. Terra hadn't seen any, but she'd read some dreadful reviews). Never mind that, decided Terra, she'd address herself to those problems once she got there. Better to be a refugee than a laboratory animal. First, she had to turn her attention to the more immediate – and very perplexing – problem of how to get to Rrth in the first place.

Could she steal a spaceship? Difficult. Each ship was biometrically linked to its owner. There was probably a way round that; she'd research it. Difficult without a slate (she was still annoyed that in her hurry to get out of the apartment she'd left it behind) but she'd figure it out.

Mind you, even if you got hold of a ship – and worked out how to fly it – space travel was heavily regulated; you'd have to get past traffic control. They could immobilise and even board you if you attempted to leave the system without the proper permits.

Stow away! That was it. Find a scheduled scientific expedition to Rrth and then sneak aboard. She could ask Lbbp when the next—

Lbbp.

Terra wept. She wept bitterly for the home she had lost, for the family she had lost. Not on Rrth, her home here on Fnrr. She'd thought she had a life, and love, and security. It had all been a lie.

Salt tears streamed down Terra's cheeks and splashed onto the rainbow sand. Terra was usually self-conscious about her tears; the sight of liquid gushing from her eyes had been so alarming to her Fnrrn friends that she couldn't help but be slightly disturbed by it herself. But not now. Now she cried, and cried, and didn't care what she looked like.

There was a distant rumble. Terra fell silent.

What was that? Tectonic activity? There wasn't a quake scheduled, not as far as she knew (Fnrrns had mastered the science of easing the tensions in their planet's crust; quakes still happened, but only minor ones, and always in controlled circumstances).

There it was again. Terra, feeling exposed out on the sand, got to her feet and scampered up the beach to the tree-line.

The rumble grew louder, or, rather, whatever it was that was making the rumble got closer.

There was a roaring, splashing sound. At first Terra thought that something big had landed in the water, perhaps a meteor, but looking out to sea she saw that something big had in fact burst OUT of the water. A huge dark blue sphere, twice the size of a house and the exact colour of Fnrrn blood, was hovering just above the sea a hundred metres or so from the shore. With another roar of displaced water, a second sphere rose up beside it. Then a third. The spheres hummed with energy as they hung in the air. As Terra watched, cowering behind a thorny bush, the spheres glided up the beach towards her. They rose with what seemed to be some difficulty above the treetops and continued to hover inland. Scared but fascinated, Terra followed them.

The three blue spheres scraped along the treetops as they progressed slowly through the air. Terra could hear the rustling of branches above the grinding of the spheres' anti-gravity engines (that was surely what the sound was, although it was much louder than any GravTech device Terra had ever heard before).

Following the spheres, Terra exited the forest and came to a stretch of meadow. She'd been here before; she and Lbbp had played with a bdkt in this place, throwing it back and forth, laughing as they ran through the wide open field.

The field wasn't wide open any more. In the middle of the space there sat a collection of squat hut-like buildings. They looked like temporary structures, sheets of rigid fabric slotted together. Around them were clustered vehicles and piles of objects. Edging closer, Terra could see that the objects were weapons: pulse-orbs, light-cannons, grav-rockets.

The spheres landed on a flat stretch of ground in the middle of the huts. Tall, muscular Fnrrns clad in plate armour rushed out of the huts and formed themselves into ranks.

Circular apertures appeared on the surface of the spheres and yet more Fnrrns emerged, also armoured. The Fnrrns on the ground let out a great hissing cheer, a guttural rasp of exultation.

The G'grk invasion had already begun.

3.6

L bbp was having a bit of trouble.

His old field-scanner had been languishing in a case in his reading room for two orbits. It had been rendered obsolete when the Preceptorate had bought a set of the newer models, but Lbbp had been allowed to keep his. Or, rather, he'd pretended he'd lost it when they asked for it back, which amounted to the same thing when you thought about it.

Now he was desperately trying to remember how to access its internal archive. Within its memory it should still retain a record of every reading it had ever given during all the expeditions and surveys on which Lbbp had used it. He needed to look back through its records, and was hoping that they went back a long way. Specifically, just over eight orbits. He jabbed at the controls and peered at the display, trying to read the tiny characters.

The fact that Lbbp was doing this outside, in the dark, while flying at reckless speed several hundred metres above open country wasn't helping in the slightest.

Success! The scanner's archives did indeed go back eight orbits, and beyond. Now he knew that, it should be relatively simple to locate the reading he was looking for. He remembered the date. He would always remember that date.

There it was. That trace of life he'd detected inside the abandoned Ymn vehicle, on that deserted road on Rrth, all those orbits ago. The scanner had logged the trace and analysed its genetic structure. Every creature in the universe has a unique genetic profile, and here, recorded in his old field-scanner, was Terra's.

As the moonlit Mlml landscape rushed by beneath him, Lbbp activated the field-scanner's sensors and instructed it to look for a match to that profile. It began scanning every living thing within range, dismissing all of them as non-Ymn. Lbbp hoped that its long-range sensors were powerful enough. He hoped that his hunch about where Terra would go was correct. He hoped he could find the words when he found her. He hoped she would be able to forgive him.

3·7

Terra scrabbled back to the trees at the edge of the field. Once she had some cover, she stood and peered towards the G'grk encampment. How was it possible that the G'grk were already building bases on Mlml? How had nobody noticed?

Since the fall of Dskt, there had scarcely been a word spoken in Hrrng on any other topic … Will the G'grk come? Can we negotiate? Could we repel them? Could we resist? For the past cycle and a half the whole nation had been preparing itself for the G'grk attack – and now it had happened and no one had NOTICED?

Those questions could wait, thought Terra. For now, someone had noticed. SHE had noticed.

But how to raise the alarm? She had no slate, no comm … her bubble's cell was exhausted and it was many days' walk back to Hrrng …

She dived back behind a tree as a G'grk sentry floated past.

Floated past …?

So the G'grk did have gravity bubbles. That would have come as a surprise to some back in Hrrng, she thought. But they obviously had the use of some sort of GravTech – something had been holding those blue spheres up, even if it sounded as if the engines had to work very hard to do so.

If the G'grk have gravity bubbles, they will have spare power-cells for them, reasoned Terra. *If I could get in there and steal one, I could get back to Hrrng and tell them that the invasion has started. Or at least find some sort of communication device.*

Keeping low to the ground, Terra crawled towards the

G'grk camp, reflecting on how this had seemed like it was going to be such a boring day.

* * *

- *Come on, come on ...*

Lbbp knew his field-scanner was not voice operated; he also knew that thumping it in exasperation wouldn't help it to function, but he couldn't help himself.

He was over the inland border of the Rfk reserve now and the scanner had not yet detected any Ymn life signs. Lbbp had been so sure that Terra would have come this way. Every time she'd been feeling sad or worried she'd asked him to bring her to Rfk. The place was like medicine for her.

Lbbp had no idea what he was going to do if it turned out he'd been wrong. No idea at all.

Pip pip p-pip.

Yes. Yes, yes, yes, yes ...

There it was. That sound, the sound that had led him to her all those orbits ago. It would lead him to her again.

Pip p-pip pip pip ...

Lbbp had no idea what he was going to say to Terra when he found her. No idea at all.

3.8

Terra crawled through the purple grass. She was suddenly very aware of how shiny her blue garment was. She looked up at the three visible moons. *I'm probably lit up like a FaZoon*, she thought. There was nothing to be done about that now. She crawled on.

Ahead of her lay one of the G'grk's huts. She could just make out an opening in its side. She waited until a sentry floated past and then scampered to the opening.

Peering inside, she saw that the hut held rows of metal shelves. On each of the shelves a G'grk drone (that was how they referred to their warriors, she remembered having read) was lying flat on his back, sleeping silently. *They sleep like Ymns,* thought Terra.

She crept inside. With extraordinary caution she examined a sleeping drone. He was asleep in full armour, she noticed. On his belt there was a holstered pulse-orb, what looked like a dagger or blade of some kind, and ... a gravity bubble generator.

It was exactly the same design as the ones Terra and her friends used. Perhaps they'd acquired them in Dskt; perhaps they'd been sold them illegally ... it didn't matter. Not right now.

Terra reached out her hand. She felt for the release catch on the side of the pod. She pressed it as gently as possible. She felt the pod click loose. She pulled it slowly, slowly, free of its holder ...

The lights switched on.

An alarm sounded.

The G'grk drones opened their eyes and sat up immediately, ready for action. The one that Terra had been in the course of robbing blinked, saw the little Ymn and grabbed her arm.

'Gkkh dkkh hrrg shk df?' he barked in her face. Then he turned to his fellow drones. 'Gkkh dkkh strrg shk df?'

The other drones clustered round her and peered at her. Another spoke.

'Nng, dkkh shk kkkh nkh … Z'ksh, shk df gkkh?'

They don't know what I am, thought Terra. *They think I'm some sort of animal. If I don't speak they might not regard me as dangerous.*

Terra stared round at the drones in dumb bewilderment. She thought about making some animal noises but didn't want to overdo it.

'Hkkh! Dkkh shk fssk sh'kst GHHH …' said one drone to the others.

'Ghhh, dkkh sk FSSK sh'kst …' agreed another, smiling. He licked his lips.

They eat animals, remembered Terra too late. *The G'grk eat animals.*

She turned and scampered back towards the doorway. It was blocked by a tall G'grk warrior with shinier armour than that worn by the drones. He wore a sword on his belt and war-paint on his face. His appearance caused the drones to snap to attention. An officer, thought Terra.

'Fsksh! Dkkh nkkh fssk sh'khhk, dkkh sh'ymn skhh. Gkkh sh'fsg-hh, T'r?'

The officer held up a small metal cube. It bleeped. The officer spoke again.

- I said, it's a Ymn, and it can speak perfectly well if it wants to. Isn't that right, Terra?

3·9

Terra was dumbfounded.

- *Give poor Z'ksh his gravity bubble back.*

Terra reached into her pocket, produced the bubble generator and handed it to the drone, who snatched it furiously and snapped it into place on his belt.

- *Foolish Z'ksh, allowing yourself to be robbed by an alien child,* said the officer. *You are G'grk! You sleep with your eyes open.*

- *Apologies, Drone Captain.*

- *No more rest for you, Z'ksh. Come with us. The rest of you, sleep! Tomorrow we march.*

The drones lay back down and seemed to fall asleep instantly.

- *Bring the Ymn, Z'ksh.* The Drone Captain strode off across the camp. Z'ksh took Terra roughly by the arm and set off after him. The Captain entered another hut, in which stood a folding table. He put his little metal cube down on the table, then sat on the edge and turned to Terra.

- *You're wondering how I know your name? You're quite famous, little monster. The alien child who tells — what do you call them? St'rss? Your reputation has reached Dskt, you will be pleased to hear.*

Terra was a little too busy being afraid to be pleased or proud. The Drone Captain went on:

- *Actually, when we arrived in Dskt, there was also much talk about the Ymn who frightened the FaZoon away. Dskt seems to take delight in Mlml's embarrassment. Just the sort of petty rivalry between nations which will soon be a thing of the past.*

Terra said nothing. There had been a time when the

thought of being a laughing stock in other nations might have felt like something to worry about, but not now.

- *But that doesn't matter. The real question is, how did you see us?*

Strange question, thought Terra. *The translator cube was obviously not working very precisely. He must mean how did I find them.*

- *I was on the beach when the spheres came out of the sea. I followed them here.*

- *Yes, yes, but how did you SEE us?*

It's not a mistranslation, thought Terra. *He really means 'see'.*

- *I'm not supposed to be able to see you ...?*

The Drone Captain thought for a moment, then laughed.

- *Those fools! So proud of their stolen light-bending machines!*

Of course, thought Terra. *They've been in Dskt. Dskt, where they perfected light-bending camouflage. They've stolen the technology. This whole camp is invisible. That's why no one in Mlml knows it's here. No one can see it ...*

-*... Except you!* said the Drone Captain, eerily completing Terra's train of thought. *You, with your little alien eyes! You can still see us! All that trouble we went to, raiding the laboratories in Dskt, persuading their scientists to help us* (Terra winced at the thought of what form such 'persuasion' might have taken), *even buying that detection suppressor field from those Kotari traders, then you just come walking along with your little blue eyes and look right at us.* He laughed again. *Remarkable. Annoying, but remarkable.*

So it was true what they said about the G'grk and technology, pondered Terra. *They get hold of it through theft and conquest but never quite figure out how to use it properly. Mind you, the need to set up their invisibility shields to work on Ymn eyes as well as Fnrrns' probably never occurred to them.*

The Drone Captain stood up. - *I must inform the Grand Marshal of our discovery. Z'ksh!* he shouted. The drone, who had been dozing against the wall of the hut, snapped to attention.

- Watch this creature. Ensure that no harm comes to it. Yet.

The Captain strode out, closing the fabric door of the hut.

Z'ksh sat on the table and glowered at Terra. He was missing his metal bed and it was all this little animal's fault.

Terra sat on the ground and smiled at Z'ksh.

Z'ksh did not smile back.

Terra kept smiling.

Terra yawned.

Z'ksh watched Terra, unmoving.

Terra yawned again. She smacked her lips. Another yawn.

Z'ksh, almost without noticing, yawned as well.

Terra gave a huge, theatrical yawn and a stretch.

Z'ksh yawned. His head lolled.

Terra closed her eyes, and waited.

After a few moments, she opened them again.

Z'ksh, his arms folded and his chin on his chest, was fast asleep.

Silently, Terra got to her feet. She felt in her pocket for the gravity bubble pod and attached it to her belt, wincing at the click it made as it snapped into place. Then she tiptoed to the fabric door and pulled it gently aside ... The fabric made the faintest rustling sound as it moved ...

Z'ksh's eyes opened. The instant it took him to remember where he was and what he was supposed to be doing gave Terra just enough time to run from the hut, hit the button on the pod and rise straight up into the air.

Z'ksh staggered from the hut. His disgrace was now complete. Punishments that did not bear contemplation awaited him. Unless he could recapture the Ymn animal before anyone else knew it had escaped ...

Z'ksh ran after Terra ... seeing her float upwards, he activated the gravity pod on his belt. The one Terra had given to him back at the hut. Her own pod. The one with the spent power-cell.

Z'ksh rose into the air ... a bit.

He rose to the height of the treetops and then started to descend almost immediately. He hurtled downwards into the forest, tumbling through branches, leaves and undergrowth before crashing to the ground in a thorny bush.

Z'ksh extricated himself from the thorns. He considered his options. Desertion? Suicide?

His thoughts were interrupted by a rustling sound. The purple grassy mound in front of him suddenly sprouted eyes and teeth. It raised its head to stare at him.

The G'grk are keen hunters, as you can imagine. For many eras they've hunted for sport and for food. Mind you, hunting has become rather less popular on the Central Plains in recent orbits. It's not as challenging as once it was, as the G'grk have hunted all the really dangerous animals of their homeland to extinction long ago. There are no fearsome predators left on the Central Plains. Which is a pity, as had Z'ksh any idea about how to behave around fearsome predators, he wouldn't have reacted as he now did.

Z'ksh stared right back at the znk. - *What are YOU looking at?* he said in G'grk.

The znk had no idea what it was looking at. But it smelled fantastic.

3.10

Lbbp stared worriedly at the power level light on his gravity bubble. He'd brought a spare cell but he didn't fancy trying to do a mid-air cell change. He'd only ever done it once. It was a long time ago, he was a student, there were girls watching …

The field-scanner's pip-pipping, which had been growing in strength as he got closer to Terra, had become more broken and hesitant, as if something was interfering with the signal. It was still strong enough to follow, though.

In fact, now it was getting stronger and stronger … As Lbbp peered at the field-scanner's display, he saw that the Ymn life-form was getting closer at a far faster rate than he was travelling. She was coming back! She was coming back to him!

Overjoyed, Lbbp peered ahead into the darkness … did he see something? The shimmer of a gravity bubble? The moonlight reflecting off shiny blue fabric?

As the shape became more and more distinct, waves of relief washed over him. He called to her.

- *Terra! Terra! I'm so glad you're safe and I'm so, so …*

- *ggggggggg*GGGGGOOOOOO AAAAAWWW*wwwa-aaayyyyy* … said Terra as she shot straight past him. Confused, Lbbp spun his bubble around and set off after her.

He could hear her shouting something. It sounded like - *No secrets! No secrets, remember? We don't need to keep secrets from each other?*

- *Terra! Look, I know you're upset, but …*

- *Upset? UPSET?* Terra stopped dead and swung round to face Lbbp. Their bubbles collided at speed and they bounced away from one another.

- You lied to me! You USED me! shouted Terra as she hurtled back towards Lbbp. *My whole life has just been one big experiment! What, are you hoping to win the Tnk Award or something? Leave me alone!* She slammed her bubble into his, bouncing him further away.

- The proposal was a mistake! cried Lbbp as he steered himself back towards her. *I was angry! I was young and stupid! I knew nothing about Ymns then! We had no right to …*

- It's just as well it was rejected, shouted Terra, surging away from him, *or I might never have been born, and then you wouldn't be able to conduct this little follow-up experiment of yours …* As Lbbp pulled alongside her, she swung her bubble sideways into his and bounced him away again.

- Did you see why it was rejected? Lbbp bellowed after her, as he regained control of his bubble. *Did you read the rejection document?*

Terra slowed down. She stopped, hovering above the trees. The sun was coming up.

- I withdrew it! I withdrew the proposal! It had to be signed by four Postulators; once I took my name off it, it wasn't a valid proposal any more. I stopped it, panted Lbbp.

Terra rotated to face him - *Why? What changed your mind?*

- The FaZoon did. Just after we submitted the proposal they turned up again. Looking at the FaZoon, I realised just how primitive we must appear to them, and I thought what if they decided we were a threat or just an encumbrance? They could wipe us out without even thinking about it.

Terra listened and hovered. The sun was peeking over the treetops.

- I suddenly knew that the Ymns had a right to make their own mistakes, to grow as a people in their own way, and if they became a problem then we'd deal with it at the time. Maybe we could even help them. And then I found you …

Lbbp reached his hand out. Slowly, so as to penetrate the bubble's field.

- And I realised everything I'd thought about Ymns was

*wrong ... As a civilisation, they've got a way to go, but so do
we all ... As individuals, you're every bit as smart, and decent,
and precious ...*

Terra reached out through the skin of her own bubble.

-*... as any creature in the universe. And yes, I've been fascinated to watch you grow up, but all parents are. And I love you
as much as anyone on this planet – on ANY planet – loves their
child. Please say you believe me.*

Terra took Lbbp's hand.

- *I believe you,* she said.

- *Thank you,* said Lbbp. *Thank you.* He pulled her to him,
and their bubbles merged.

Terra looked into Lbbp's eyes. Her expression changed.

- *We have to go.*

- *I know,* said Lbbp, *it's freezing up here.*

- *No, we have to go NOW,* and she turned and sped back
towards the city.

- *Why?* said Lbbp, his words suddenly drowned out by a
low rumbling sound. He looked around but saw nothing.

- *Just take my word for it!* screamed Terra. *Don't look back!
Just move, now!*

Lbbp set off after Terra. She cast a glance back at him,
her eyes full of panic.

- *What's happening?* shouted Lbbp, barely audible over
the mysterious rumble.

From nowhere, a tangle of threads enveloped his bubble
and stopped him dead. He was being pulled backwards. He
had been caught in a net, and was being reeled in towards
... what? There was nothing in the sky except him and
Terra. Looking across to her, he saw that she too had been
netted.

Terra called out to him but he couldn't hear. As they
were pulled closer together by the mysterious nets, her
voice became clearer.

- *It's the G'grk! The G'grk are here!*

A circular door opened in the sky, and they were hauled
through it.

Hands grabbed them and switched off their gravity bubbles. They dropped hard onto a metal floor.

- *I take it you were on your way to the city, little animal?* asked the Drone Captain. *It will be our pleasure to give you a ride.*

3.11

The sphere travelled judderingly through the air, gravity engines grinding away.

Lbbp and Terra sat on the floor, their wrists sealed in binding gel.

The Drone Captain stood over them. He seemed glad of the company. G'grk drones are not bred for conversation.

- Tell me, little animal, just what did you do to poor Z'ksh?

- Did you find him? asked Terra.

- We found some of him. Extraordinary. You don't look capable of it. Still, I had something far worse in mind for him. He should be grateful.

The Drone Captain bent to examine Terra. *- What a fascinating, surprising species. I look forward to getting to know it better.*

- Don't touch her! said Lbbp.

The Drone Captain smiled. *- That's the spirit! If your compatriots show such defiance, who knows, there may even be some fighting left to do by the time we get there.*

Terra was confused. *- What do you mean?* she asked.

The Drone Captain smiled cruelly. *- Foolish child. Did you think this was the spearhead of the invasion? The front line? The first wave? This is the rearguard!*

Lbbp and Terra exchanged horrified glances.

- Your friends in the city will have the honour of greeting the spearhead any moment now ...

3.12

Preceptor Shm was not having a good morning. He'd been in the Forum until very late the previous night, and now, no satisfactory resolution having been reached, he was there again, far too early for his liking. The fact that Lbbp was nowhere to be found wasn't helping his mood, either. Shm made a mental note to have strong words with Lbbp when he turned up.

Meanwhile, he had strong words for the civilian government, and they weren't going to like them.

- *Chairman ... Chancellor ... Senators ... I can only reiterate what I told you yesterday. This war cannot be averted by any action we take. The G'grk may yet decide against invading Mlml but that will be entirely a matter for them. Nothing we say or do can influence that decision on any meaningful level. We have nothing to offer them which they do not believe they can take by force. We have nothing with which we can threaten them which they fear in any way.*

The assembled senators shuffled uneasily and low, discontented mumblings echoed around the floor. Shm went on.

- *The G'grk have been in complete control of Dskt for over a cycle. We already know that any invading army would vastly outnumber our own defensive forces and it is reasonable to expect that their weapons would be at least comparable to our own. If the G'grk attack, we cannot repel them.*

- *So what then?* asked a robed senator. *We surrender?*

- *The G'grk despise surrender,* said Shm, *and regard those who capitulate as beneath contempt. If we surrender now they would exterminate us on principle.*

Gasps of shock.

- The FaZoon! Contact the FaZoon! The FaZoon will save us! cried another senator. Shouts of agreement from around the Forum. *- FaZoon! Bring the FaZoon back!*

- Attempts have already been made to contact the FaZoon, said Shm. *They have not been successful. Either they can't hear us or they're not listening. Besides,* Shm went on, *even if we could persuade the FaZoon to get involved, who's to say which side they'd be on?*

Murmurs of discomfort. No one had thought of that.

A pause.

- Senators, I'm sorry if this isn't what you wanted to hear. I know you were hoping we'd come up with some brilliant solution. That's what you want from us, the clever ones, the thinkers, the Postulators, I know. And I could just make something up, something that sounds ingenious, and be hailed as the saviour of Mlml, and let's face it, if I were wrong I probably wouldn't be around long enough to have to explain myself. But I'm not a hero. I'm a scientist. I have to follow the evidence and form my conclusions, and then present those conclusions as honestly as possible. And that's what I'm doing today.

- Is there then no hope at all? asked the Chancellor, weakly.

- One hope. Retreat, regroup, resist, said Shm. *First, we evacuate. Get everybody out of the major cities and coastal areas. Remove or destroy anything that the G'grk might be able to use against us. Hide out in the hills and forests, reassign the military commanders to train all able-bodied civilians as resistance cells. Then fight back. Attack supply convoys, blow up bases, make life as difficult as possible for the invaders, until one day they decide that occupying Mlml is more trouble than it's worth. There, you asked for my recommendations, senators, and that's all I've got for you. I'm sorry.*

The idea sank in. It was a desperate plan, but it was a plan.

- How much warning are we likely to get of a G'grk attack? asked an elderly senator.

Shm was about to reply when he felt a tingle in his feet. The tingle grew stronger. The crystal lanterns hanging from

the Forum ceiling started to rattle. The building was vibrating.

Shm sighed. It had been a good plan. He'd almost been
looking forward to it.

- *Not enough,* he said sadly.

The senators ran to the windows and looked out. With
a great crackle of energy, hundreds of blue G'grk spheres
deactivated their invisibility shields and appeared hovering
above the city.

One senator just had time to say - *It's the G'grk! They're
already*— before the ceiling fell in.

3.13

- What was THAT?

- Sit down, Fthfth, and come away from the window . . .

Bsht had just got the novice class settled when the first explosions were heard. She didn't bother trying to convince herself that it was an unscheduled quake, or a rogue thunderstorm. She knew exactly what it was. She'd hoped they'd get more warning than this.

- Everybody stay in your seats, she said as she went to the window.

Blue spheres hung over all quarters of the city. How had they got so close? Plumes of smoke rose from strategic targets; the Forum was already gone, the barracks at Gst-Fnchst, it looked like the fusion station was under attack, the information centre as well. *They knew where to hit us,* she thought.

Occasional bursts of grav-rocket fire would issue forth from the ground and hit the spheres. It didn't seem to be having much effect.

- What's happening, Bsht? asked Thnst.

- Don't be stupid, said Yshn, *you know what's happening. They're here. They're here and we're all going to die!*

- Nobody's going to die, said Bsht. *Just let me think for a moment.*

The building shook. The children screamed. Bsht ran to another window. A G'grk sphere was firing what looked like small rockets into the side of the Lyceum tower. *Why haven't they just flattened it with light-cannons?* wondered Bsht. *They could destroy the tower if they wanted to. They don't want to. Why not?*

The building shook again. *Why hasn't anyone given*

the evacuation order? wondered Bsht. Then she thought, *Evacuate to where?* and finally, *Who's 'anyone'?*

There was no plan. You couldn't plan for something like this. No one was in charge. It was up to her to save the children.

From the corridor outside, the sound of pupils and staff fleeing for the exits. Everyone else seemed to have come to the same conclusion. It was time to go.

The building shook again, and again. The children yelped and whimpered with fear.

- *Everybody listen to me!* Bsht called out above the noise and panic. *Listen to me! It's not safe here any more. We need to get out of the Lyceum, maybe even out of the city. Now come with me and STAY TOGETHER. Pktk, Fthfth, wait until last and keep an eye on the littler ones.*

Bsht led the children out into the corridor. The building shook violently, seeming almost to lurch. They passed lectoriums and laboratories, all deserted. From a room at the end of the corridor, Bsht heard a frantic voice.

- *Can anyone hear me? There are children in this building! Cease your fire! There are children here! Anyone?*

Looking in, she saw Vstj yelling desperately out of the window.

- *Vstj! What are you doing! Get away from the window!*

- *I've got to talk to them! I've got to find someone to negotiate with!*

- *It's the G'grk, Vstj. They don't negotiate. Come with us.*

Keeping low and gibbering with fear, Vstj scampered out into the corridor and joined the line of children.

- *Get to the back, make sure we don't leave any behind,* said Bsht, leading the way once more.

Vstj crawled to the back of the queue. - *Fthfth, isn't it? How nice to see you again. How's your mother?*

Bsht rounded a corner. Ahead of them was an emergency grav-chute, down which – if it was working – they could slide straight to the main atrium on the ground floor. What they would find down there, Bsht didn't want to contemplate yet. They'd deal with that in due course.

She saw the grav-chute portal. On his knees, next to the portal, was Pshkf. He had a box of tools and was tinkering frantically with the chute controls.

- *It's fried,* he said, *I reckon I can fix it, though.*

- *How long is that going to take?* asked Bsht, annoyed by the squeaky tone of her voice.

- *Why, do you have something you'd rather be doing right now?* retorted Pshkf. *Anyway it'll be quicker if you give me a hand.*

Bsht sighed. - *Everybody wait here a moment. Vstj, keep the children together. No wandering off, and that includes you.*

The building shook again. - *We'll be right here,* said Vstj airily. *Take your time.*

- *What exactly are you doing?* Bsht whispered, passing Pshkf a vibro-spanner.

- *Ripping out the fused circuits and bypassing them with circuits from the lights. Here we go . . .*

Pshkf touched the chute activation switch (which was now dangling from the wall on a bit of loose cabling) and the chute hummed into action.

Bsht turned to address the children. - *Right, listen to me. One at a time, and walk—*

The corridor exploded. Whatever those missiles were that the G'grk were firing at the building, one had hit the floor above them. With a roar of displaced matter, the ceiling collapsed between Vstj and Bsht. Vstj and the children were blown over one way by the blast, Bsht and Pshkf the other.

Bsht was first back on her feet. - *Vstj! Vstj! Are you there?*

Vstj's voice came through the rubble. - *Yes, we're all right. But we can't get through to you now.*

Bsht felt a sharp sting of despair and shame. She was cut off from the children, the children she was sworn to protect. Then Vstj's voice came again, and it had a quality Bsht had never heard before.

- *It's okay. I've got the children. I'll get them out of here.*

- Vstj, I...

- Go. Get to the ground floor. Bring help if you can. We'll be fine, I'll keep the children safe.

Something in Vstj's voice told Bsht that he believed what he was saying. And stranger still, so did she.

- Good luck, Vstj, she said.

- It's me, said Vstj, *I've always been lucky.*

Bsht turned to Pshkf. *- It's still working?* she said incredulously, hearing the hum of the grav-chute.

- When I fix something, it stays fixed, smiled Pshkf. *Now come on,* he said, picking up his toolbox, and a large bag which he slung over his shoulder. It took some effort; whatever he had in there was obviously very heavy. Bsht realised what it was.

- Is that ... oh, you have got to be crazy ...

- That's what you do in a crisis, isn't it? said Pshkf. *Grab your most prized possession and run? Not my fault if my prized possession weighs a bit.* He patted the bag containing his lovingly restored vintage thirty-first-era infralight drive, and stepped into the chute. Bsht shook her head and stepped in after him.

3.14

Security Chief Fskp had waited for a moment like this his whole life, and now that it had arrived, he was disappointed to find he wasn't enjoying it in the slightest.

It had been, by and large, a relaxing job being in charge of the Preceptorate Retinue. Policing a temple of learning and contemplation; keeping the peace in a place where the peace kept itself. There had been the occasional interesting moment, he supposed – that time when that skinny f'zft had turned up with an alien baby sprang to mind – but nothing you could base a thrilling memoir on, certainly.

He'd been trained for battle and seen none; six orbits he'd spent in the Mlml Space Infantry with not so much as a scratch on him. Peace. Overrated.

Finally he reasoned that if the nation were to be mired in permanent serenity, then he might as well spend it at home. He resigned from the infantry with full honours, took up the Preceptorate job and his boots had rarely left his desk since.

Now battle had found him at last, and he was beginning to see what it was that everybody liked about peace so much.

He crouched behind the reception desk in the main atrium of the Preceptorate complex. Beyond the crystal doors of the atrium, a giant blue sphere throbbed and hovered. Fskp aimed his pulse-orb at the sphere. He had few illusions about being able to do it much damage. He held his aim and waited for the sphere to do something.

What it did was speak. A voice, harsh, guttural, deafeningly loud.

- *MLMLN SLAVES! YOUR MASTERS HAVE*

ARRIVED! EMBRACE YOUR DEFEAT AND RE-CEIVE THEIR MERCY!

- *We've heard about your mercy!* shouted one of Fskp's guards. He had no idea if the G'grk could hear him but didn't care. *My brother was in Dskt!*

The Retinue had taken positions behind any upright structure they could find. They trained their pulse-orbs on the sphere, and waited.

The tension was broken by the swish of the grav-chute door opening. Fskp wheeled round as if to fire, but lowered his weapon on seeing Bsht and Pshkf.

- *Get down, the pair of you! Take cover!*

Bsht and Pshkf dropped down behind the reception desk, alongside Fskp.

There was a pause. - *They've stopped,* noticed Bsht.

- *What?* asked Pshkf.

- *They've stopped firing.*

- *The Wrath of The Occluded Ones,* muttered Fskp. *That's what they call it. It's how the G'grk began the assault on Dskt. Massive aerial bombardment just to show them who was boss. Then once everyone was terrified and disorientated they sent in the ground troops.*

- *Cowards,* muttered Bsht.

- *It's war,* said Fskp.

The voice came again.

- *TEACHERS! LECTORS! EDUCATORS! YOUR WORK HERE IS FINISHED! A NEW ORDER BEGINS! HISTORY STARTS AFRESH!*

Bsht and Pshkf glanced at each other, wondering.

- *SEND THE CHILDREN OUT TO US!*

Bsht closed her eyes. Pshkf's jaw clenched. That was why they hadn't destroyed the building. They wanted the children.

- *THERE IS NOTHING MORE YOU CAN TEACH THEM. YOU CAN NO LONGER PROTECT THEM. THEY BELONG TO US NOW. THEY WILL NOT BE HARMED. SEND THE CHILDREN TO US AND THEY WILL BE SAFE.*

- *Pshkf,* whispered Bsht, *that infralight drive of yours …*

- *I know, I know, I should have left it behind …*

- *Shut up a moment and listen. A ship can only engage its infralight drive once it's in space, am I right?*

- *That's right; you use bubble generators to get off the planet and fire up the drive once you're in orbit, why?*

- *What would happen if you were to start up the drive while on the planet's surface?*

- *Something bad.*

Bsht gestured towards the blue sphere. - *Bad for whom exactly?*

Pshkf smiled.

3.15

In the belly of another blue sphere, still travelling towards the city, Lbbp and Terra sat huddled together on the floor.

- *I've just figured it out.*
- *What?* said Terra.
- *How you managed to get the proposal document open when it was supposed to be secret,* said Lbbp.
- *Good for you,* muttered Terra.
- *Your slate was connected to our home terminal. The Source opened the document because it thought it was me trying to look at it, not you. Since I'm one of the signatories, it . . .*
- *Can you really be thinking about that at the moment?* asked Terra incredulously.

Lbbp looked around him. - *Well, what else am I going to think about?* he said miserably.

- *You! Mlmln! No talking!* barked the Drone Captain.
- *Or what?* snorted Lbbp. *Bad things might happen?*

The Drone Captain bent down and hissed in Lbbp's face.

- *I have orders to keep the little one alive. For you I have no such orders.*

Lbbp fell silent. The sphere juddered on.

3.16

- *So where are we going?* asked Shnst and Thnst simultaneously.

- *Erm ...* replied Vstj decisively. Then, realising how much he sounded like his old self, the self he didn't want to be any more, he said, - *If we can get to the practical science laboratory, I may have an idea.*

- *Practical science is through there,* said Pktk glumly, pointing at the rubble.

- *There's bound to be another way through. This building is over six eras old, it's full of passages, corridors and tunnels that everyone's forgotten about,* said Vstj. *I don't think anybody knows the complete layout.*

Fthfth had an idea. - *Not yet they don't. Come on, back to the lectorium!*

- *But we just came from there!* protested Pktk.

3.17

- TIME GROWS SHORT. IF YOU TRULY CARE FOR YOUR CHILDREN YOU WILL SEND THEM OUT TO US. OUR PATIENCE IS SPENT AND OUR VENGEANCE WILL BE SWIFT AND TERRIBLE. YOUR CHILDREN CAN LIVE UNDER OUR PROTECTION OR DIE UNDER YOURS. YOU WILL CHOOSE NOW.

- What are you doing with that thing? hissed Fskp. Pshkf and Bsht had cracked out Pshkf's tools and were making adjustments to what looked to Fskp like some sort of antique cleaning device.

- Almost done! replied Pshkf.

- We're refocusing the drive's displacement field, said Bsht. *Instead of throwing the field around itself, it will throw it around something else.*

- I didn't understand a word of that, said Fskp, *will it annoy the G'grk?*

- Severely, said Pshkf, *and it's ready.*

- Let me do this bit, said Bsht.

Slowly, she got to her feet, holding up both hands to show she was unarmed.

- I'm coming to talk! she shouted.

To everyone's surprise, the sphere answered.

- NO TALKING. THERE IS NOTHING TO TALK ABOUT. THE CHILDREN. NOW.

- The children are being gathered together. They will be brought to you in a moment. First, we offer this tribute to our new masters. Hail the G'grk!

She looked over her shoulder.

- *Hail the G'grk*, said Fskp, without even feigned enthusiasm.

Pshkf now walked to the crystal doors, carrying the infralight drive. It hummed gently. *Eight, seven*, thought Pshkf.

- *Please accept this tribute in the spirit in which it is given!* he shouted, with absolute sincerity. The drive hummed more loudly. *Five, four . . .*

Pshkf walked slowly backwards. *Three, two, one . . .*

- *NOW!* shouted Pshkf, diving behind the reception desk. Bsht did likewise.

There was a bright flash. The crystal doors shattered.

The sphere, enveloped in the displacement field, became massless. Its own gravity engines, which until that moment had been struggling to keep it off the ground, now repelled it away from the planet at almost the speed of energy. A few of the G'grk on board survived the trauma of the acceleration long enough to see the sphere, which was not built for extra-atmospheric travel, split apart in the pressureless vacuum of space. They hurtled out into the freezing void, giving thanks to The Occluded Ones for granting them such an interesting death.

3.18

- *We don't have time for this!* said Pktk.

- *We don't have time NOT to do it,* replied Fthfth crossly. *Now are you going to help me or not?*

Fthfth had set up the Interface on Bsht's desk. She was powering it up and adjusting the dome to her height.

- *Might I ask what's going on?* enquired Vstj as diplomatically as possible.

- *It's simple,* said Fthfth. *We need to find our way around this building. It's possible we're going to be trapped here for some time and need to find places to hide, possibly for days. As you point out, nobody, not the G'grk, not us, knows the whole layout of the place. So anyone who DID have that information,* she patted the dome of the Interface, *would have a distinct advantage.*

- *That's a lot of information,* said Pktk warily.

- *We'd better get on with it then,* said Fthfth, jamming her head into the dome. *Pktk, files, please. Complete schematics and architectural history of Hrrng Preceptorate to the present day.*

- *Er, shouldn't I ... I mean, wouldn't it be better if ...* Vstj pointed to his own head, then to the Interface, then his head again.

- *No,* smiled Pktk. *She knows what she's doing.*

- *Well, I will in a moment,* said Fthfth from inside the dome. *Start the programme! Now!*

Blip ... blip ... blip ...

3.19

Down in the atrium, the celebrations had been short-lived.

The disappearance of the sphere had brought hisses of triumph from the Retinue guards, who now fell silent.

Another sphere descended slowly from the sky, to take the place of the vanquished (and vanished) one. Then another, then another.

The spheres landed a hundred metres or so from the atrium entrance. Circular apertures appeared on the blue surfaces and ranks of G'grk drones emerged, armoured, painted, fearsome. They began to march towards the building.

- *Hand to hand,* muttered Fskp. *They only fight hand to hand with those they consider their equals. You've impressed them,* he said to Pshkf. *Don't suppose you could do it again?*

- *No, sorry,* said Pshkf, looking sadly at the twisted, blackened remains of the infralight drive. Two whole orbits' work. Worth every moment. *At least we gave them something to think about, and we may have bought the children some time,* he said.

Bsht shivered as she looked at the advancing phalanx. Some of the G'grk drones activated gravity bubbles and ascended the outside of the building. *That's why they've been blowing holes in the walls,* thought Bsht. *Run, children, run and hide. I'm so sorry.*

- *Any of those going spare?* asked Pshkf, indicating Fskp's pulse-orb. Fskp handed his spare side arm to Pshkf; another guard handed his to Bsht.

- *Know how to use that?* asked Pshkf.

- *Of course,* said Bsht quietly. She looked at the pulse-orb.

How hard could it be? She looked at the advancing G'grk. What difference would it make?

- *I'm glad I finally got to know you, Bsht,* said Pshkf.
- *Me too,* said Bsht.

They took aim.

3.20

- *What was that?* asked Yshn.

- *Orb-fire. The G'grk are inside the tower,* said Pktk. *Come on, Fthfth!*

- *We have to go!* urged Vstj. *Get her out of there!*

- *Not while the programme's running! You'll cook her brain,* said Pktk.

The programme finished. The dome dimmed. Fthfth didn't move.

- *Fthfth ...?* said Pktk quietly. The sound of battle was getting nearer. *Seriously, Fthfth?*

Fthfth flung the dome from her head and announced:
- *Hrrng Preceptorate was founded in the seventeenth era by Bft-sh-Bft of Hrrng and was relocated to its present site in the twenty-fourth era. Renowned as the birthplace of GravTech, it is regarded as one of the ...*

- *I think it worked,* said Pktk. *Fthfth ... Fthfth ... SHUT UP, Fthfth. Thank you. Now can you get us to the practical science lab?*

- *Of course!* said Fthfth, skipping into the corridor. *The practical science lab is situated on level thirty-one. Opened by Preceptor Hsk in orbit forty-one of the twenty-fifth era, it ...*

3.21

- *I think we're landing,* whispered Lbbp to Terra.

- *What will they do to us?* Terra asked, trembling.

- *If they wanted us dead they'd have killed us when they found us,* said Lbbp. *They must want us alive, and while we're alive, there's always hope.*

The sphere jolted as it touched down. A circle of bright daylight appeared in the side of the vessel, causing Terra to blink.

- *On your feet!* barked the Drone Captain.

Standing, Terra could see that the sphere had landed in the middle of the Preceptorate itself.

- *Move! Outside!*

Terra and Lbbp shuffled out into the light. Terra gasped as she saw the Lyceum tower. Smoke billowed from great gashes in its side. What had become of her friends?

Lbbp scanned the city skyline. Plumes of smoke, flames. Sounds of panic and distant explosions. *I thought I was rescuing her by taking her away from Rrth,* he pondered sadly. *Away from savagery, from brutality ... What do you call this?*

- *Lbbp ... look ...* Terra gazed tearfully at the courtyard in front of the atrium. Tnk's statue had been smashed; metallic blue pieces of it now whirled crazily in mid-air.

- *March!*

- *Where are we going?* asked Terra. Lbbp gave her a not-now look and one of the drones turned towards her, savagely.

- *Silence, beast!* He raised his hand; Terra flinched but no blow came.

- *Unharmed, drone, remember. The alien is to be unharmed.*

The Drone Captain's voice was commanding. Terra looked at him in confusion.

- *You are to be presented, little monster. The Great K'zsht himself wishes to see you. Now march!*

3.22

- ... *and although the practical science laboratory itself retains that name, the Practical Science department was amalgamated with Life Science and Theoretical Science in orbit sixty-one of the thirty-second era. And here we are!*

Fthfth had hardly paused for breath since the gaggle of fugitive children had left the lectorium. She'd opened secret doorways, led them through abandoned passageways, through crawlspaces and maintenance hatches, all the while narrating their route like a hyperventilating tour guide.

Pktk seized the momentary lull in the commentary. - *Do you have to do that?*

- *Yes. I think so. It helps me sort through all the new information. It's annoying, isn't it.*

- *Just a bit. But at least we're here now.*

At the far end of the corridor in which they now found themselves, lay the practical science lab. Vstj looked at the door and swallowed hard. His plan was coming together, and there was still a chance that he wouldn't have to ...

A high-pitched buzzing filled the air. It was coming from the floor. Someone was cutting through the floor.

- *What's that?* asked one of the little ones.

- *Are we being rescued?* asked another.

- *There's no one left to rescue us,* said Pktk. *Run!*

They ran towards the laboratory door. The first of them reached it just as the G'grk Drone Sergeant burst up through the corridor floor. Vstj stayed at the doorway, ushering the children through. A squad of G'grk drones emerged behind their sergeant; they formed a rank and began to run down the corridor, weapons raised.

- *The children are to be taken alive!* barked the Drone Sergeant.

- *In here!* said Vstj, pushing the last of the children through the door and rushing in behind them.

Once inside, he hit the orange paddle which activated the laboratory's lockdown mechanism. This sealed the lab in the event of a dangerous leak or other such accident. The laboratory door slammed shut and locked itself with a clunk that didn't sound nearly solid enough.

- *That won't hold them for long,* said Pktk.

- *Long enough,* said Vstj. *Now, Fthfth, does your newly installed knowledge of the Preceptorate layout extend underground?*

- *Yes it does,* said Fthfth proudly. *There is an extensive network of tunnels underneath the Preceptorate complex, some dating back to before the ...*

- *Yes, yes, that's all very commendable,* said Vstj. *Here.* He wrenched open a stiff metal shutter in the wall. It revealed a blackened chute, which descended in a spiral pattern off into darkness. *This leads to the old incinerator.*

- *Incinerator?* said everybody, alarmed.

- *Relax, it's been deactivated since orbits ago.* Vstj knew this; he'd been responsible for turning down the request to have it repaired. Pointless, now they had matter scramblers. Would have been a waste of time and resources. Just one more wise decision for which he'd never be recognised.

- *If you slide down there you can climb through the incinerator into the disused service tunnels ...*

- *... which were built in the twelfth era to facilitate repairs to the old generators, before the fusion system was installed in the thirty-first era,* said Fthfth, unable to help herself. She was getting less and less keen on the Interface.

- *Whatever. Once down there you can find your way outside the city without ever coming above ground. Here, take this.* Vstj handed a small metal tube to Pktk.

- *What is it?*

- *The key to my house. It's the big one on top of Hrrnf-Kth*

Hill. Pktk had often wondered who lived there. *You'll find everything you need there to hide out for a few days. I hope you like configurations four and twelve, though.*

– *Will you come and meet us there?* asked Shnst.

– *Well, that'd be lovely, wouldn't it,* replied Vstj. And indeed, the thought of that big draughty house being full of children – and him not being there to see it – added another twinge of regret which he immediately shoved to the back of his mind. No time for any of that now; the G'grk were hammering and orb-blasting away at the laboratory door.

– *Quickly, in you go,* said Vstj, and the children climbed one by one into the chute, Pktk staying until last to help the little ones in.

As the last of the children slid away, Pktk climbed into the chute and turned to Vstj. – *You're not ...?*

– *You have to take care of them now, Pktk. I'm sorry.* Vstj shoved Pktk down the chute and slammed the shutter closed.

Vstj looked at the equipment scattered around the lab and racked his memory. The hammering on the laboratory door was very distracting, but looking around, he was fairly sure he had everything he needed.

3.23

The G'grk tend to favour brute force when confronted with obstacles. Had they thought of finding a way to override the laboratory's lockdown system they might have opened the door rather sooner, but they preferred the direct approach. After a shade or so of battering and blasting, the door gave way.

The Drone Sergeant led his troops through the doorway. There was no sign of the children. The adult Mlmln had his back to them.

- *Where are the children?* growled the Drone Sergeant.

- *Children aren't allowed in the lab outside of class time,* replied Vstj calmly, surprising himself with his own composure.

- *You will tell us where the children are,* hissed the Sergeant. Still Vstj didn't turn round. He sighed.

- *Yes, yes, I imagine I will. Sooner rather than later, I should think. You won't get much resistance out of me, boys, sorry about that.*

The G'grk exchanged puzzled glances. This wasn't how this part usually went.

Vstj went on. - *Different story if my old mother were here, I can tell you. Oh yes, she'd have kicked your brf-shrfs into the middle of next cycle. Don't really take after her side of the family.*

The Drone Sergeant lost patience. - *You will tell us NOW!* He grabbed Vstj by the shoulder and spun him round.

- *Mind you,* said Vstj after a moment's hesitation, *I don't really get much from my father's side either. Brilliant scientists, you know. All of 'em. You couldn't move for awards in our house. Not me, though. Can hardly do a thing in a lab. I mean look at this ...*

Vstj gestured towards the work bench behind him. A blob of grav-matter was spinning in a containment field. A crystal projector was bombarding it with high-frequency energy waves. Very high frequency.

- *It's not supposed to look like that, now is it?* asked Vstj.

The Drone Sergeant's eyes widened. He didn't know exactly what he was looking at but he suddenly knew why Vstj had been stalling. He turned to flee and fell right over the drone standing behind him. This drone in turn knocked another over, and, as the grav-matter started to spin out of control, the tightly disciplined G'grk squad was reduced to a tumbling scramble of bodies in the laboratory doorway.

Vstj's penultimate thought was: *So, is this what bravery feels like?*

Vstj's final thought, as the containment field collapsed, was: *Bravery hurts.*

3.24

Pktk was ushering the last of the children through the hatch which led out of the incineration chamber and into the service tunnels. There was a distant sound from high above them, a sort of 'whump' and a great gust of wind blew through the chamber and into the chute, as if sucked up towards the laboratory.

Fthfth figured it out first. - *Vstj!* she gasped. *He ... he's ...*

- *Come on,* said Pktk.

3.25

Terra marched through the antechamber of the council dome. She remembered the last time she'd walked through this room, on her first day at the Lyceum. She remembered the thrill and excitement of that occasion. A lifetime ago. A million lifetimes.

- *March!* shouted one of the G'grk drones, entirely unnecessarily. The binding gel had completely solidified around her hands and she was aware of a horrid itching at her wrists. She glanced up at Lbbp. He smiled reassuringly at her but there was fear in his eyes. Proper grown-up fear.

They entered the council chamber. Blue G'grk banners fluttered from the ceiling. The council members were seated in their usual rows of seats but rather than sitting upright and alert, as they had been on that faraway day, they were slumped and bowed. Some of them were bruised and bloodied, blue stains on their shimmering robes. In front of the seats, kneeling on the floor, were yet more Mlmlns. Lbbp recognised some of them as members of the civilian government. They too looked wounded and battered. Ranks of G'grk drones stood watch over them all.

Approaching the rows of kneeling Mlmlns, Terra saw Preceptor Shm himself. He sat slumped in his usual place, blue blood trickling from a fresh wound in his scalp. He looked up as Terra passed; there was a flicker of recognition, followed by a terrible sadness in his eyes.

A high-pitched ranting voice was echoing through the chamber as they were shoved to the front of the crowd. - *Kneel!* barked the drone again, pushing Lbbp down to his knees. Terra knelt unbidden, to Lbbp's relief.

- *It'll be okay,* whispered Lbbp.

- *Quiet, slave!* shouted the drone. He kicked Lbbp hard in the lower torso. Lbbp doubled over in pain but did not cry out. Neither did Terra, though she trembled violently and tears welled up in her eyes. The drone glowered at her.
- *Disgusting,* he muttered, then turned his attention to the centre of the room.

The ranting voice, which had continued all this time, came from a tall young G'grk warlord who paced back and forth in front of the chamber's central dais. He wore shining plates of armour over his bare skin, and his face was striped with war paint. Looking up, Lbbp recognised him as Sk'shk, Grand Marshal K'zsht's deputy and herald.

- *The Occluded Ones have seen your weakness and decadence! Rejoice that they send their avatars to cleanse and redeem you! You will be returned to the true path! K'zsht the Righteous will purge you of your sickness! K'zsht the Just will heal you through pain and fire! Your screams of anguish will be pleasing to The Occluded Ones! They will hear your cries of repentance!*

On the dais behind Sk'shk, silent and unmoving, stood K'zsht himself. He looked exactly as Terra had seen him on the lectorium visualiser all those cycles ago. His skin was tough and wrinkled, criss-crossed with the scars of a hundred battles. He too wore armour but unlike Sk'shk's gleaming plates his was scratched, scorched and dull. He held his ceremonial lance – the one that tradition required should never leave his grasp as long as he lived – and stared impassively out into the room as Sk'shk paced and bellowed.

- *For many of you it is too late!* cried Sk'shk. *You are too sunk in luxury and depravity. You are too sick, too weak to be saved. You will suffer, and when death comes you will welcome her. But for your children there is hope ...*

The mood of the crowd, until then one of numb despair, now tightened into horror, and just a hint of anger. Terra sensed it immediately.

- *Your children will receive the blessings of hardship and ordeal! They will grow strong! Their spirits will harden with their flesh! They will be saved! They will be purified! They will be G'GRK!*

Uproar. Noise from every quarter. A victorious cheer from the G'grk, cries of fury and defiance from the Mlmlns. One council delegate, a rudimentary bandage over one eye, pushed his way to the front of the crowd and yelled directly at Sk'shk.

- *Every one of us will die before we let you take our children!*

Sk'shk stared back at him with the merest hint of a smile.

- *Yes, you will,* he hissed, and nodded almost imperceptibly to one of the waiting drones.

The drone reached for his belt, to which was attached a row of little metallic spheres. In a single fluid action he snapped one of the spheres off, crushed it between his thumb and finger, making it crackle and fizz with a nasty energy, and hurled it at the delegate who had challenged Sk'shk. It struck the delegate square in the chest; he lived just long enough to feel his component atoms begin to lose their cohesion and fly apart in all directions. His scream of terror and agony was still resounding around the quartz dome as the last trace of him disappeared.

The cries of horror and alarm stifled themselves to whimpers and moans as the drones turned their fierce gaze upon the surviving Mlmlns. *Anti-matter grenade,* thought Lbbp. *Invented right here in Mlml a few orbits ago. Outlawed immediately. Some fool obviously went ahead and made some anyway and somehow the G'grk got hold of them. Maybe we deserve this.*

Lbbp could feel Terra shivering beside him and thought he would explode with impotent fury. He'd heard reports about individuals who, in moments of extreme stress or rage, had suddenly performed terrific feats of strength and saved the day. He knew now such tales were myths; if anger could bring strength, he would have snapped free of the binding gel and torn the G'grk limb from limb. As it was, he fought to maintain focus and stay alert for a chance – ANY chance – to change the situation in their favour by even the slightest degree.

Terra closed her eyes tight and tucked her chin to her chest ... she wanted desperately to hide and this was as close as she could get. She clung to the hope that if she could get to the end of this ... meeting, rally, conference, whatever it was – without attracting attention to herself, then maybe, just maybe ..

- *THERE it is ...*

No. Oh no.

- *Now we see how far you have strayed. NOW we see how low you have fallen. That you would accept this ... THING into your midst, that you would dress it up in clothes and treat it as one of your own ... Have you no pride? No honour? No SHAME?*

Terra looked up through her tears and saw Sk'shk peering down at her. She found the strength to whisper.

- *Please,* was all she could say, *please ...*

Sk'shk seemed taken aback. - *It speaks ...*

- *Yes,* said Terra, *I can speak.*

- *How revolting,* said Sk'shk. *Bring it!*

Two drones seized Terra's arms, yanked her to her feet, marched her to the dais and threw her down before K'zsht.

- *There, Grand Marshal. See the alien wretch that these weaklings have cosseted!* He turned to the cowering prisoners once more. *This ... beast, this animal ... You have not only allowed it to corrupt your land with its presence, but you have permitted it to infect your very minds with these ... f'k-shnns, these st'rss ... Such weakness! Such vice! You are indeed fortunate that we, the G'grk, choose to deliver you from your own frailty and wickedness.*

K'zsht peered down at Terra. He did not speak and his face showed no clue as to his thoughts. Terra knelt up and made as if to address K'zsht.

- *You will not speak to the Grand Marshal, beast!* screamed Sk'shk. *You will not defile his hearing with your screeches. See, Great K'zsht,* he went on, turning back to his leader, *what filth and putrescence pollutes the stars. But no longer!* He spun around to address the Mlmln prisoners. *Now your nation has fallen, its bounty shall be ours! We will harness your space-bending technology and make it our own. We will set out and take the G'grk's gifts of purity and death to all the worlds of the universe! Starting,* he hissed, turning back to glower at Terra, *with the forsaken rock which spawned this vile creature . . .*

Rrth, thought Terra. *They're going to Rrth. They only know it exists because of me. What have I done?*

- *Rejoice, little beast,* hissed Sk'shk. *You will be the first of billions of your kind to die at the hands of the G'grk.*

- *She's my responsibility!* shouted Lbbp. The drone nearest to him made as if to strike him but hesitated at a gesture from Sk'shk.

- *I brought her here,* said Lbbp. *If her being on this planet is a crime then the crime is mine. Take me.*

Sk'shk gestured again. A drone stepped forward and produced a small vial of fluid from a pouch on his belt. He poured a drop of the fluid onto the binding gel encasing Lbbp's hands and it dissolved away. The drone beckoned to Lbbp to stand and he did so, rubbing his wrists.

- *You would assume responsibility for this creature?* asked Sk'shk, pointing towards the kneeling Terra.

- *Always.*

Sk'shk glanced towards K'zsht, then turned back to Lbbp.

- *K'zsht the merciful offers you a boon. You have a chance to make amends for your offence.*

Sk'shk drew his sword, a heavy bronze blade with a curved serrated edge. He flipped it over and offered the jewelled handle to Lbbp.

- *Kill her.*

Lbbp stared wordlessly at the sword. Terra turned her head to look up at Lbbp. She could read no emotion in his face.

- *This place is to be consecrated as a temple to the Occluded Ones,* announced Sk'shk. *This demands an act of sacrifice. You will now atone for your blasphemy in polluting their chosen world with this deviant filth. Spill her foul alien blood and you will be spared. Do it not, and you and all your compatriots,* he gestured around the chamber at the cowering masses, *will die today.*

A moment's pause which lasted an age.

Lbbp reached out and took the sword.

He examined the exquisite scrollwork engraved along the blade. *Strange that they should put so much effort into decorating it,* he thought. *They obviously have a sense of beauty somewhere among all the hatred and fury. How odd. How sad.*

Terra looked up at Lbbp, desperate to see some sign of his thoughts in his expression. Lbbp did not meet her eyes but stared fixedly at the sword in his hand.

Lbbp sighed.

- *You know,* he said looking up at Sk'shk, *I really should take a swing at you with this but I'd probably miss, and besides, I want you to hear what I have to say right now.*

He tossed the sword down at Sk'shk's feet.

- *I'm not doing it. I don't care any more. Kill me, kill all of us, it doesn't matter. Even if I believed you were serious about letting these people go, and I don't, we're better off dead than ruled by you. But any killing you want done, you'll have to do yourself. I'm not your instrument. We're not your slaves.*

Lbbp exhaled hard. He felt neither fear nor pride, just a peculiar calm.

- *As you wish,* hissed Sk'shk. *But first you will watch her die.*

Two drones seized Lbbp by the arms. Sk'shk bent down to retrieve his sword, bristling at the indignity of having to do this himself. At that instant, Terra realised that no one was watching her. She scampered away on all fours between armoured legs. Shouts of - *Catch her!* and - *Go on Terra!* came from above her. Her hands still held together by the binding gel, she could only manage a loping, tripedal crawl; moreover, she realised with rising panic, whatever she did there was nowhere to go.

A strong hand seized the back of her garment and lifted

her off the floor. Terra dangled helplessly as a G'grk drone brandished her triumphantly above his head. She let out a wail of terror.

- *Hear how it howls!* laughed Sk'shk. *Hear how the beast howls!*

Suddenly Terra's mind was somewhere else.

The terror was just too intense for her conscious mind to process, so her mind did something different.

It remembered.

It remembered the last time she'd felt such abject despair. The kind of despair a new-born baby feels the first time it knows pain.

Terra was tiny. She was dressed in soft clothes. Her little limbs were curled up uselessly across her body. She was held in strong but gentle arms and her tummy ached. The pain was the first she'd ever felt, and it was terrifying to her brand new mind. She screamed, and screamed, and screamed.

The arms began to rock her, and a sound came to her ears. A voice, soft, soothing, a beautiful sound that eased her pain and banished her fear. Her mother's voice.

* * *

Back in the council chamber, back in reality, the gloating G'grk heeded Sk'shk's command to listen to Terra's cries, but what they heard was not the howling of a terrified beast.

Terra, only dimly aware of her surroundings, half in the present and half in the past, did something neither she nor anyone else on Fnrr had ever done before.

Terra sang.

Her clear little voice rang out, resounding through the quartz dome of the chamber. A tune she'd long forgotten, in a language she barely understood. The first music ever heard on Fnrr, heard now by Mlmln and G'grk together.

'Do not cry
Do not weep

Floating gently off to sleep
You are loved and safe from harm
Sleeping sound in Mummy's arms ...'

The song ended. Silence.

A sound. A metallic, clattering sound.

Then a voice. A new, thin, papery voice. The voice of someone very old.

- *Let her make that sound again,* said Grand Marshal K'zsht. *Let her do it again,* he said, pointing at Terra with his right hand. The hand which a moment earlier had dropped his sacred lance to the chamber floor.

The drone holding Terra lowered her to the floor.

- *Come here, child,* said K'zsht. Sk'shk made as if to protest but thought better of it.

- *That sound,* said K'zsht. *Does it have a name?*

- *I don't know,* said Terra. *I've never done it before.*

- *But you could do it again?*

- *I'll try,* said Terra, and she sang the song once more.

G'grk and Mlmlns listened to the song in silence. K'zsht closed his eyes until the song was over.

- *I have fought so many battles, both large and small,* he said quietly. *I have fought for survival, for advancement, I have fought to attain the position of Grand Marshal and I have fought to keep it. Many, many more have died at these hands than have ever grasped them in friendship.*

K'zsht reached out and took Terra's small pink hands in his gnarled old grey ones.

- *On the eve of each battle, as is our custom, I would commune with The Occluded Ones and ask that my army be victorious.*

Terra listened. Lbbp listened. Everyone listened.

- *I am told that some of my predecessors could hear The Occluded Ones reply to them. I never could. But then battle would be joined, we would prevail as always and I would consider my request granted. Do you understand, child?*

- *I think so,* replied Terra quietly.

- *Before we mounted this campaign I communed with The*

Occluded Ones as usual. But this time I asked for something different. This time I asked them to send me a sign, to tell me whether we were indeed on the true path. Not whether we were capable of victory, but whether we were deserving of it, and our enemies deserving of death and defeat.

K'zsht's black eyes gazed into Terra's blue eyes.

- *Are you that sign, child?*

- *I don't know ... I've often wondered if I was brought here for a reason ...*

- *When I heard about the child from another world, I was curious. I saw you in this place and I was fascinated, but now I have heard this sound ... The Occluded Ones could never be pleased by the destruction of such beauty. They must surely have sent you to this place as their emissary.*

- *An emissary from The Occluded Ones!* shouted one of the G'grk drones. A charge of excitement passed around the ranks of G'grk; the Mlmln prisoners, sensing that things were changing, remained silent.

- *I don't know why I'm here,* said Terra bravely, *but I do know that I've learned a lot from being here. And I think those who've known me have learned a lot, too.*

She looked into K'zsht's eyes, searching for a connection.

- *I've learned what it is to be looked down on, to be thought of as savage and primitive. And my friends and I, we've learned what it is to surprise each other, to be better than we're expected to be ...*

K'zsht seemed to understand.

- *Most of all,* said Terra, *I've learned that the things that make us the same matter more than the things that make us different ... That the things that bind us together ...*

- *... are stronger than the things which set us apart ...?* said K'zsht.

- *Exactly,* smiled Terra.

A smile began to form on K'zsht's face. It looked like it might have been his first.

- *Perhaps we have much to learn from each other ...*

- *We do,* said Terra. *We all do.*

Terra looked round and saw Lbbp, his face beaming with pride. She beckoned to him and he stood beside her, placing his hand on her shoulder and squeezing it.

K'zsht rose to his full height, and made as if to address the crowd. But another voice rang out first.

- *NO!*

Sk'shk stood in front of the dais. He shook with rage as he spoke.

- *How many? How many of my brothers have fought and died at your word? How much G'grk blood has been spilled for you? We have followed you across the face of this world, killing and dying at your command and now you betray your birth right, your heritage, your PEOPLE for the mewlings of a frightened animal? Weakling! Traitor! Coward! HERETIC!*

Too late, everyone noticed what Sk'shk had in his hand. He had picked up K'zsht's lance, and now drew it back, aiming it at the Grand Marshal himself.

Terra saw Sk'shk's arm flash forwards, loosing the lance. Lbbp saw it too, and without a moment's thought he pushed Terra aside and threw himself in front of K'zsht.

The lance struck Lbbp in the upper torso with such force that it lifted him off his feet and propelled him backwards into K'zsht. K'zsht's bodyguards, bewildered by the rapidity of events (and perhaps, until now, a little conflicted as to where their loyalties should lie) snapped back to attention and fell upon Sk'shk, beating him to the floor. One of them drew his sword and swung it high into the air, meaning to cleave Sk'shk's head off, but paused at the sound of the Grand Marshal's voice.

- *No! No one else dies today!*

Everyone turned to see K'zsht cradling Lbbp. The lance had buried itself in Lbbp's shoulder and protruded from his upper back. Thick blue blood soaked Lbbp's garment and a thin trickle ran from his mouth. Terra rushed to him.

- *I'm so proud of you* ... said Lbbp faintly. *So proud* ...

- *Please*, wept Terra. *Don't leave me now!*

She felt K'zsht's hand on her arm. - *I said no one else*

would die today, and I meant it, said the Grand Marshal. *Bear him to my ship! Alert my personal physicians! And bind that one!*

As K'zsht's bodyguards gelled Sk'shk's wrists and dragged him away, both G'grk and Mlmlns rushed to Lbbp's aid. Preceptor Shm, still bleeding himself but no longer bowed, was the first to reach him. The Drone Captain, the one who had captured Lbbp and Terra, was the second.

- *We can't move him with this,* said Shm, indicating the lance.

- *Don't pull it out! He'll bleed to death where he lies!* said the Drone Captain, who knew about such things.

- *Wait,* said K'zsht. He grasped the lance just above the point where it entered Lbbp's body, and grunting with effort, snapped off the shaft. Everyone gasped; the G'grk at K'zsht's destruction of his own sacred emblem, and the Mlmlns at how much stronger the old warrior was than he looked.

- *Go! Quickly!* said K'zsht.

The last thing Lbbp knew before unconsciousness washed over him was that he was being borne aloft by both robed Mlmlns and armoured G'grk.

3.26

The next thing Lbbp saw was orange sunlight streaming through the window of his own room, and Terra's face smiling at him.

- *You're awake!*

- *It would seem so. How long have I ...?*

- *Don't move. The physicians said it'd hurt for a while. The G'grk physicians didn't have any pain-relieving medicine, of course. They think it's for the weak. We had to send to the Nosocomium for some.*

- *Are the G'grk still here?*

- *Some of them. K'zsht has gone on permanent retreat to the desert moon of Jsk Four to spend the rest of his days in contemplation or something.*

- *And Sk'shk?*

- *Banished.*

- *Where to?*

- *No one knows, which I think was the idea.*

Lbbp looked around him. He and Terra were alone in his room.

- *How many did we lose?*

- *We don't know yet. They're still counting. Many are still missing but more turn up alive every day. Fthfth and Pktk are okay; they were setting up a camp in the hills above the city. My whole class were hiding out there. They were the only ones to get away! All the other pupils got rounded up, but thankfully peace broke out before the G'grk could ... do anything to them.* Terra shuddered.

- *The whole novice class hiding out in the hills ...* pondered Lbbp. *I imagine Fthfth was in charge.* He smiled.

- *Actually Pktk was,* said Terra. *I know!* she responded

to Lbbp's incredulous expression. *I think he was a bit disappointed when they were rescued; he was looking forward to being a plucky resistance fighter. Oh, but Lbbp ... There's no sign of Bsht. Anywhere. I'm sorry.*

Lbbp let this sink in for a moment. Then he said, - *She'll turn up. You wait and see. I know Bsht.*

- *Of course, you're right*, said Terra, not believing this. *But there's one bit of good news ...*

- *Yes?*

Terra held up a glittering gold star in one hand and a jewelled dagger in the other. - *You're the first Fnrrn in history to be honoured for bravery by both the Mlml government and the G'grk High Command. Thought you'd like to know.*

Lbbp smiled ruefully. Bravery. Bravery? Him? Bravery, really?

He sighed.

- *Listen, Terra ...*

Terra sat up, listening keenly.

- *I have to tell you something. Something I figured out before the war started. Something I couldn't tell anyone, not even you. But now I can, in fact I think I have to.*

Terra's nose wrinkled.

- *It's about the night I found you*, began Lbbp.

228

3.27

A few days later, Lbbp stood alone in the council chamber. The blue G'grk banners had been taken down and most of the debris of the brief war had been cleared away, but the council had not been reconvened. Some councillors had died in the initial assault and successors had yet to be found.

An uneasy truce persisted; no one was sure what the long-term resolution would be. There was talk of the G'grk being placed in charge of planetary defences in return for withdrawing their troops back to the Central Plains, and even of assigning G'grk officers to train the armed forces of Mlml and Dskt. Lbbp had no doubt the politicians would figure something out. And when that didn't work they'd figure something else out.

In the silence of the chamber, Lbbp could almost hear Terra's voice, still echoing around the quartz dome. Music, that was what it was called. He'd looked up the word while recovering from his injury. The Source contained quite a lot of information on the use and meaning of Ymn words, gathered from the broadcasts received from Rrth over the last era. Lbbp now realised he'd heard such 'songs' before, while studying these broadcasts himself ... Ymns had such a strange up-and-downy way of talking that he'd never really noticed the difference. It was only when he'd heard Terra's sweet little voice ringing out in this room that he'd understood what music was. A form of communication, one that bypassed the intellect and spoke straight to the core of one's consciousness. Remarkable.

Lbbp rubbed his sore shoulder and looked around the high white walls. He spoke.

- So how much of this did you see coming?

There was no reply. He'd expected none. He continued.

- The war? The invasion? The song? All of it?

No response but the echo of his own voice.

- Is that why you let me keep her?

He paused before going on,

- So is that it now? Prophecy fulfilled? Do we get to live the rest of our lives as we please or is there more?

Echoes, then silence.

- Well, it doesn't matter now anyway.

The silence was broken by a scraping, rattling sound. Lbbp turned to see a young Fnrrn, clad in a white garment, pulling a metal trolley full of cleaning tools and products. The trolley scraped along the floor; it was designed to hover just above it but Lbbp could see that its power cell had gone flat. Power had not yet been restored to the whole city, people were having to make do.

- Here, let me help you with that, said Lbbp. He proffered his good arm and helped the grateful young Fnrrn pull his cleaning trolley into the chamber.

The cleaner took a long-handled brush from his trolley; he was about to set to work when he paused. He turned to Lbbp.

- I'm sorry, he said, *but are you Postulator Lbbp?*

Lbbp sighed. Since he'd been strong enough to leave home he'd spent much of his time being thanked and congratulated by strangers for his heroic actions. It was all very well meant, he knew, and he supposed he should be pleased, but he was growing very weary of having the same conversation over and over again ... Yes, he had been scared, yes, the Ymn girl was fine, yes, it had hurt a lot ...

Lbbp took a deep breath and was preparing to run through the story one more time, when he had an idea.

- No, said Lbbp. *A lot of people have asked me that. I think I must look like him.*

- Oh, said the young cleaner, disappointed. Odd, this tall Fnrrn did look a lot like Postulator Lbbp, he was standing in

the very place where Lbbp had performed his now famous feat of bravery, he even (the cleaner now noticed) seemed to have a sore shoulder much as Lbbp would certainly have, but he'd said he wasn't Lbbp, so he obviously wasn't. He wouldn't say it if it weren't true, would he? Why would anyone do something like that?

That was easy, thought Lbbp. He turned to go. He had a lot to do; in the immediate aftermath of the extraordinary events in the council chamber, Terra had been promised a reward. She'd made a request, the request had been granted and tomorrow it would be honoured.

Lbbp wasn't looking forward to it.

PART FOUR

Forbidden Planet

4.1

The SETI laboratory at Hat Creek, California, was a quiet place. SETI stood for Search for Extraterrestrial Intelligence, and so far nobody, either here at Hat Creek or at any of the other SETI observatories around the world, had ever found any. Many people thought that the whole thing was a giant waste of time and money. Most scientists and astronomers insisted that, on the contrary, intelligent life was certain to exist somewhere out in space, and that it was only a matter of time before they found it. The cleverest of the scientists and astronomers admitted – privately at least – that any really intelligent life would be smart enough never to allow its presence to be detected by the human race. It wouldn't have cheered these scientists and astronomers up one bit to know that they were right.

This particular morning at 5.21 a.m., the extremely bored and poorly paid scientist, whose job it was to stay awake as hours of unremarkable data poured in from the huge radio telescopes towering over the building, was suddenly awoken by the sound of a dozen computers clicking into furious activity, the hum of printers switching themselves on and the glare of many screens banishing their swirly screensavers and flashing up instead rows and rows of numbers.

Rubbing his eyes, the scientist looked at the computer screens. Not just numbers; the same numbers. The same four numbers, over and over again. He phoned the SETI labs at Ohio State University, the Parkes Observatory in Australia and Jodrell Bank in England and was told that they were all indeed receiving the same signal. Then he made himself some coffee and phoned some rather more important scientists than himself to come in and help him, since he wasn't being paid nearly enough to handle this sort of thing on his own.

At 5.45 a.m. the important scientists finished their coffee and played rock paper scissors to see who had to phone the government. The losing scientist drained his cup, took a deep breath and picked up the phone.

At 6.01 a.m. the first phone calls came from the TV news people. The signal was now so strong that anyone with a radio could pick it up, and people were wondering where it was coming from and what the four numbers meant. The government released a statement saying it was a routine communications test. Nobody believed this for a second.

At 6.44 a.m. the Air Force officers who, much to the scientists' annoyance, seemed to have pretty much taken over the running of the Hat Creek laboratory realised that the four numbers were probably latitude and longitude readings. The numbers were giving a location, a special place on Earth where ... nobody knew what would happen there, but it seemed obvious that something would, and soon. One of the Air Force officers hurried off to get a map while the scientists made more coffee.

At 6.52 a.m. the map location given by the mysterious signal was identified as an unremarkable stretch of road, passing through an uninteresting bit of countryside. The Air Force officers hurried back to the helicopter they'd arrived in, while the scientists played rock paper scissors to see which one would get to go with them.

At 7.25 a.m., somebody – nobody knew who, but they would be SO fired when they were found out – told the TV news people what was going on. The stretch of road was already crawling with news vans, cameras and expectant onlookers by the time the soldiers arrived to clear the area.

At 7.45 a.m. the signal changed suddenly. Instead of the four numbers there was now just one: nine. Over and over again, the number nine. Everybody now knew that whatever was going to happen, it was going to happen at nine o' clock. Pessimists all over the world decided they had an hour and fifteen minutes left to live. A radio breakfast show DJ played a record with a chorus that went 'It's the end of the world as we know it' several times in succession until he was forcibly ejected from the building. He didn't seem to care.

At 8.51 a.m., as more or less the entire population of Earth sat watching their TVs in varying states of fear and excitement, a missile early warning station reported that something had entered the upper atmosphere directly above the suddenly very special location. The military jet planes which had been circling the area for nearly two hours reported that they couldn't see anything.

By 8.58 a.m. the soldiers had managed to clear a space about thirty metres wide at the location. While the TV news reporters babbled into their cameras, many of the onlookers started singing. Some sang solemn hymns, some – the ones who'd brought beer – sang rude songs. It sounded terrible.

At 8.59 and 50 seconds someone in the crowd started counting down from ten like it was New Year's Eve. Nobody joined in, so after 'Seven!' he stopped.

At 9.00:00 ... nothing happened.

At 9.00:02 Lbbp remembered to switch the invisibility shield off.

At 9.06 a.m. people were still screaming.

By 9.07 a.m. they'd started to calm down a bit.

At 9.08 a.m. the soldiers holding back the crowd began to notice that their mood had changed; no longer were they surging forwards and backwards, their singing and shouting had faded away and the air of fear and excitement had dwindled down into a sort of numb acceptance that whatever was going to happen, was going to happen.

So when at 9.09 a.m. a beam of white light burst from the underside of the strange hovering lemon-shaped object, there were no screams of alarm, just the sort of 'ooh' a crowd watching fireworks might make. Even the soldiers stood in silent anticipation, their weapons lowered.

The light faded.

The crowd – and via the TV, the human race – stared at the ground beneath the hovering object. Something was there. No, not something, someone ... small, dressed in a curious shimmering blue garment, but definitely a person rather than a thing. What at first looked like a halo of light around its head proved to be honey-blonde hair, and the face beneath was pink, heart-shaped and ... human?

'Hello,' said Terra brightly. 'Perhaps you can help me. I'm looking for my mummy and daddy.'

4.2

There were two things Mrs Bradbury hadn't done for a long time. One was argue with Mr Bradbury. The other was laugh.

The initial searing pain of their tiny daughter's disappearance had long since faded to a dull ache of loss which they knew would never go away. They'd had no more children; neither of them had ever even suggested it. It wasn't so much that the Bradburys didn't want to be parents again; it was more that they didn't feel that they deserved to be.

The small upstairs room which had been set aside to be the nursery still looked exactly as it had twelve years previously. The nameless baby had never slept there; she was still sleeping in a basket beside Mrs Bradbury's bed at the time of her disappearance. The cot still bore its first clean sheet, the little dangly musical mobile had never turned, the cupboards still contained the few toys that her parents had bought for her, alongside the empty spaces meant for the toys that they'd intended to buy.

Mr and Mrs Bradbury would occasionally admit to each other that keeping the nursery like this was foolish; to be reminded of their lost baby every day only made it harder on them and it really was time to convert the little room into an office, or spare bedroom, or something. That would be the right and sensible thing to do, they would agree. Yet it never happened; neither of them could bear to change a single thing in that room. So there it stayed, as perfect and as empty as it had ever been.

Mrs Bradbury would only go into the nursery now to clean it; she would be sure to do this when she was alone in the house. She didn't want her husband to find her sat crying on the floor, as would always happen for a few minutes before she collected herself and finished the job in silence.

On this particular morning Mrs Bradbury finished cleaning the nursery, wiped her eyes, blew her nose and went downstairs to make some coffee. She was working from home today and had the house to herself. The TV was on in the living room but the sound was turned down. People on TV annoyed Mrs Bradbury. Always talking, talking, yammering on about things that just didn't matter at all. So few things really mattered. Mrs Bradbury knew that now.

Mrs Bradbury was still wiping the last smudges of moisture from her eyes as she passed through the living room on her way from the kitchen.

The people on the TV were particularly over-excited this morning. Newsreaders whose faces on other days were smooth masks of professional calm babbled away to the camera and each other, their eyes glinting with both terror and joy. Reporters in the streets tried to interview passers-by, but the conversations all seemed (Mrs Bradbury still had the sound down) to dissolve into hysteria. And it was all because of – what did that caption say? Appearance? Mysterious? Extra-what?

Then she saw the shape.

The shape that had appeared to her every time she closed her eyes in the last twelve years. Except now it wasn't flickering away inside her head or tormenting her in a dream. It was right there on her TV screen.

Mrs Bradbury's coffee cup slid from her fingers and landed with a thud-splash on the carpet. She didn't hear it.

4.3

Mr Bradbury very nearly hadn't made it into work that morning. The traffic had been – quite literally – crazy, with people leaping out of their cars for no obvious reason and screaming at each other. Mr Bradbury turned the radio on to see what was happening but couldn't make sense of anything anyone was saying. One station was just playing an old REM song over and over. By the time he arrived at his office building he was feeling agitated and bewildered.

The front lobby of the building was deserted; usually there was a uniformed guard to greet him but today there was no sign of him at his desk; just a half-full cup of still steaming coffee and a half-eaten breakfast muffin.

Going up in the elevator Mr Bradbury heard waves of unusual sounds as he passed through each floor of the building. Singing, crying, laughing, screaming … What was going on?

The elevator arrived at his floor and the door opened. A wave of noise hit Mr Bradbury as he ventured into the office.

He saw his boss yelling frantically into a phone, his jacket off and his tie loose (already?); he saw his own secretary waving at him, with a huge smile and tears streaming down her cheeks; he saw two of his colleagues beckoning him towards the TV, he saw …

Mr Bradbury stood silent and open-mouthed amid the commotion. A single tear rolled down his cheek. His fingers fumbled inside his pocket for his phone. He dialled his home number without looking, his eyes still fixed upon the

TV screen. He heard a click and knew his wife had picked up the phone.

They didn't say a word to each other. They didn't have to.

4·4

Two days later, Lbbp was wishing he'd borrowed a bigger ship.

His own little lemon-shaped spaceship was now quite cramped and uncomfortable, being fuller than it had ever been before, but Lbbp was determined not to let that ruin what promised to be a very special day. One way or another.

Lbbp and Terra had been joined on board by a very impressive and serious young Ymn in a smart blue uniform who had been introduced to them as Major Hardison, and a rather less smartly dressed and considerably less serious Ymn called Professor Steinberg. Professor Steinberg, they had been assured, was one of the very cleverest Ymn scientists on the whole planet Rrth, but today he was simply overcome with excitement. He talked and giggled almost non-stop while on board the ship, asking questions in his funny up and downy Ymn voice that neither Terra nor Lbbp had time to answer before he asked another. They'd used the Interface to install Ymn language learning patches before leaving Fnrr, but they still had a lot of difficulty understanding Professor Steinberg. Occasionally Major Hardison would shoot Professor Steinberg a stern look, and Professor Steinberg would fall silent for a moment. Just for a moment.

The days since their arrival on Rrth had passed in a flurry of meetings, examinations and interviews, with impressively commanding Ymns in blue and green uniforms, clever-sounding Ymns in white coats, and finally an extremely important-seeming Ymn in an expensive-looking grey uniform, who was addressed by his many helpers as Mizzer Prezden. Mizzer Prezden had his picture taken with Terra and Lbbp and then asked Terra if she still wanted to find her parents. When Terra replied that yes, she did, Mizzer Prezden asked one of his helpers if Terra's parents had been identified and contacted, and he was told that yes, Mizzer Prezden, they had. More pictures were taken and Mizzer Prezden said how much he wished he could travel with them in Lbbp's ship to the meeting; one of Mizzer Prezden's helpers persuaded him that this would NOT be a good idea, Mizzer Prezden, and Mizzer Prezden agreed, although his disappointment was obvious. As she waved goodbye, Terra reflected that maybe Mizzer Prezden wasn't really that important after all.

The location of Terra's parents' house had been kept absolutely 100 per cent classified and top secret, so naturally by the time the little spaceship arrived overhead, the street was crammed with news reporters and onlookers.

Terra looked down from one of the ship's windows and frowned. She didn't like those machines that some of the crowd were pointing up at the ship. She knew they were just for taking pictures but there was still something threatening about them. 'Make all these silly people go away,' she muttered crossly.

Major Hardison coughed. 'Um, that could be difficult, ma'am.' He'd been calling Terra 'Ma'am' all day. Terra had no idea what it meant but she had decided she rather liked it. 'The street is a public right of way; I could request a special security order but it would have to be ...'

'Oh I'm sorry,' smiled Terra, 'I wasn't talking to you.'

Terra nodded to Lbbp, who had already reconfigured the displacement field generator to its external setting. There was a hum, a flash, and the street below them was deserted. The old Bsht-Pshkf manoeuvre, as it was now known on Fnrr.

Bsht. Lbbp missed Bsht.

Professor Steinberg burst out laughing, but Major Hardison seemed very concerned. 'Where have they gone?'

'Somewhere else,' replied Terra matter-of-factly. 'They'll be all right.'

And indeed they were all right, although they weren't really dressed for mountain climbing and it took them AGES to get back down again.

The little ship descended silently to hover a few metres above the surface of the street. Terra could see a tall Ymn standing in front of the house's main door. She breathed hard.

Major Hardison insisted on being the first to go down to speak to the Bradburys, but seemed very nervous about using the gravity beam to do so. Professor Steinberg, on the other hand, couldn't wait to give it a try. He chortled all the way down to the ground and as soon as he touched down, shouted something about 'another go'.

Terra watched Major Hardison walk up to the tall Ymn. At first she thought he was handing something over to him but then she saw that the two Ymns were just holding each other's hands and sort of wobbling them a bit. She'd seen Ymns doing this a lot since their arrival; she supposed it was some sort of greeting. She liked it; it looked friendly.

Lbbp put his hand on her shoulder.

- *Are you sure you want to do this?*

- *I can't disappoint them now. Not today. Not again.*

Lbbp gave Terra's shoulder a pat. - *I'll go first.*

* * *

Mr Bradbury had never known how he'd feel if he ever met the being who'd taken his child away. When it had first happened, the grief had been too intense to leave any room for anger. When, some time later, the anger came at last, sadness and shame soon overwhelmed it. Since the arrival of the spaceship he'd heard Lbbp's side of the story – everyone on Earth had – and now they were face to face he found himself looking at someone who, for all the physical differences between them and the extraordinary distance between the places they called home, was much like himself ... an ordinary person who tried to do the right thing and sometimes made dreadful mistakes.

Lbbp extended his hand in imitation of the Ymn gesture he'd observed. 'I ...' he said, the unaccustomed sound stretching his mouth uncomfortably. 'I'm ...' He tried to access the Ymn language learning patch but now he needed it, the information seemed vague and jumbled. Useless Interface, thought Lbbp.

'I'm ... sor-ry ...'

Mr Bradbury took Lbbp's hand and shook it gently.

'I'm sorry too.'

There was a momentary glow behind Lbbp. Mr Bradbury swallowed, and Lbbp stepped to one side.

Mr Bradbury studied the little face that now looked up at him. His own eyes, his wife's face ... If there had been any doubt in his mind – what doubt could there have been? – it was gone now. His mind raced in search of something, anything to say.

Terra spoke first, in slightly accented but perfect English. 'Am I supposed to call you Daddy?'

Mr Bradbury laughed tearfully. 'You can call me whatever you want ...'

He took a step towards the child; he only meant to stoop down to bring their faces level but his legs buckled and he found himself on his knees before her. For a moment his lips moved silently. When the words came, they poured from him in a great shuddering cry.

'We never even gave you a name ...'

Terra put her arms round his head and stroked his hair as his tears dampened her shiny blue suit.

'Terra,' she said softly. 'My name is Terra.'

* * *

A minute or so later, a calmer and more collected Mr Bradbury was leading Terra through the front door. Terra looked around her. She knew that it was unlikely she'd recognise anything, but she hoped to see something, anything that might trigger a memory of some kind. But there was nothing. A twinge of disappointment; Terra had expected the Bradburys' house to feel at least a little bit like 'home', but now she was standing here she felt every bit as alien as she'd ever felt on Fnrr.

Major Hardison was sat in a chair, deep in conversation with a female Ymn who sat opposite him in a similar chair.

The Ymn woman turned her head, with what seemed to be some difficulty, to look at Terra for the first time.

Hope is a terrifying thing sometimes.

In the days since the ship had arrived and changed the world, so many people all over the planet had been hoping for many different things. Scientists had hoped for great leaps forward in technology; the sick had hoped for miraculous new medicines, military leaders had (secretly) been hoping for devastating new weapons, religious zealots had been hoping for confirmation of their preferred ancient prophecy, and a lot of people on the internet were hoping that the next ship to arrive would bring Elvis back.

Only one person on Earth hadn't been hoping for anything at all.

Mrs Bradbury did not hope, because she would not allow herself to hope. Every time the thought that she was about to get her little girl back entered her mind, she furiously suppressed it. Even if this child was her own lost baby – and it seemed certain that she was – how could it possibly be as simple a matter as her lost child coming home? Coming home? Home? This house had never been her home. This planet had never been her home. She and Mr Bradbury had never been her family. The child had another life, another family, another world to which she belonged. How could she slot back into their lives as if nothing had happened? Why would she even want to?

Mrs Bradbury had been working very hard to stop hope from taking root in her mind, for she knew that when the hope proved false – as she felt sure it would – the pain of losing her child all over again would literally be more than she could bear.

Right now the thought Mrs Bradbury was trying not to have was that the girl now standing in her living room was every bit as bright, alert and pretty as she'd dreamed her child would be by now.

A moment's quiet.

Mr Bradbury was waiting by the door. This was something he wasn't going to be able to help with. Professor Steinberg, despite his excitement, sensed that now was not a moment for enthusiasm. For politeness's sake, he introduced himself quietly to Mr Bradbury.

'I remember reading about what happened,' he said. 'It's amazing anyone believed you.'

'They didn't,' said Mr Bradbury.

Professor Steinberg was going to say 'I did,' when he noticed that Mrs Bradbury was about to speak.

'It was your birthday. Two weeks ago.'

'How old am I?' Perfect English; a hint of an accent. Mrs Bradbury composed herself and went on.

'Twelve. You ... you're twelve now.' Nearly said 'would have been'.

'Really? I'm still eight back – back on Fnrr. The years. They're a little longer.'

'I see.'

Terra had been about to say 'back home'. She'd caught herself just in time. She hoped her mother hadn't noticed. She knew she had.

'Can I see my room?'

'Of course.'

Mrs Bradbury led Terra to the bottom of the staircase. *Oh yes, stairs,* thought Terra. *I hope I can use them correctly. Should be easy, they're like the Forum steps in Hrrng but much narrower.* Watching her mother's actions carefully, she followed up behind her. It felt strange, and yet entirely natural.

Mr Bradbury watched his wife and daughter ascend the

stairs, then turned to the others and spoke. 'I'd ... I'd bet-ter ...'

Major Hardison nodded and Mr Bradbury climbed the stairs. Professor Steinberg had been about to follow when Major Hardison shot him a glance which he and even Lbbp understood immediately. Professor Steinberg sat in one of the armchairs and beckoned to Lbbp to sit in the other.

'So ...'

'So?'

'So, um, not your first time on Earth, then ...'

'No. First time among Ymns, though.'

'And how are you finding us?'

'Fascinating.'

Professor Steinberg let out an involuntary yelp of laughter. Major Hardison glowered at him. 'Oh come on,' pleaded Professor Steinberg, shaking with suppressed mirth. 'Fascinating,' repeated Professor Steinberg in a deep voice, raising one eyebrow. 'Far out ...' he chuckled. Major Hardison shook his head sadly. Lbbp had absolutely no idea what was going on, but at least Professor Steinberg seemed happy.

* * *

Mrs Bradbury pushed the nursery door open. Yellow sunlight poured through thin curtains. Terra took a step inside. Shelves, a few brightly coloured books, some simple plastic toys, all obviously intended for the baby she had once been and could never be again. In the corner, what looked like a tiny cage; on closer inspection, a little bed surrounded by wooden bars. *To stop me rolling out in my sleep,* thought Terra. *To keep me safe. Like the straps in the car. Just to keep me safe.*

Mrs Bradbury stood behind Terra, longing to speak but with no idea what to say.

'Did I sleep here?'

'No.' Mrs Bradbury swallowed and went on. 'You were still too tiny. You slept in a basket beside my bed. We were going to move you in here when ... when it ... when you went away.'

Terra thought.

Mrs Bradbury waited.

Mr Bradbury silently entered the room and put an arm round his wife's shoulders. She was shivering.

Terra spoke.

'This isn't going to work.'

Mrs Bradbury shuddered and her husband's arm tightened around her. 'No, of course it isn't.'

Terra turned round. 'If I'm going to be living here from now on, I'll need a much bigger bed,' she said.

Mrs Bradbury let out a great sob, which turned into a laugh, and back into a sob, and she was laughing and crying all at once, and her husband joined in, and they both wrapped their arms around their little girl like they would never ever let her go again.

* * *

Downstairs, Professor Steinberg listened to the sounds of joy and laughter coming through the ceiling.

'Well ... I guess she's staying.'

Even Major Hardison smiled, and shook Professor Steinberg's hand.

Lbbp sat alone. He tried his best to be happy. He knew he would be one day.

4·5

Terra dreamed.

In her dreams she was flying, flying over rainbow beaches and deep pink seas. Flying over spires of crystal and steel, flying through soft clouds, soft downy clouds, clouds that tangled around her limbs and pulled her off course until she crashed down onto the carpeted floor of her bedroom.

Duvets.

Like everything else in Terra's new world, duvets were going to take some getting used to.

One thing Terra was sure she'd never get used to was having to wash herself before getting dressed. It was all so much fuss and bother. She had to admit that showers felt fantastic, though.

She trotted down the stairs – she could take them at quite a pace now without stumbling – and greeted her parents. She sniffed the air.

'Pancakes!' she said happily.

'Of course,' smiled her mother.

The car arrived just as Terra was finishing her pancakes. She got into the back with her parents on either side of her. Terra still found travelling by car bumpy and noisy, but at least it didn't make her sick, as she had feared it might when she first tried it.

'How long is this going to take?' she asked her father.

'About an hour.'

About ten minutes by bubble, reflected Terra, *but never mind.*

* * *

Fifty-eight minutes later, the car passed through a security checkpoint manned by young soldiers who seemed quite excited to see them, and drove on into the airbase.

Terra was delighted to see Lbbp's little ship, hovering above a flat stretch of runway. She hadn't seen it for three weeks and now there it was, surrounded by all that bulky, messy Ymn technology. It looked so ... simple.

Major Hardison stepped forward to greet them as they got out of the car. He was dressed not in his smart blue uniform, but in the shimmery one-piece garment of a Fnrrn. Behind him, and similarly dressed, was Professor Steinberg. His garment looked rather tighter on him than Major Hardison's. Behind him stood Lbbp. Terra raced to Lbbp and flung her arms around him.

- *I'm so happy to see you! How have you been?*

- *Not bad. The gravity gets to me occasionally. I'll be glad to get home, although it'll be so ... quiet.*

- *You'll have lots to do, though. The treaty with the G'grk, the rebuilding of the Forum, establishing ... what was it again?*

- *Proper cultural and diplomatic relations with Rrth,* said Lbbp, *although that will be Major Hardison and Professor Steinberg's job more than mine. I'll just be advising.*

Terra looked over her shoulder at her parents. They were talking to Major Hardison.

- *Anyway, never mind me, how are YOU getting along?* asked Lbbp.

- *I'm getting the hang of it,* replied Terra. *I'm starting Ymn school in a month. I'm not looking forward to that.*

- *It can't be any harder than starting the Lyceum was, and you managed that okay,* said Lbbp. *It should be less eventful, at least.*

- *I'm not sure,* said Terra. *We've changed so much about these people's lives just by coming here. I think Rrth has some interesting times ahead.*

- *Well, you can keep me informed with the infralight comm. You've kept it hidden?*

- *Yes,* said Terra, *I know, we don't want them tinkering*

252

with it before they know how it works. I haven't even switched it on yet. I'm dying for news from Fnrr. Have you heard anything?

- *Well, let's see,* said Lbbp ... *The terms of the peace treaty are still being discussed, which is fine, the Dsktn refugees are nearly all home, which is better, and Pktk and Fthfth have written a play. About you. It's a musical.*

Terra said nothing, but was suddenly quite glad she was twenty-eight light years away from Fnrr. - *So when will you be back?*

- *Six, oh, whatever it is they call cycles here ...*

- *Months?*

- *That's it.*

Terra hugged Lbbp again. - *I'm not sorry, you know.*

- *What?*

- *I'm not sorry you did what you did. Not sorry I grew up with you. And Mum and Dad* (Lbbp had got used to hearing Terra call them that now) *say they're not sorry anymore either. They're always saying they're much better parents now than they would have been.*

- *It's very kind of them to say so,* said Lbbp, even though he didn't believe a word of it.

- *And anyway, I don't need to have the best Mum and Dad in the world,* said Terra, *because I'll always know that somewhere up there, I've got the best stepfather in the known universe.*

- *I'm so proud of you,* said Lbbp. He held up his hand. *Always here.*

Terra touched her fingertips to his. - *I'm so proud of YOU ... Always here.*

Ten minutes later, Terra stood with her parents either side of her as the little lemon-shaped spaceship rose gently into the air.

Onboard, Major Hardison and Professor Steinberg did their best to get comfortable in the flight seats that had been rather haphazardly installed. Lbbp turned to address them.

'Ready?'

Major Hardison nodded. Professor Steinberg gestured with his fingers.

'Engage!' he said, and giggled.

Major Hardison sighed. It was going to be a long trip.

As Terra, her parents, and a few dozen extremely important military and scientific personnel watched, the little spaceship shot upwards and disappeared from view.

There was a pause.

'What happens now?' asked Terra.

4.6

Once in deep space, Lbbp had transmitted a message to Fnrr, saying that Terra was settling in and that he and the Ymn envoys were on their way.

The message passed at infralight speed through wormholes, spatial folds and interstitial vortices and was received by the Preceptorate's extraplanetary communications array. There it was relayed, as was all information, to the Extrapolator.

The Extrapolator assimilated the news and processed it with what, in an organic brain, would be called contentment. All was proceeding as the Extrapolator had foreseen. The war had been averted, the planet was safe, and the Ymn child was back where she needed to be.

For now.

Acknowledgements

A few without whoms:

Thanks to Simon, Jon, Genn, Mark and the rest of the Gollancz gang. Thanks to Greta for being Terra AND Fthfth, and to Astrid for being Astrid. Big thanks to Ken and Liz Bartlett for the use of The Barn and Hilary Bartlett for unfailing moral support. Thanks to Max Leadley-Brown and Lee Budgie-Barnett for unpaid editorial duties and moral support. Thanks to Dad for turning me into a science-fiction freak and Mum for letting him. Thanks to Ian Wilson for managing to manage managing me. Finally, thanks to Neil Himself Gaiman for being an inspiration on so many levels, and to Clara Benn for literally EVERYTHING else.